OREO

Oreo

by

Fran Ross

with a foreword by Danzy Senna
and an afterword by Harryette Mullen

A NEW DIRECTIONS PAPERBOOK

First published as a New Directions Paperbook in 2015
Manufactured in the United States of America
Designed by F. D. R.

Library of Congress Cataloging-in-Publication Data
Ross, Fran, 1935–1985
Oreo / Fran Ross ; foreword by Danzy Senna ; afterword by Harryette Mullen.
pages ; cm
ISBN 978-0-8112-2322-5 (alk. paper)
1. Racially mixed people—Fiction. 2. African American girls—Fiction.
3. New York (N.Y.)—Fiction. 4. Race relations—Fiction. 5. Jewish girls—
Fiction. 6. Birthfathers—Fiction. 7. Domestic fiction. I. Title.
PS3568.O8433O74 2015
813'.54—dc23   2015016209

10 9 8 7

New Directions Books are published for James Laughlin
by New Directions Publishing Corporation
80 Eighth Avenue. New York 10011

In memory of my father, Gerald Ross;
and my great-aunt Izetta Bass Grayson (Auntie)

Oreo defined: Someone who is black on the outside and white on the inside

Oreo, ce n'est pas moi. — F.D.R.

A likely story. — FLAUBERT

Burp!* — WITTGENSTEIN

Epigraphs never have anything to do with the book

---

*Anything this profound philosopher ever said bears repeating. — Ed.

CONTENTS

Foreword

The first time I read Fran Ross's hilarious badass novel, *Oreo*, I was living on Fort Greene Place, Brooklyn in a community of people I thought of as "the dreadlocked elite." It was the late 1990s, and the artisan cheese shops and organic juice bars had not yet fully arrived in the boroughs, though there were hints of what was to come. Poor people and artists could still afford to live there. We were young and black and we'd moved to the neighborhood armed with graduate degrees and creative ambitions. There was a quiet storm of what Greg Tate described as "black genius" brewing in our midst. Spike Lee had set up a production studio inside the old firehouse on DeKalb Avenue. Around the corner on Lafayette Street was Kokobar, a black-owned espresso shop decorated with Basquiat-inspired paintings; there were whispers that Tracy Chapman and Alice Walker were investors. Around the corner on Elliott Street, Lisa Price, aka Carol's Daughter, sold organic hair oils and creams for kinky-curly hair out of a brownstone storefront.

Years earlier I had read Trey Ellis's seminal essay "The New Black Aesthetic" from my West-Coast dorm room, curled beside my dreadlocked, half-Jewish boyfriend. We saw glimmers of ourselves in his description of a new generation of black artists. We, too, had been born post-Civil Rights Movement, post-Loving, post-soul, post-everything. We were suspicious of militancy, black or otherwise, suspicious of claims to authenticity, racial and otherwise. We were culturally hybrid—"cultural mulattos," as Ellis put it— whether we had one white parent or not.

Now, in nineties Fort Greene, we had arrived. Many of the black kids in our midst were recovering oreos: they'd grown up listening to the Clash, not Public Enemy, playing hacky sack, not basketball. They were all too accustomed to—as my friend Jake Lamar once put it—being "the only black person at the dinner party."

Only now we were throwing our own dinner party. We were *demi-teint*—half-tone—a shade of blackness that had been formed in a clash of disparate symbols and signifiers, nothing pure about us. We were authentically nothing. Each of us had experienced a degree of alienation growing up—being too black to be white, or too white to be black, or too mixed to be anything—and somehow at the same moment in time we'd all moved into the same ten-block radius of Brooklyn together.

Oreo came to me in this context like a strange uncanny dream about the future that was really the past. That is, it read like a novel not from 1974 but from the near future—a book whose appearance I was still waiting for. I stared at the author photo of the woman wearing the peasant smock and her hair in an Afro and could easily imagine her moving through the streets of Fort Greene. She belonged to our world. Her blackness was our blackness.

Oreo, its first time around in 1974, had disappeared as quickly as it had appeared. It got a few amused and somewhat confused reviews in *Ms. Magazine* and *Esquire* but apparently didn't speak to the wider cultural landscape of the moment. It came out only two years before that other novel, the cultural sensation, Alex Haley's *Roots: The Saga of An American Family.* While *Oreo* may have been one of the least-known novels of the decade, *Roots* went on to become the single most popular novel of the decade, black or white. It occupied the number one spot on the *New York Times* bestseller list for twenty-two weeks. It was adapted into one of the most-watched television miniseries of all time.

For most Americans my age—particularly if you are black—*Roots* is part of our childhood iconography. We can all trade stories of sitting on the family-room floor, watching with a mixture of rapture and disbelief. I remember weeping when Fiddler died, because I too played the fiddle. I remember how at school, the day after the miniseries aired, a white girl walked up to a table of black kids in the cafeteria and said, with tears in her eyes, that she was so sorry about slavery, and could she please empty their lunch trays for them?

The titles themselves of these two texts—*Roots* and *Oreo*—imply the profound gap between the works—giving us a clue into the kind of black narratives we like to celebrate and the kind we've tended to ignore. *Roots* looks toward the past. It offers black people an origin story, an imagined moment of racial purity—when the Mandinka warrior Kunte Kinte is kidnapped off the shores of Gambia. It constructs a lost utopia for us and a clear fall from Eden, Africa. *Oreo,* from the title alone and its first loony pages, suggests murkier, more polluted racial waters.

Indeed, Oreo's origin story is one of gleeful miscegenation. The moment Samuel Schwartz falls for Helen (Honeychile) Clark, it's too late to look back. An "oreo" is, of course, a cookie, white on the inside and black on the outside; it is also the taunt of choice for black people who appear to "act white." Fran Ross embraces this epithet, embraces the idea of falling from racial grace. But it's no mulatto sentimentalism—no "ebony and ivory" simplistic tale of racial mushiness. From page one, both sides of Oreo's family—the black and the Jewish—are equally horrified by their children falling in love. In fact, James Clark, Helen's father, Oreo's black grandfather, is so horrified by his daughter's coupling with a Jewish guy that his actual body becomes encoded by hate—paralyzed into the shape of a half-swastika.

Oreo, born Christine Clark, the biracial progeny of the fall, is our heroine, and like all good heroes and heroines, she's on a quest. But unlike Alex Haley, Oreo is trying to find her white side—her missing Jewish father. Her absent father is no site of longing; he's a voice-over actor in Manhattan who has left her an absurd list of clues to help her locate him. He's a bum, according to her mother. "I'm going to find that fucker," is how Oreo sets out on her search, which feels more like an excuse to wander away from her home than a real desire for a father.

Oreo is cheeky, mischievous, a trickster—or, as one uncle says of her: "That girl's got womb ... she's a real ball buster." She is radically, almost aggressively mixed; within one passage she can and does code-switch with ease between a multitude of tongues— from Yiddish to so-called Ebonics to highbrow academic jargon. She's tainted from the get-go, a mad-cap play on Dubois's "double-consciousness." Only in this case it's not doubled, it's tripled, qua-drupled, and on. This multiplicity she inhabits is not a "burden" that she must fight to keep from tearing her "asunder." Rather, it's a source of strength and agility. Her twoness keeps her on her toes, enables her to move between multiple worlds. She is as Jewish as she is black; there is nothing tragic about this mulatto. She is, if any-thing, a comic mulatto, turning the world on its head with a verbal precocity and wit that sharpen her ability to shape-shift and pass.

Aesthetically, *Oreo* has all the hallmarks of a postmodern novel in its avoidance of profundity and its utterly playful spirit. The novel draws no conclusions and the quest leads to no giant revelatory payoffs. The father and his secret about her birth constitute, in the end—and without giving anything away—as absurdist and femi-nist a send-up of the patriarchal myth as one could hope to find. The novel at every turn embraces ambiguity. Its quest-driven plot is at every step diverted by wordplay and metareferences to itself. It feels in many ways more in line stylistically, aesthetically, with Thomas Pynchon and Kurt Vonnegut than with Sonia Sanchez and Ntzoke Shange, to name two other black female writers of Ross's time.

Oreo never becomes a fully believable character, and this feels appropriate to the work's spirit. The novel does not strive for realism; Ross is not trying to construct a seamless, plot-driven narrative, or a sympathetic, three-dimensional main character. We are always aware of Oreo as a construct, and her story as a construct. Puns, wordplay, stand-up comedy riffs, menus, charts, tangents: the journey to find the father is just a chance for Ross to meander through her wicked and free imagination and to push us toward a hyperawareness of language itself. "Christine," Ross writes, and she could be writing of herself, "was no ordinary child.... She had her mother's love of words, their nuance and cadence, their juice and pith, their variety and precision, their rock and wry."

Alongside the feminist standards we had lying around my house when I was a kid, *Our Bodies, Ourselves* and Erica Jong's *Fear of Flying*, there was this anthology of black literature called *Dark Symphony: Negro Literature in America,* which always seemed to be in the kitchen. It was one of the early canonizing texts of the burgeoning African-American Studies departments. On the cover was a silhouette of a black male face, foreboding and sad, surrounded by a circle of red. I guess that male profile was supposed to be taken literally, because inside, of the thirty-four authors included in the book, exactly four were women.

Oreo was published seven years after this anthology; the second-wave feminist movement had come of age, and women were beginning to find their voices, cracking open the male literary establishment bit by bit. By the 1980s, black literature was a dark male symphony no longer. Black women writers had come into vogue. And yet even by the 1990s, as I read *Oreo* in my apartment in Fort Greene, the birthplace of post-soul black bohemia—and even now, so many years after the fact, as the Brooklyn I once knew sits in gentrified, glittery ruins—Ross feels to me like part of some future that still has yet to arrive.

Oreo resists the unwritten conventions that still exist for novels

written by black women today. There's nothing redemptively uplift-
ing about her work. The title doesn't refer to the Bible or the blues.
The work does not refer to slavery. The character is never violated,
sexually or otherwise. The characters are not from the South. Oreo
is sincerely ironic, hilarious, brainy, impenetrable at times. Oreo's
mother is mostly absent. She dumps Oreo and her sweet, eccentric
brother with their grandparents so she can go on the road. She writes
the children mawkish, insincere letters from different places. Oreo
replies with letters written backwards. When held up to a mirror,
Oreo's words read: "Cut the crap mom." Her mother does just that
and begins to get real with her daughter. She explains in one letter
why women are oppressed. After an elaborate theoretical analysis,
she concludes: "I have been able to synthesize these considerations
into one inescapable formulation: men can knock the shit out of
women." In the same letter, her mother tears to hell the stereotype of
the black matriarch: "There's no male chauvinist pork like a black
male chauvinist pork."

Like the best satire, nobody is safe, nobody is spared. The humor
is low at times, scatological and plain silly, and the humor is high,
sophisticated wordplay and clichés flipped on their heads. Ross is
a hard sell for February, black history month, and a hard sell for
March, women's history month. Hers is a postmodern text; it is a
queer text, it is a work of black satire; it is a work of high feminist
comedy; it is a post-soul text. Her novel is multifaceted, multilin-
gual, which still makes it an awkward presence on the landscape of
American fiction, where "ethnic" literature can be put into kiosks
like dishes at a food fair, and consumed just as easily.

After *Oreo*, Fran Ross never wrote another novel. She died young
of cancer in 1985, anonymous from a literary standpoint, but surrounded by friends. We know only scattered details about her life,
tidbits about who she was as a person. When she first came from
her hometown of Philadelphia to New York City, she lived in a
boarding house in midtown, the Webster Apartment for Women. A

friend who met her there recalls her from the start as brilliant and warm and extremely funny. Ross was fascinated by Jewish culture and the Yiddish language; several professors encouraged her in her studies at Temple University, where she graduated magna cum laude. She loved Mark Twain, Oscar Wilde, Jean Genet, and James Baldwin. She went to hear Baldwin speak at various venues around the city. In her social world, she was often the only black girl at the white feminist dinner party.

Once, with a group of these friends, she looked up the famously reclusive Djuna Barnes in the phone book. Together they all went to the listed address, and, standing outside the apartment door, they heard classical music playing inside. When they knocked, Barnes, an old woman already, opened it and simply said to the circle, "I don't see people anymore," before shutting the door in their faces.

Ross's middle name was Delores and she signed all her letters FDR, amused by the presidential echo. She was intensely close to her family, particularly her mother. She was disappointed by the way *Oreo* was ignored. She tried to find another home for her talents and went out to Los Angeles in the late 1970s, with a deal to write for Richard Pryor's television show. Perhaps a stand-up comedian, especially somebody as out there as Pryor, would have appreciated her disregard for social propriety, her outrageousness, her loyalty to nothing but the workings of her own startlingly original mind. But when she arrived, she found herself disillusioned by the people in Pryor's circle—and the show was canceled. She returned to New York City and her day job in publishing, still searching for a genre in which her voice could be heard—a space where she could be true to her own fierce contradictions.

—DANZY SENNA

PART ONE: TROEZEN

1 Mishpocheh

First, the bad news

When Frieda Schwartz heard from her Shmuel that he was *(a)* marrying a black girl, the blood soughed and staggered in all her conduits as she pictured the chiaroscuro of the white-satin *chuppa* and the *shvartze*'s skin; when he told her that he was *(b)* dropping out of school and would therefore never become a certified public accountant — *Riboyne Shel O'lem!* — she let out a great *geshrei* and dropped dead of a racist/my-son-the-bum coronary.

The bad news *(cont'd)*

When James Clark heard from the sweet lips of Helen (Honeychile) Clark that she was going to wed a Jew-boy and would soon be Helen (Honeychile) Schwartz, he managed to croak one anti-Semitic "Goldberg!" before he turned to stone, as it were, in his straight-backed chair, his body a rigid half swastika, discounting, of course, head, hands, and feet.

Major and minor characters in part one of this book, in order of birth

Jacob Schwartz, the heroine's paternal grandfather
Frieda Schwartz, his wife (died in paragraph one but still, in her own quiet way, a power and a force)
James Clark, the heroine's maternal grandfather (immobilized in paragraph two)
Louise Butler Clark, the heroine's maternal grandmother (two weeks younger than her husband)
Samuel Schwartz, the heroine's father
Helen Clark Schwartz, the heroine's mother
Christine (Oreo), the heroine
Moishe (Jimmie C.), the heroine's brother

Concerning a few of the characters, an *aperçu* or two

Jacob: He makes boxes ("Jake the Box Man, A Boxeleh for Every *Tchotchkeleh*"). As he often says, "It's a living. I *mutche* along." Translation: "I am, *kayn aynhoreh,* a very rich man."
James and Louise: In the DNA crapshoot for skin color, when the die was cast, so was the dye. James came out nearest the color of the pips (on the scale opposite, he is a 10), his wife the cube. Louise is fair, very fair, an albino *manquée* (a just-off-the-scale −1). James is a shrewd businessman, Louise one of the great cooks of our time.
Samuel Schwartz: Just another pretty face.

Helen Clark: Singer, pianist, mimic, math freak (a 4 on the color scale).

Colors of black people

white	high yellow (pronounced YAL-la)	yellow	light-skinned
1	2	3	4

light brown-skinned	brown-skinned	dark brown-skinned
5	6	7

dark-skinned	very dark-skinned	black
8	9	10

NOTE: There is no "very black." Only white people use this term. To blacks, "black" is black enough (and in most cases too black, since the majority of black people are not nearly so black as your black pocketbook). If a black person says, "John is very black," he is referring to John's politics, not his skin color.

A word about weather

There is no weather per se in this book. Passing reference is made to weather in a few instances. Assume whatever season you like throughout. Summer makes the most sense in a book of this length. That way, pages do not have to be used up describing people taking off and putting on overcoats.

The life story of James and Louise up to the marriage of Helen and Samuel

In 1919, when they were both five years old, little James and little Louise moved to Philadelphia with their parents, the Clarks and the Butlers, who were close friends, from a tiny hamlet outside a small village in Prince Edward County, Virginia. When they were eighteen, James and Louise married and had their first and only child, Helen, in the same year.

During World War II, James worked as a welder at Sun

Shipyard in Chester, Pennsylvania. Every morning for three years, he would stop at Zipstein's Noshery to buy a pickle to take to work in his lunchbox. He would ask for a sour. Zipstein always gave him a half sour. From that time on, James hated Jews.

After the war, James had enough money saved to start his own mail-order business. He purposely cultivated a strictly Jewish clientele, whom he overcharged outrageously. He researched his market carefully; he studied Torah and Talmud, collected *midrashim,* quoted Rabbi Akiba — root and herb of all the jive-ass copy he wrote for the *chrain-*storm of flyers he left in Jewish neighborhoods. His first item sold like *latkes.* It was a set of dartboards, featuring (his copy read) "all the men you love to hate from Haman to Hitler." No middle-class Philadelphia Jew could show his face in his basement rec room if those dartboards weren't hanging there.

With this success as a foundation, James went on to tie-ins with other mail-order houses. He was able to offer his customers cheese blintzes for Shevuoth, handkerchiefs for Tisha Bov ("You'll cry a lot"), *dreidels* for Chanukah, *gragers* and *hamantashen* for Purim, wine goblets for Passover, honey for Rosh Hashanah, branches for Succoth ("Have the prettiest booth on your block"), and a recording of the Kol Nidre for Yom Kippur ("as sung by Tony Martin"). Next to each item in his catalog was a historico-religious paragraph for those who did not know the significance of the feasts and holidays. "You have to explain everything to these *apikorsim,*" he told Louise, who said, "What say?" Over the years, his steadiest seller was the Jewish History Coloring Book series, including "the ever-popular Queen Esther, Ruth and Naomi, Judah and the Maccabees (add 50¢ for miniature plastic hammer), the Sanhedrin (the first Supreme Court), and other all-time Chosen People favorites." At last, his money worries were over. He was able to send Helen to college and buy Louise the gift of her dreams: a complete set of Tupperware (5,481 pieces).

Temple University, choir rehearsal

As Helen sang her part in the chorale chorus *Jesu, Joy of Man's Desiring*, she constructed one of her typical head equations, based on the music's modalities and hers:

$$BTU = \frac{3 \times 10^8}{\sqrt{\epsilon/\epsilon_0}} \quad \text{m/sec}$$

where B = Bach
T = time
U = weight of uric acid, ml

Simple, she conceded, compared with the overlapping fugal subject-answer-countersubject head equations that were her favorites—elegant, in fact, but not quite absorbing enough to keep her mind off the fact that she was perspiring and wanted desperately to pee.

Samuel, passing through the rehearsal hall, caught a glimpse of Helen's face and, mistaking her expression of barely controlled anguish for religious fervor, was himself seized with an emotion that mystics have often erroneously identified as ecstasy-*cum*-epiphany (*vide* Saul on the road to Damascus, Theresa of Ávila every time you turn around): the hots. His accounting books fell to the floor.

Decisions, decisions

After much soul- and *neshoma*-searching, respectively, Helen and Samuel decided to marry and live in his hometown, New York City. Samuel wanted to be an actor. Furthermore, because

Helen was a math freak, obviously gifted, Samuel wanted to have Helen's child—or, rather, he wanted *her* to have her/their child. Helen did not mind. Pregnancy, she felt, would give her time to sit and play the piano and do her head equations while Samuel was studying Intermediate Walking and Talking at drama school.

Birth of the heroine

A secret cauled Christine's birth. This is her story—let her discover it. Helen named the baby girl in a moment of pique after a fight with Samuel in the hospital. They made up before the ink was dry on the birth certificate. Although Samuel was a nonobserving Jew and did not give a fig that his daughter was named after Christ, he playfully extracted a promise from Helen that he could name the next child.

Helen and Samuel

Later that year, Samuel stroked Helen's thigh and joked, "Now let's try for the Messiah."

Helen and Samuel *(cont'd)*

They fought Mondays and Thursdays. Finally, Samuel said, "When Christine is old enough to decipher the clues written on this piece of paper, send her to me and I will reveal to her the secret of her birth." He handed Helen the paper, adding a lot of *farchadat* instructions it is not necessary to go into here. "I still hope to see you from time to time," he said.

"Later for you, *shmendrick*," said Helen.

Samuel left to work on a scene in drama class in which he was to play Aegeus.

Helen goes home

After the breakup but before the divorce, Helen moved back to

Philadelphia. She was with child again. In the fullness of time, a son was born, in circumstances neither more nor less unusual than those that attended the advent of Christine. Samuel sent Helen a one-word telegram: "MOISHE." He thought it was funny to name a black kid Moishe. It was the name on the birth certificate, but everyone called the child Jimmie C., after his maternal grandfather and, inadvertently, after his paternal grandfather (James = Jacob).

A peek at Jacob

Jacob lived on the Upper West Side of New York City. The first thing you noticed about him was that his upper middle incisors did not line up with the center of his face. A line drawn through the interstice of the two teeth would bisect not the septum but his left nostril. This gave the impression either that his face was off-center or that his false teeth had not quite settled around his gums. But his teeth were his own. Had they been false, he would have had a better set made. All his life, everybody and his brother had driven him *meshugge* cocking their heads this way and that whenever they talked to him. Everybody, that is, except his Frieda, rest in peace, whose neck and therefore head had been permanently set at an angle on her shoulders ever since her Uncle Yussel, klutz, had missed when he was playing upsy-daisy with her when she was six months old.

"Another year, another *yahrzeit,*" he sighed. "Two years already have passed and still I can't bring myself to go into my Frieda's room. In there are all her plants. She loved plants." He gestured helplessly to his neighbor, Pinsky, apartment 5-E. "Pinsky, she would talk to them, what can I tell you, like she was having a *shmooz* with her friends." He wept yet again when he thought of his wife's devotion to her greenery.

An hour later Bessie, the cleaning woman, came in to do her

daily chores. She decided to take care of the dead lady's plants first, before her corns started tom-tomming (''Sit down — *bam!* — 'fore you — double *wham!* — fall down — *boom!* Would I — *boom-boom!*—treat you this way?—*wham-boom-bam?*''). ''Lord have mercy, that woman *do* have some plants,'' she said as she took out her feather duster and opened the door on one of the largest collections of plastic plants in America.

2   The Cube and the Pip

Food

Louise Clark's southern accent was as thick as hominy grits. No one else in the Philadelphia branch of the family had such an accent. Her mother and father had dropped theirs as soon as they crossed the Pennsylvania state line. Her husband could have been an announcer for WCAU had they been hiring 10's when he was coming up. While all about her sounded eastern-seaboard neutral, why did she persist in sounding like a mush-mouth? One reason: most of the time her mouth was full of mush or some other comestible rare or common to humankind.

Louise was once challenged to name a food she did not like. She paused to consider. That pause was now in its fifteenth year. During that time, she spoke of other things, lived her life, paid attention to what was going on, to all appearances; but all the while—simmering on a back burner, as it were—she was trying to bring to the boil of consciousness the category of food she had once tasted at Ida Ledbetter's second child's husband's cousin's wake after Ida Ledbetter's second child's husband's cousin's mother had collapsed after dishing out the potato salad. She would go to her reward without putting a name to that food, which was not food at all but a frying pan full of Oxydol. Why the Oxydol was in the frying pan in the first place is beyond the scope of this work, but when Louise had walked by the stove, she had hand-hunked a taste. Her judgment was that, whatever it was, someone had been a mite too heavy-handed with the salt. Thus, this was not truly her first antifood opinion but, rather, her first (and only) anti*seasoning* decision, an important subcategory.

She always looked with perfect incomprehension on those finicky eaters who said that so-and-so's spaghetti sauce was too spicy, her greens too bland, her sweet potatoes too stringy. For Louise, nothing to eat was ever too sour, salty, sweet, or bitter, too well done or too rare, too hot or too cold. Anything that could be subsumed under the general classification "Food" was exempt from criticism and was endued with all the attributes of pleasure. Consequently, anything Louise liked was compared, in one way or another, with food. A free translation of what she said on her wedding night after James went into his act would be: "The blacker the berry, the sweeter the juice."

Aside on Louise's speech

From time to time, her dialogue will be rendered in ordinary English, which Louise does not speak. To do full justice to her speech would require a ladder of footnotes and glosses, a tic of apostrophes (aphaeresis, hyphaeresis, apocope), and a Louise-ese/English dictionary of phonetic spellings. A compromise has been struck. Since Louise can work miracles of compression through syncope, it is only fair that a few such condensations be shared with the reader. However, the substitution of an apostrophe for every dropped *g*, missing *r*, and absent *t* would be tantamount to *tic douloureux* of movable type.

To avoid this, some sentences in Louise-ese have been disguised so that they are indistinguishable from English. In other cases, guides to pronunciation and/or variant spellings are given parenthetically whenever absolutely necessary to preserve the flavor and integrity of the Louise-ese or, antithetically, translations are provided for relict English words, phrases, or sentences that survive her mangle-mouth.

Back to food

Fortunately for her family, who did not share her universal palate, Louise was a cook for the ages, adept at unnumbered ethnic and international cuisines, her shrewd *saucisson-en-croûte* surviving even her attempts to pronounce it to take its place on the dining-room table, in due course, beside her butter-blinded *pommes de terre Savoyard*, her brave corn pudding, untouchable beef curry, toe-tapping hopping john, *auto-da-fé paella*, operatic *vitello tonnato*, and soulful hog maws.

One of Helen's earliest memories was of sitting on her mother's lap and being urged to "tayce dis yere tornado Bernice" (taste this here *tournedos Béarnaise*) as she looked over her mother's shoulder to compare Louise's startlingly white face with the portrait of her grandfather, a 1 if there ever was one. The portrait hung in an oval frame in the dining room. Helen's grandfather had been the offspring of an enterprising African woman who had immigrated to New York in 1869 and had had a hand in the somewhat unfortunate attempt to corner the gold market ("Black Friday" was named after her) and a Richmond bugler who had been a turncoat during the Civil War and was vamping in the Bronx until he felt it was safe to tootle back to Virginia. Her grandmother was said to be half Cherokee and half French — hence the influence of French cuisine in the family, the oldest handed-down-from-generation-to-generation recipe being a providential dish called rabbit-on-the-run *suprême*, in commemoration of the French and Indian Wars. The last joke James Clark heard before his immobilization was his daughter's rather feeble "Just think, Daddy, now I can call myself Hélène Sun-See-A-Ray Schwartz."

More about Louise

Louise went gray at thirty-two trying to understand what her husband and child were saying when they talked that foolish talk they talked sometimes. ("You're *draying* me such a *kop* with that racket, Honeychile," said the father. "*Kvetch, kvetch,*" said the daughter under her breath.) She had her "good" hair dyed auburn, a color and texture that she never failed to compare favorably with the dull black kinks of her neighbors as she waited her turn while the beautician straightened their nappy heads with the hot comb (or "cum," as Louise pronounced it, with the *u* of "put"). "I thank you, Father," she would pray, "fo' gib'm me de gray hairs, but I *truly* thank you fo' gib'm folks de knowledge so I don' hafta hab'm. I'd look like a *f*-double *o-l* walkin' 'round yere wif a gray head, young's I am."

Louise talked in generalities that required the listener to fill in the who, what, where, when, why, and how. She rarely bothered to remember names ("Dere go Miz What-cha-cawm an' her daughter"), or she made two or three tentative tries at capture before the killing pounce ("Yoo-hoo, Jenkins . . . I mean, Mabel . . . I say, *George!*") or substituted names that were close (the "Jolly" of "Go to de sto' and git me some-a dat dere Jolly" meant Joy dishwashing liquid). She was vague about time. She never gave you the hour or the minute. It was always "ha'p pas'," "quart' to," or "quart' afta." Thus any time from 3:01 P.M. to 3:24 P.M. was merely "quart' pas'." No one knew from whom she had expropriated the southern expressions that seasoned her speech. When Helen was growing up, Louise would tell her that as long as she had two holes in her nose, she would "be John Brown" if she would ever understand "why de ham-fat" a daughter of hers was so "slub'm" (slovenly), that her hair looked like a "fodder stack," her room like a "debbil's hurrah's nest," that she lacked "mother wit," acted sometimes like a "fyce dog," was a "heathen" because she refused to go to Calvary Baptist Church, and, as for her day-to-day actions, well, everybody knew that "God don' like ugly."

In her later, more corpulent years, Louise liked to sit on the front porch rocking in her rocker or gliding in her glider. She sat and rocked and glided and judged. Of a woman wearing a riotous flower print: "Look at dat gal goin' by. Dere she. Look like any Dolly Vahd'n [Varden]. And she in the fam'ly way fo' sho." Of a prosperous dentist: "His money's awright, but he sho-god is *ugly!*" She covered her face. Every once in a while, she would open her fingers, peek at Dr. Bruce, shudder, and close them again, gliding, gliding.

Louise was very lucky. Forget the odds against hitting the numbers; she hit them virtually at will. Two of her regular numbers were 595 (her brother Herbert's old standby) and 830 (given to her by Helen when she was just a toddler and babbling anything that came into her head), which seemed to come out every August.

The immobilization of James

After James was afflicted, whenever Louise wanted his tip on a number, she would first adjust the asafetida bag she had put around his neck. (Asafetida headed her list of panaceas. The others sounded like ingredients in a you-are-what-you-eat recipe/cure for a constipated, sickly child with rickets and a chest cold: mustard plasters, Epsom salts, cod-liver oil, castor oil, cambric tea.) Then she would point to the numbers she had written down that morning after consulting her dream book. When her husband grinned like a "Chessy ket" (Cheshire cat), she would play that number — in the box, to be on the safe side. On the very day after he was stricken, she had played 421, the number for paralysis, and hit for three hundred dollars.

What she did not know was that James was not paralyzed. When Honeychile had broken the news about Samuel and called herself Hélène Sun-See-A-Ray Schwartz, she had also broken a blood vessel in her father's brain. James's affliction was a bad case of retrograde amnesia. As Louise would have said, he remembered the past like white on rice, but he could not hold on to the present for more than a few seconds at a time. He would start to get up, for example, then forget what he was doing before he had moved perceptibly. He could have talked, but he just had not tried.

For years, Louise had commandeered any help she could get from passersby, neighbors, relatives, and friends to help her carry James into the back yard for exercise and hosing off. The exercise consisted in pushing his head toward his knees and pulling his legs out in front of his body, but he always snapped back into his half-swastika pattern. James's clothes mildewed after the first few months, and there was always the danger of his catching a chill after the hosing. Louise solved that problem by making him a line of stylish ponchos (different materials, patterns, and colors to change with the seasons), which she could just whip off and on whenever he had to be hosed. Louise's brother Herbert had devised a jar-and-bucket contraption for James's waste, and she herself fed him her latest recipes. According to her readings of his facial twitches, veal stuffed with ham mousse barely beat out lamb *bobotie* as his postaffliction favorite.

To Louise, a Jamesian grin meant "yes," and she consulted

her husband on all household matters. She was not far off, since James grinned only when he was having a particularly pleasant memory of the past or had thought of a new way to run a game on Jews. He was, of course, unaware that he kept thinking of the same swindles over and over again and would forget them before he had had time to stand up and get the shells moving. One of his schemes, which recurred every time Louise asked him to give her a tip on the number, was of somehow revising dream books and palming his product off on ignorant Jews as gematria. "Did you dream about a visit from your cousin Sarah?" his copy would read. "Turn to SARAH in the list of names at the back of this numerology book. The number next to that name is G 18-6, which means Genesis 18:6. This verse from the Five Books directs you to 'Make ready quickly three measures of fine meal, knead it, and make cakes upon the hearth.' If you do as directed, such *mazel* you wouldn't believe! If for some reason you cannot do as the verse directs, find other entries in this book that have the number 18-6 or 1-86. Look for hidden clues that will tell you how Sarah's visit will turn out. See also VISIT."

His mind usually jumped then to ways in which he could take advantage of Jewish children. Why stop with the parents? He thought immediately of the local yeshivas. Was there a way, he wondered, to convince them of the need for a know-your-opposition unit on Jesus as a historical figure, using materials that he, of course, would supply them with? What about some *bobbe-myseh* about the day-to-day life of Jesus, tied in maybe with some *shlock* toys and games? As for educational value— hoo-ha! He would devise a series of short-answer quizzes to be used at the end of the unit. When the little *bonditts* of the yeshiva were through with these quizzes, they would be able to tell the *goyim* a thing or two about the Nazarene. "Do you know in what New Testament verse Jesus makes a pun?" the little smart-asses would say. "I'll give you a clue—the name Peter means 'rock.' Give up? Nyah-nyah, Matthew 16:18!" Or they would sidle up to a gentile and whisper, "Nobody knows what Jesus did on the Wednesday before he died." Twenty years later, a Jewish art historian would owe this revelation to James: "Byzantine mosaics, the earliest representations of Jesus, will one day prove to be not just an art technique but an accurate rendering of the cracks in [Christ's] face." James did not remember, of course, but every day he devised the same quiz:

JESUS THE CARPENTER

The purpose of this quiz is to find out what you know about Jesus as an ordinary laborer. Did he do good work? [For the teacher's edition, James planned to add his educator's joke for the day: "Did Jesus know his adz from his elbow?"] Pretend you are a citizen of old Galilee, and answer the following questions:

1. How would you rate Jesus on over-all workmanship?
   ( ) A *balmalocha* ( ) Good ( ) Fair ( ) All thumbs
2. Do you have to wait in for him all day?
   ( ) Yes ( ) No ( ) Sometimes
3. Are his hourly rates ( ) high ( ) average ( ) a bargain?
4. Does he have good work habits?
   ( ) Yes ( ) No ( ) Can't say
5. Is he good at Jewing-down [mental note of James: "Change this phrase in final draft"] his suppliers and thereby passing on a savings to you?
   ( ) Yes ( ) No
6. In cleaning up after a job, how does he rate on a scale of 1 to 10, in which 1 = You could eat off the floor and 10 = Very messy? Insert number here: _____
7. Does he render bills promptly?
   ( ) Yes ( ) No
8. Would you hire him again?
   ( ) Yes ( ) No

James, a memory

James grinned. He was thinking now about his childhood. His earliest memory was of the day his family and the Butlers left the village of Gladstone to go North. The village idiot had waved at them and smiled his sweet but dumb smile. Little James's parents never tired of talking about their adventures in Gladstone.

Gladstone was blessed not only with a village idiot but with a village moron and a village imbecile. They were brothers. Each day they would go to their jobs on the village green. The people of Gladstone felt that it was good for the three boys to work outdoors. The fresh air would do them good. In bad weather, the village moron, with his superior intelligence (IQ 53), could be seen herding his less advantaged brothers and co-workers in out of the rain and under the lean-to that the village had built for them with the proceeds of the triquarterly fish fry and census.

The Gladstonites liked to see what — or, rather, who — was new every nine months. The fish fry was an important part of this head counting, since it was the testing ground for determining which proportion of which kind of fish would give the greatest boost to the fertility curve of Gladstone. Some Gladstonites felt that the matter was already settled, that a 3:1 ratio of porgies to smelts had given sufficient proof of its power back in the summer of 1906. Others plumped for a 5:4:3½ mixture of mackerel, cod, and striped bass or — six of one, half a dozen of the other — an 8:7 blend of smelts and catfish, pointing to the fact that census-taking methods in 1906 were somewhat hit-or-miss and that the years of *their* compounds, 1907 and 1908, had each been only one off the high-water mark. These latter factions, countered the porgy-smelt bloc, could talk all they wanted, but they could not argue with the record book. It was infantile to deny the part their formula had played in the Baby Boom of Aught Six.

By 1919, the total population of Gladstone—not counting the Butlers and the Clarks, who were leaving and who, technically, lived on the outskirts of the restricted and segregated village, but counting the three village dogs—was twelve. The nine people included Josh and Lettie Jones, who were the parents and next-door neighbors of Jed Jones and his wife-sister Maybelle, who were the parents and next-door neighbors of Jody Jones and his wife-sister Lulu, who were responsible for the Baby Boom of Aught Six and also the boomlets of 1907 and 1908. It was Jody and Lulu who, in 1906, had produced twins Clyde and Claude, who were, respectively, the village imbecile and idiot. In 1907, Clarence I was born but succumbed to the croup at three months. In 1908, Clarence II, the pride and joy of the Jones family, was born. Although he was the youngest, Clarence II's natural ability soon evidenced itself. From shoe tying to vacant staring, he was more adept at age nine than Clyde or Claude would ever be.

Clarence II led his older brothers to the green each morning, sat them in their spots in the middle of the sward, made sure they had all their materials, and settled next to Clyde. The brothers made moccasins, at the rate of one-half a day. They made only one size (ladies' 6½B) and for the left foot only. Lulu, their mother-aunt, undid their output every day, but it kept them off the streets. At first it was thought that Claude, the idiot, would hold the others back in any joint endeavor, since all he could do well was drool. But drooling turned out to be an important aspect of moccasin production. While Clyde and Clarence II stared into space waiting for the production line to gain momentum, Claude began chewing and drooling on the piece of leather Lulu put in his mouth on the way to the green each morning. This drooling-chewing process softened the leather, which had become hard and stiff after drying out from the previous day's drooling-chewing, so that Claude's twin brother could more easily fold and crease it in four places and hand it on to Clarence II, who would stitch through the holes that his mother-aunt had punched for him, totally absorbed as he shoved and hauled on the leather thong tied to the small stick.

By the time Clarence II got halfway around with his stitching, the clock in the church tower, had there been a church with a tower with a clock, would have struck three. As it was, the only way to tell it was three o'clock was that the town drunk, Jed Jones, grandfather and great-uncle of the Jones boys, would come stumbling toward the one tree on the village green, would circle around the two-year-old sapling in confusion, and, thinking he was lost in the woods, begin sobbing uncontrollably. Whereupon, all the village Joneses would stop whatever they were doing, look up, and say, "Jed's lost. Must be nigh onto three o'clock." For Lulu, it was time to go pick up her three children-nephews-craftsmen.

James had heard this story about Gladstone and the Jones boys at least one and a half times. And at least that often he had wondered what had happened to the porgy-smelt bloc. And the mackerel-cod-bass people—his favorites—what of them? No matter. He would never forget Claude's incoherent little wave and smile as the Butlers and the Clarks left town. Outsiders, numb to nuance, often ascribed more intelligence to Claude's smile than he was, by Stanford-Binet standards, entitled to. "Look at that moron grin," a wagonload of Jukes once said as they went creaking and kallikaking past the village green. But it could not be doubted that this scion of Virginia aristocracy had the family smile. It was rumored that Claude and his brothers were related on both sides — that is to say, on one side — to the Randolphs. Thinking of little Claude, James daily reproduced the patrician simper of one of the F.F.V.

How James's affliction affected Helen

"I don't have *eppes* an idea of how to support my children," Helen said as she sat down to assess her situation after the breakup with Samuel. "How long can we go on living on the proceeds from Daddy's backlist? It would be an *averah* if I can't get up off my rusty-dusty and come up with an idea for making some heavy *gelt*." Her monologue over, she listed her talents on a piece of paper:

1. Mimicry
2. Making head equations
3. Singing
4. Piano playing

As far as she knew, there was no great call for black female impressionists. ("And now, my impression of James Cagney showing Mae West how to do the buck-and-wing." Cagney: *Tappety-tap, tappety-tap.* Mae West: *Humpety-hump, humpety-hump.* Cagney: "You, you, you dirty rat—I said the *buck*-and-wing!") As for her head equations, she refused to commercialize them. Operating on numbers 3 and 4 were all the pluses and minuses of cliché, but she picked number 4.

As she began practicing, her head equation was:

$$88BW = \infty M + R$$

where B = black keys (or Helen's folly), reminders
W = white keys (or Samuel's head), poundings
M = Money, dollars
R = road, years

3 Helenic Letters

The first letters

When Christine was a year old and Jimmie C. a baby, Helen began sending them letters, which Louise read to them. The letters always said the same thing:

Chicago [or wherever]

Dear Kids—

Mommy misses you and sends you ∞ love.

Louise sometimes read "∞ love" as "lazy-eight love" and sometimes as "scribble love," until Helen, home on one of her rare visits, straightened her out. Then she read it as "infanty love," thinking it was a special term for babies.

The children paid no attention to Helen's letters.

When Christine was three and Jimmie C. two, Helen's letters read:

Pittsburgh [or wherever]

Mommy would give anything to just stay at home and take care of her precious babies.

One day, Christine looked up from her coloring book (a left-over copy of her grandfather's best-selling *Esau Gets a Shave*) and snatched the letter from her grandmother's hand. Louise let the child play with the letter and went into the kitchen to prepare *sop buntut Djakarta*. Christine stared at the letter for some time, then, carefully selecting her Crayolas (a huge set that boasted exotic colors like red, green, and blue as well as the standard mauve, puce, chartreuse, and oregano), she composed a reply:

philadelphia

dear mom cut the crab

Helen made a moue of wry appreciation when she got her daughter's letter, wrote her by return mail that intentional mirror writing had gone out with Leonardo, and began sending the kids letters about her own childhood remarkable for their Helenic this and that.

Selected excerpts from Helen's letters to her children: the first twelve years

Minneapolis

Kindergarten! The smell of finger paints at George Brooks Elementary School: wet plaster going sour. Every afternoon at two, we would have a container of piss-warm milk and three graham crackers. Every afternoon at fourteen minutes after two, Roselle Morgan would spit up. We left a big space around her and went to sleep on our little rag rugs, our little noses twitching like rabbits', our tender sinuses cleared.

Des Moines

My first boyfriend was a *nayfish* named Roger. I sat next to him in Miss Barton's first-grade class. One day Roger said to me, "Malvina is my girlfriend. I like Malvina." I looked at

Malvina, the most beautiful first-grader in America. "Frankly, I don't see what you see in her," I lied. "Why don't you like me instead?" "Okay," he agreed, and I took him home with me for lunch. Louise made *coq au vin* that day, as I recall. Roger asked for a peanut butter sandwich, which he dipped in that divine sauce. A *chaloshes!* I dropped him at recess the next day and gave him back to Malvina.

Boston

Time: World War II. *Place:* Mrs. Dannenbaum's room, Shoemaker Junior High School. As the scene opens, the students are singing patriotic songs.

"We're the Seabees of the Navy. We can build and we can fight!"

". . . oh, nothing can stop the Army Air Corps — except the Seabees."

Mrs. Dannenbaum's husband was a Seabee.

San Francisco

TV? Feh! In my day we had THE MOVIES! In our old neighborhood in West Philadelphia, we had the Cross Keys, the Nixon, the State, the Belmont, the Mayfair, and—bedbuggiest of all—the good old Haverford, affectionately known as the Dump. At the Dump, we ate until we thought we would *plotz.* Do they still make Grade A's, Baby Ruth, Payday, Milk Duds, Rally, Hershey (with and without almonds), Butterfinger, Tootsie Rolls, Jujyfruits, Mr. Goodbar, Oh Henry, Raisinets, Good and Plenty, Dots, Milk Shake, Sno-Caps, Goobers, Chuckles, Hershey's Kisses, Nestlé's Crunch, and Goldenberg's Peanut Chews? Mounds, Almond Joy, polly seeds, candy corn, candy buttons, candy-in-the-tin-fluted-cups-with-the-little-tin-spoon, Mary Janes? What about jelly apples, wax lips, fudgicles, ice cream cake?

For eleven cents we could see a double feature, five cartoons, a serial, and a footrace. We had cowboys like "Wild Bill" Elliott, Johnny Mack Brown, Bob Steele, Don "Red" Barry, Tim McCoy, Tim Holt. I can't relate to a generation that thinks that the real Tarzan is Gordon Scott. *We* had the only real Tarzan — Johnny Weissmuller — and Jane and Cheetah and Boy. (The guys in the background saying "Ooga-booga" were jazz musicians who didn't have a gig that week.) We had Maria Montez and Jon Hall, Sabu and Turhan Bey. We had *Spy Smasher*. But best of all, we had *Perils of Nyoka,* known to the neighborhood kids, of course, as *Pearls*.

Every week we'd leave Nyoka, Queen of the Jungle, and her boyfriend Larry in a *mess*, honey—they were sure to die. We'd rush to the Dump the next Saturday—and the episode would start practically in the middle of the previous week's chapter. That way, only half the new chapter was really *new*. As for the "impossible" situation—a *nebbech* would have sneered at it. Something would always be added that hadn't been shown the week before. Suppose old Nyoka was in a room with steel spikes sticking out of the walls. Suppose the room was getting smaller and smaller. Suppose you *knew* she was about to be iron-maidened to death. The next week the spikes would be about as close as Camden, New Jersey, when Larry, who was supposed to be *in* Camden (or thereabouts), would rush in, throw a piece of bubble gum into the machinery — and away all spikes. We fell for this week after week.

Then there was the footrace — a short feature of a *ridiculous* cross-country race with a lot of wildly dressed, scrocky-looking competitors cheating their way toward the finish line. When you first went into the Dump, you got a stub with a number on it. If your number matched the number of the nerd who won the race, you got a prize — a bicycle or something. Nobody I knew ever won anything. The movie manager's son opened a bicycle shop on his fourteenth birthday. He was found Schwinned to death on the day after his fourteenth birthday.

Aside from the Scheherazade Perplex (Maria-Jon-Turhan-Sabu), over the years I had two movie idols: Jane Powell and Barbara Stanwyck (weep, Yma Sumac, over the range of Helen Clark!). I could be as moved by *Song of the Open Road* as by *The Strange Love of Martha Ivers;* by *Rich, Young, and Pretty, A Date with Judy, Luxury Liner,* and *Small Town Girl* as by *Double Indemnity* and *Sorry, Wrong Number. Nu,* what moves you kids? Road Runner and Coyote!

Wapshot-on-the-Chronicle, Mass.
What ever happened to Toughie Brasuhn?

Baltimore
I wonder if the sign I used to see on Spruce Street is still there? It read: LITTLE FRIENDS DAY SCHOOL. I always expected a bunch of dwarf Quakers to run out of the building.

Denver
Scene: Overbrook High School homeroom. Brenda Schaeffer is telling her classmates Arlene Melnick and Helen Clark about her weekend. How she and her family were invited for Friday-night dinner to the home of a business acquaintance of her father. How at this house, a little old lady with the burning eyes of a fanatic was lighting candles. How this same L.O.L., when she lit the candles, did this also. *(She demonstrates for Arlene and Helen, drawing her arms toward herself over the imaginary flame of the imaginary candle.)* "Now, what was that all about?" says Brenda, daughter of the biggest pretzel maker in Wynnefield (it was her sacred duty to provide free pretzels for all her friends' pajama parties). Arlene shakes her head like an ignorant *shiksa.* It is left for Helen the *shvartze* to explain to

these *apikorsim* the tradition of the *shabbes* candles. "Oh,"
says Brenda, her curiosity quenched, her religiosity quashed, "I
just thought it was some weird European way of warming your
hands."

Cincinnati

My Worst School Assignment: Mr. Storch, criminally insane
English teacher, told our class that we should get to know our
city more intimately. "I volunteer to fuck Market Street,"
whispered Joey Hershkowitz, class clown. This was my assignment: to do a first-hand report on all the statues in center
city, from river to river, from Vine to Pine. Yes, he did mean
first hand. Yes, "river to river" did refer to our beloved
Schuylkill and our renowned Delaware. Yes, Vine Street is not
exactly cheek by jowl with Pine Street. Yes, it was the dead of
winter. Yes, I did freeze my *kishkas*. Yes, Storch is probably
still at large in the Philadelphia school system.

New York

Advantages Philadelphia Has Over New York: Fairmount Park
(more than four times bigger and better than Central Park). The
park's colonial houses: Strawberry Mansion, Lemon Hill, Belmont Mansion. The weeping cherry trees of George's Hill, the
Playhouse in the Park, Robin Hood Dell. Hoagies (more than
four times better than heroes). Steak sandwiches (they don't
make them here the way they do at home: layers of paper-thin
beef smothered in grilled onions; melted cheese, optional; cat-
sup, yet another option!). People who wait for you to get off the
subway before they try to get on. Smoking on the subway plat-
form. Row houses. The Philadelphia Orchestra. Mustard pretzels *with* mustard (in New York—would you believe?—they
sell mustard pretzels *plain*). Red and white police cars so you
can shout, "Look out, the red devil's coming!"

Things I Miss About Philadelphia That Are Long Gone: Woodside Amusement Park. The Mastbaum movie theater. The Chinese Wall. Schuylkill Punch (no soup in the country is as chunky, as stick-to-your-ribs as the witches' brew we called water). The raspy spiel of a huckster named Jesus.

Detroit

We have had two ashtrays for as long as I can remember. One says: *Honi soit qui mal y pense.* The other one is my favorite. It says: *De robe flétrie/nul ne souci.* The *flétrie* ashtray is off-white ceramic. Two brown slashes at each of the corners accent the four depressions for cigarettes. Rounded red and green leaves sprig each of the four rim sections. The message is on the floor of the ashtray; it is painted in two lines in brown handwriting. Another sprig of rounded red and green leaves is just under the words. Touch it, children, and think of me.

Chattanooga

A Job I Had Before Going on the Road: I am working in a dry cleaner's. A member walks in. She is huge and powerful. She is permanently ready to take offense. Her eyes slit in indignation, her lips form a sullen pout.

SHE *(with eye-slitting and pouting):* Where mah clo'es? They **been** here since Tuesday! *(This is Wednesday.)*

ME *(placatingly):* The tailor will get to your alterations as soon as his fracture heals, his wife gets out of the hospital, and the baby's funeral is over.

SHE *(the standard slit/pout):* Don' gimme no scuses. Y'all must think I'm simple. They better *be* here t'morra, two-three o'clock. *(She lumbers out.)*

The expression on her back shows that she likes me, else I would now be on the floor with a broken nose.

I close the shop and walk across the street to catch the trolley.

I am standing directly opposite the shop when along comes Mr. Johnson with a huge pile of dirty clothes. I can smell them from where I stand. I stagger and hold on to a telephone pole for support. Mr. Johnson looks disconcerted. The shop is obviously closed. He stares at the door. Obviously, the thought of turning around and going back home, a matter of about fifty feet, does not occur to him in his disoriented condition. Oh-oh. He spots me. A relieved smile lights up his face. I look down the trolley tracks. I can see the trolley coming, but I can't quite hear it. Meanwhile Mr. Johnson has dashed across the street.

HE: Hi.

ME: Hi.

HE *(smiling):* Glad I caught you.

ME: Oh?

HE: Could you do me a favor?

ME *(trying to get downwind of the funky* shmatte *he is waving under my nose):* What?

HE: Could you check these in for me?

ME *(flabbergasted):* Look, Mr. Johnson, the store is closed. I've had a hard day and I'm anxious to get home and my trolley's coming.

HE *(considering the reasonableness of my speech):* I see. Well, couldn't you just open the door and throw them in on the floor? I don't mind. They're dirty anyway.

ME *(lying):* If I open the door any time between now and eight o'clock tomorrow morning, the alarm will go off.

HE *(disappointed):* Oh. *(Then, brilliant idea!)* Tell you what. Why don't you just take these home with you and then bring them in with you in the morning?

The trolley rattles toward us, its metallic jig fortunately out-clamoring my words as I tell Mr. Johnson where to go, what to do, and what to kiss. He is still standing there cradling his redolent bundle as I settle back and watch him recede until he is a raggedy blue dot.

Davenport
Pensées d'Hélène: I used to think that Rudy Vallee was short for Rudolph Valentino. He is.

Minneapolis
Jobs I Have Had *(cont'd):* I once demonstrated fill-in painting at a ten-cent store. I would gather a crowd around me and take out my Sylvan Scene Number 10 cardboard with its jigsaw of shapes, all numbered. For about three minutes, I would do my cyborgian routine, showing the shoppers how to put bleeding-gum crimson in all the 5's — never in a 7 or a 2. Then, all of a sudden, I would go crazy. I could not bring myself to stay within the lines. My blind-man blue would stray from the 52-to-75 lower-sky section, where it belonged, and would begin to invade the cavity yellow of the 45-to-48 cloud tinge. But the management kept me on. They merely warned against sloppiness, saying prissily, "Neatness counts, neatness counts."

I kicked at the traces. I started to seek out the potential artists among the old men and housewives who were my students. I told them not to bother with these *shlock* paints, to save up and buy some real oils or watercolors or even crayons. I showed them how to mix pigments, stretch canvas, keeping just ahead of them by studying at night. For my first life class, I invited the harridan whose regular mooch was ten feet on either side of the double doors of that Woolworth's to come in and pose for us. Each of my students gave her ten cents. The total take was more than she could have hustled outside in the cold. In the middle of their first fumbling attempts at what critic Bernard

Mosher has called "gesture drawing," I was fired. "Don't stay in the lines!" I managed to shout over my shoulder as I was thrown out.

Because of my experience with painting-by-numbers (I didn't bother to mention that I'd been fired), I had the perfect background and experience for my next job. Heshie Herschberg, dress wholesaler *extraordinaire,* was faced with a Chicken Little disaster. A five-thousand-lot shipment of sky-blue summer cottons had arrived with a piece of sky missing. With an empty display of resistance, each of the dresses, stewing in celestial juices, had refused to dye. There it was—a bull's-eye about the size of a dime that would, if given a chance, ring the size 12 average whatsis of the size 12 average shopper (the biggest market for this simply cut basic that you could shop anywhere in).

As Heshie outlined it, this was my job: "Listen closely, girlie, this particular number, it's my bread and it's my butter. And to me a life isn't a life without it should have bread and butter. If, God forbid, I shouldn't be able to unload this number as per usual, my wife Sadie will never let me hear the end of it that 'Revka-down-the-block-she-should-drop-dead was able to go to Florida and get a nice tan and me—whose husband is supposed to be such a big deal in the garment world, yet—I can't afford to go around the corner.' Now, this number is going to roll past you at a rate of, oh, one every five seconds, but we can adjust—faster, slower, you name it. I want you should wash your hands real good. I want people that they are walking down the street and never saw you before in their lives that they should take time out to pass a remark that such clean hands they have never before seen on a person, except maybe on a surgeon as he slips into the rubber gloves, and what with the dope and *dreck* that they had when they saw it on the surgeon, his hands were pretty blurry, but on a bet they would say yours were cleaner. With these clean, clean hands, I want you should gently grasp each of these number 12 regulars here, pull it tenderly toward you, and then with these No. 2 Magic Markers that my brother Morris, he should live and be well, has seen fit to provide me with at a special discount, with these No. 2 Magic Markers, you should with a swish and with a swash fill in that little dime-size white spot just below where the *pupik* should be. Sam Spade—pardon me—with an X-ray machine should be able to look at this dress and not see dark edges from where the Magic Marker overlapped onto the part that's already blue. He should not be able to see one little hint, one little breath, one little zephyr of a white spot left over from where the No. 2 Magic Marker, God forbid, missed. Have I conveyed the importance of this task? Yes? Well, then, begin. I will stand here until I see that you've got the hang of it, the swing of it, the *art* of it. Good, good. I knew you were the one for the job when I saw you walk in. I will come back in an hour to check on your progress. I figure that with hard work and steady effort, you should be able to say to me at six o'clock on the dot, just before I am ready to lock up and go home to Sadie the *nudzh,* 'Mr. Herschberg, I have the honor of informing you that I have finished my appointed task and the number 12 average is, thank God, ready for shipment.' "

Well, children, the finish is, I walked out of there cross-eyed. Before I had gone three feet, I had to resist the impulse to color the spots before my eyes. That cleared up after a block or two, but now if I see a white spot on a dog, I want to fill it in.

I saw Sadie Herschberg as I was leaving. She was so fat she could have used a bra on her kneecaps — about a 38D. I mean to tell you, she was 360 *degrees* fat. Herschberg himself was a beanpole — a *loksh.* When they went down the street together, one streaking, one shloomping, they looked like a lame number 10 or maybe an 01, depending.

Newark

A few minutes ago, I was listening to the local TV newscast, and the announcer said something like: "Fred Jones of Rahway, New Jersey, has been indicted for milking a bankrupt kosher meat company of thirty-three thousand dollars." *Milchedig* and *fleishedig!* A *frosk in pisk* to Fred.

Happiness, Montana

What am I doing in Montana? What am I doing in a town called Happiness? Nothing. So I make long-distance calls to the circulation departments of the *New York Review of Books*, the *Partisan Review,* and *Commentary.* I say, "Hello, [*name of magazine*]? This is Miss Cream at your fulfillment house in Iowa [all fulfillment houses are in Iowa]. Could you please give me a list of your subscribers in Happiness, Montana? Our computer has gone haywire, and we are double-checking our records." There is a short wait, and I look out the window at the pyorrheic mountains while New York checks its records. New York comes back on the line with a list of two names. In each case, they are the same two names.

Then I call up the local newspaper, the *Happiness Chronicle*, and speak to the editor-publisher-reporter-layout man. I say, "Hello, *Chronicle?* This is *Life* magazine calling. Miss Sweet here. We are doing a survey on ethnic and religious groups in Montana and want to include your town in the survey. We know you're on top of things out there, and if you can help us we'd be glad to mention your name in the piece we're doing. Our question is twofold: *(a)* How many members of the Jewish faith are there in Happiness? And *(b)* What are their names?" The editor-publisher-reporter-layout man says, "Well, yes, there's a Jewish fella out here—Mel Blankenstein. He's the only one of Jewish persuasion in this town. A real nice fella too. Keeps to himself. Joe Kerry down to the superette does land-office business on farmer's cheese because of Mel, I hear tell.'' Then I say, ''Thank you so much for your cooperation, sir. Look for your name and the name of that fine paper you're running in the pages of *Life* magazine.''

I hang up and I compare my *Partisan Review–New York Review – Commentary* list. Yes, Mel Blankenstein, reader of the above-named magazines, is one and the same Mel Blankenstein that is the nice fellow who has a taste for pot cheese. But— wait a minute. There is another name on my magazine list. What of that? I stare at the name. The name is Leonard Birdsong III. Leonard (surely Lenny) Birdsong (Feigelzinger, perhaps, or is the last name simply a flight of Wasp-inspired fantasy?). And III, of course just means third generation on Rivington Street. I now know something that nobody else in town knows — not even Mel. I know that Leonard Birdsong III is a crypto-Jew. My God, he's passing—the *geshmat!*

I look at the two-page phone book and, yes, there they both are, the proud Jew and the *meshumad*. I decide to send Lenny a note before I leave town. My note will say: ''Dear Lenny: Can you come over Friday night? My wife will fix you a meal like in the olden days. A little *gefilte* fish, a little *chrain*, some nice hot soup, a nice chicken. Who knows? Maybe a *kugel* even. Come on, Lenny, enough shlepping *trayf* home from Kerry's Superette (though the pot cheese is unbeatable — imported from New York). It would be an *averah* if we Jews didn't stick to- gether, especially way out here. I am so sick and tired of look- ing at *goyim* I could *plotz!* We'll expect you early. Best, Mel. P.S.: If you like pepper, please bring your own. We don't keep it in the house. It's such a *goyische* thing, pepper, but to each his own. M.B. P.P.S.: Bring this note with you. I am writing my autobiography and ask all my friends to save any invitations, postcards, etc., I send them. I could have sent you a carbon, but I feel it's so much nicer to receive an original. So bring it with you and I'll keep it on file under *F* for Feigelzinger. You can refer to it whenever you wish to — if you happen to be writing your memoirs also. M.B.''

I feel I have performed a real *mitzvah* for Lenny, and I look up at the clock and see that if I hurry, I just have time to make it to the local movie house for the cultural event of the season. They are having a John Agar Festival.

4 Pets, Playmates, Pedagogues

Christine and Jimmie C.

From the Jewish side of the family Christine inherited kinky hair and dark, thin skin (she was about a 7 on the color scale and touchy). From the black side of her family she inherited sharp features, rhythm, and thin skin (she *was* touchy). Two years after this book ends, she would be the ideal beauty of legend and folklore—name the nationality, specify the ethnic group. Whatever your legends and folklore bring to mind for beauty of face and form, she would be *it*, honey. Christine was no ordinary child. She was born with a caul, which her first lusty cries rent in eight. Aside from her precocity at mirror writing, she had her mother's love of words, their nuance and cadence, their juice and pith, their variety and precision, their rock and wry. When told at an early age that she would one day have to seek out her father to learn the secret of her birth, she said, "I am going to *find* that motherfucker." In her view, the last word was merely *le mot juste*.

Where Christine was salty, Jimmie C. was sweet. He was a 5 on the color scale and was gentle of countenance and manner.

He had inherited his mother's sweet voice, and he was given to making mysterious, sometimes asinine pronouncements, which he often sang. From Louise he had inherited a tendency to make up words. Thus this exchange between Louise and her grandson:

LOUISE: Dessa cream on your boondoggle? *(Trans.: "Condensed milk on your boondoggle?")* How 'bout some mo' ingers on dem dere fish eggs, sweetness? *(She points to the onions on the red caviar.)*

JIMMIE C. *(looking sweetly at his plate):* I have never had such a wonderful dish. It is like biting into tiny orange-colored grapeskins filled with cod-liver oil. *(He snaps his fingers.)* I know! These wonderful little things here before me in the bowl of my grandmother are like *(and he sings, in the key of G)* tiny little round orange jelly balls. *(On a letter scale with legatos indicated by hyphens and rests by commas, this phrase would be GG-CC-G, FF, EDC.)* From now on I shall call these good things trevels.

Christine loved her younger brother, but often she was exasperated by him. Every day she would sit on the bottom step in the living room and read to Jimmie C. He stopped her gently once and sang, "But nevertheless and winnie-the-pooh" — which was one of his favorite expressions — "I get Christopher Wren and Christopher Robin confused."

Christine looked at him and, in a rare instance, made up her own word. "You are a stone *scrock*, boy."

The family liked Christine's new word and gave it inflections for various occasions:

LOUISE: Mayhaps if I'm careful, I won't scrock up dis yere recipe. Las' time, it turned out right scrockified, dey tell me. *I* liked it, though. Thought it tayce real good.

JIMMIE C. *(gently):* Uncle Herbie can be just a tiny bit scrocky sometimes.

HELEN *(by letter):* The TV set in my hotel room just scrocked out.

CHRISTINE: Oh, fuck scrock!

Louise's dream

When Christine was about two and a half, she got her nickname. It came to Louise in a dream. Louise was walking down a dusty road with Christine on a gray, overcast day, when suddenly the clouds parted and a ray of sunshine beamed down right in front of the child. Out of this beam of sunshine came a high-pitched, squeaky voice. "And her name shall be Oriole," squeaked the voice.

When Louise woke up that morning, she went straight to her dream book. Next to the word ORIOLE was the number 483. Louise played it in the box for three days. On the third day, it came out and she hit for five hundred dollars, her first hit in more than three weeks (the longest dry spell she could remember). She had told James about her dream on that first day, when she was hosing him off, and he had grinned. She had told her whole family and all her neighbors, as she usually did with her important dreams. Sometimes the entire neighborhood hit if they could figure out what Louise was saying.

Everyone thought that Louise had found a great nickname for Christine. People had been calling the child various things as she toddled down the street after Louise, cursing them under her breath. They called her Brown Sugar and Chocolate Drop and Honeybun. But when they looked at Christine's rich brown color and her wide smile full of sugar-white baby teeth, they said to themselves, "Why, that child does put me in mind of an Oreo cookie — side view." And that is how Oreo got her name. Nobody knew that Louise was saying "Oriole." When, through a fluke, Louise found out what everyone thought she was saying, it was all right with her. "I never did like *flyin'* birds, jus' eatin' ones," she said. "But I jus' loves dem Oreos." And this time she meant what everyone else meant.

Pets

Naming was very important in the Clark family. Here are two other instances. Herbert Butler, Louise's wandering brother, brought back a parakeet for the children after one of his journeys. It was powder blue. Only its color (Louise's favorite) saved the bird from her total disdain ("He ain' eem a flyin' bird, jus' a settin' one"). Oreo called the parakeet Jocko, Jimmie C. sweetly called him Sky. Louise, because she could not bother to remember either of these names, called him "bird," not as a name but as a category, just as she called various other pets of friends and family "cat," "dog," and "goldfish." She sometimes had to call all the categories before she got to the right one: "Take dat go'fish . . . I mean, cat . . . I say, *dog* out fo' a walk." After two months, in confusion over his true name, Sky-Jocko-bird died, a living (or rather, dead) example of acute muddleheadedness.

That was also the year that Oreo and Jimmie C. had the German shepherd. Everyone said he was the smartest German shepherd anyone had ever seen in the neighborhood. He could do anything — fetch the paper, roll over and play dead, shake hands. He would romp with the children for hours on end, and they would take turns riding on his powerful back. He ran back and forth between the children, his handsome eyes shining, his powerful muscles rippling as he leaped a fence to get a ball Oreo or Jimmie C. had thrown. His papers said his name was Otto, followed by a string of unpronounceable names, but the family decided to call him something else. This time they quickly agreed on a name, one that Helen suggested. They called him Fleck. "A German shepherd should have a German name," Helen had written to them when the family consulted her, getting her jollies over the fact that she had named the princely German shepherd plain old ordinary Spot. Louise said, "Dat Fleck, he eat like any starve-gut dog," and she delighted in fixing him special meat dishes that no German shepherd before him had ever had, dishes like *daube de boeuf à la Provençale* and *kofta kari*. Then misfortune struck — or, rather, bit. Fleck got into the habit of biting strangers, and the Clarks had to get rid of him. The whole family was sad. Jimmie C. summed up their feelings when he said, "He was a nice guy, that Fleck. If he could cure himself of that bad biting habit, brought on by homesickness, I'm sure, he might be able to find a suitable flock—maybe out West, where the employment situation for shepherds is better—and be able to bring his wife and children over from the fatherland."

"*Auf Wiedersehen,*" said Fleck when it was time to go. "*Ein feste Burg ist unser Gott.*" (It was not clear whether he feared Bach or Luther more—the old Rodgers-or-Hart dilemma.)

Oreo and Jimmie C. had to find a new playmate.

Other playmates

One of their playmates was their grandfather. As soon as the children were big enough, they would tumble James to the floor and play with him as if he were a piece of eccentric cordwood. Whenever Louise waxed the kitchen floor, they would get James onto a throw rug and drag him into the kitchen, where they would give him a nice spin and watch him revolve, his half swastika doubling in the shininess.

Once when Louise saw them doing this, she admonished the rambunctious children. "Y'all play nice, you yere me? Hard head make soft behind. Don' make me nervy. Doct' say I got high pretension." She went on fixing the *tamago dashimaki* she was taking to her friend Lurline at Mercy-Douglass Hospital. She decided to eat the omelet herself, since it would not survive the journey. Then she put on her hat and said, "Now, Oreo, you and Jimmie C. put James back in de lib'm room right now. He had 'nough 'citement fo' one day. 'Sides, look like to me he right dizzy." She paused to think. "I greb'mine take the G bus [I've a great mind to take the G bus], 'cause it fasta dan dat ol' trolley. I will cenny be glad to see Lurline on her feet again. Thank de good Lord her sickness not ligament."

"Malignant," Oreo said mechanically.

"Moligment," Louise amended. "Oreo, you in charge. Take care yo' sweet brother and stay in de back yard."

The children wiped the excess wax off their grandfather and put him back in his corner in the living room. They went into the back yard to play. Mrs. Dockery, their next-door neighbor, was in her yard watching her brindle tomcat fight with an alley cat. She watched for some time, then she turned to Oreo and Jimmie C. and said, "My cat's a coward." Jimmie C. had his fingers in his ears at the time, and he heard Mrs. Dockery's simple sentence as "Mah cassa cowah." Jimmie C. was delighted. He decided to use this wonderful new expression as the radical for a radical second language. "Cha-key-key-wah, mah-cassa-cowah," he would sing mysteriously in front of strangers. "Freck-a-louse-poop!"

Oreo recognized the value of Jimmie C.'s cha-key-key-wah language over the years. For her, it served the same purpose as black slang. She often used it on shopkeepers who lapsed into Yiddish or Italian. It was her way of saying, "Talk about mother tongues — try to figure out *this* one, you mothers. If you guess *this* word, we'll ring the changes on it until it means *that*."

Whenever they played together, if Oreo thought her brother

had said something silly or stupid or sweet, she would make one of her savage "suppose" remarks. Both children had the habit of, in Jimmie C.'s phrase, "jooging" (the *o*'s of "good") in their ears—to get at an itch that ran in the family. Once when they were both doing this, Jimmie C. said, quite seriously, "Let's put our wax together and make a candle."

Oreo answered, "Suppose you were sliding on a banister and it turned into a razor blade."

Jimmie C. fainted.

Oreo was very sorry when that happened. She did not really want to be mean to her sweet little brother, but sometimes it was a case of simple justice. When Jimmie C. asked her whether there was such a thing as an emergency semicolon (of course!), she answered, "Suppose you were putting Visine in your eyes and it turned into sulfuric acid."

Jimmie C. fainted.

Oreo resolved to give up her "suppose" game until she found a less deserving person to use it on.

One day Jimmie C. came to Oreo and said gently, "Suffer the little children to come unto me." This was his derivative way of asking her to gather all the kids on the block for a special outing. Soon there were eighteen children of eighteen colors, sizes, shapes, and ages milling about in the Clarks' back yard. (The eighty-one-year-old qualified on the grounds of demonstrable dotage.) Jimmie C. explained to them that his grandmother was at that moment making a six-foot-long hoagie à la Louise that could be cut into as many sections as there were children and that he knew of a great place to have a picnic.

All the children jumped up and down shouting that they did not want to go. Oreo gave them a threatening look, and they gave in.

Jimmie C. ran into the house and came back with a plastic bucket. He went to the side of the house and turned on the garden tap. And, lo, the bucket did fill up with foamy orange Kool-Aid.

The children gasped. Petey Brooks, the eighty-one-year-old, said wistfully, "In my yard it always comes out water." All assembled thought they had witnessed a miracle.

But honest Jimmie C. laughed his tinkly, musical laugh and sang, "The Kool-Aid was already in the bucket." Oreo thought her brother was a prize scrock for letting the kids know this, but she kept her peace.

And so they set off. All the children took turns carrying the Kool-Aid bucket and slopping it all over their sneakers and jeans. They had been walking for about fifteen minutes when Petey Brooks, who was in bad shape for his age, said diplomatically, "Where the fuck *is* this park?"

"You'll see, you'll see," said Jimmie C. "It's near nobby."

"I don't remember any park near here," said Petey.

And Jimmie C. said unto them, "O ye of little faith, it's just around the grabus."

They turned the grabus, or corner, onto another street. A plain street. No park. "So where's the park?" Oreo asked.

Jimmie C. looked stunned. "It *should* be right nobby."

But it wasn't.

"I'm tired," said Petey.

"So am I," said seventeen other voices.

Oreo took over. "Let's sit down here." They ranged out over the steps of a row of row houses. Oreo opened her paper bag and took out her section (the best) of the hoagie à la Louise. She dipped her paper cup into the half inch of Kool-Aid that had not spilled on the way. Everyone else did the same. Then they stared at Jimmie C.

He smiled sweetly at them. Finally, when they were almost through chewing and swallowing and staring, a glow transfigured Jimmie C.'s face. "I know what!" he exclaimed. He chuckled musically to himself.

"What, fool? Speak up," said Oreo.

Jimmie C. ascended to the top step, stretched out his arms to the multitude, and sang, "I dreamt the park!"

Oreo looked at him in disgust, then she had to turn and protect him from thirty-six fists, handicapped though they were by the remnants of the hoagie à la Louise they were still clutching. Jimmie C. thoughtfully advised them to hold on to this sustenance, for they would need nourishment on the long journey back home.

Oreo expressed the sentiments of the whole group when she looked at her little brother and said slowly, "You are a *yold.* You and your jive dream parks."

Oreo's tutors

Oreo did not go to school. With the income from James's backlist, Louise's numbers, and Helen's piano playing, the family was able to hire special tutors for Oreo. Professor Lindau, renowned linguist and blood donor, was her English tutor. He spoke in roots. He would come in after his daily blood-bank appointment mumbling, "How are you this morning, my vein, my blood?" which was not a comment on his most recent donation but a greeting to Oreo. He would then toss Oreo a volume of one of his two idols, Partridge or Onions, and Oreo would have to figure out what he meant by consulting the book. Thus his greeting was a simple "How are you this morning, macushla?" Professor Lindau talked so much about Partridge and Onions that Louise was inspired to invent *perdrix en poirier à l'oignon.*

One day, Professor Lindau came in, in a bad mood. He ranted fitfully about his girlfriend. "That wedge!" he shouted. "What can one do with a wedge like that?" he asked rhetorically.

Oreo was puzzled, so the professor tossed her the desk copy of

Partridge. After following a trail of false roots and camouflaged cognates, she came to Partridge's assertion that *cunt* (or, as Partridge put it, *"c*nt"*) derived from the Latin *cunnus,* which was related to *cuneus,* or "wedge." Eric went on to say that the word had been considered obscene since about 1700, adding that "the dramatist Fletcher, who was no prude, went no further than 'They write *sunt* with a C, which is abominable', in *The Spanish Curate.* Had the late Sir James Murray courageously included the word, and spelt it in full, in the great O.E.D., the situation would be different; . . . (Yet the O.E.D. gave *prick:* why this further injustice to women?) . . . (It is somewhat less international than *f**k,* q.v.)"

Oreo fell off her chair laughing at this witty entry in Partridge. When she got herself together, she shook her head. Her *sprachgefühl* told her that Eric was stretching a point (or, rather, a wedge) and that the professor was perpetuating Partridge's error by persisting in this pie-eyed usage. She had never been misled by her *sprachgefühl,* and as she thumbed through a later edition of Partridge, she found that that worthy had corrected himself in a supplement: "*cunt* (p. 198) cannot be from the L. word but is certainly cognate with O.E. *cwithe,* 'the womb' (with a Gothic parallel); cf. mod. English *come,* ex O.E. *cweman.* The *-nt,* which is difficult to explain, was already present in O.E. *kunte.* The radical would seem to be *cu* (in O.E. *cwe*), which app. = quintessential physical femineity . . . and partly explains why, in India, the cow is a sacred animal."

Oreo fell off her chair laughing at the part about the cow. She was, after all, just a child in her mid-units. Then she pointed out the passage in the supplement to the professor.

"I know, I know," he said, dismissing her quibble. "But I like the *idea* of wedge. It whips." When Oreo looked puzzled again, he tossed her volume 12 of the O.E.D.

Oreo became adept at instantaneous translations of the professor's rhizomorphs. "Mr. Benton is worn out by child-bearing. Of course, his paper was an ill-starred bottle. I don't wonder he threatened to sprinkle himself with sacrificial meal."

"You mean," said Oreo, "that Benton is effete, his paper was a disaster, a fiasco, and he wanted to immolate himself."

The professor was impressed but not struck dumb. "I am phonofounded," he said logodaedalyly.

Once in an adjective-adverb drill, Oreo wrote: "He felt badly." The professor was furious and viciously crossed out the *ly*. He was ashamed of Oreo.

Oreo looked him dead in the eye and said, "I am writing a story about a repentant but recidivous rapist. In the story, this repentant rapist catches his hand in a wringer. Therefore, when he goes out, recidivously, to rape, he feels both bad and badly."

The professor kissed Oreo on both cheeks.

Oreo was still angry with him for doubting her, and in her story about the rapist she added such abominations as: "The Empire State Building rises penisly to the sky. As architecture, manurially speaking, it stinks." She felt it appropriate to employ genito-scatological adverbs to express academic vexation.

The professor wept and promised never to cross out her *ly*'s until he was sure of her intentions.

A few months later, the professor's gait was bouncier as he came up the front steps. His blood donations seemed to be more and more a source of comfort and anemia to him. Oreo found out that much of the credit for the new Lindau belonged to his latest girlfriend, a wedge of a different fit. Oreo overheard him mumbling happily to himself about the many joyous conflations he and his new friend had had together. That one was easy for Oreo to figure out. "Conflation, from *conflare*, 'to blow together,' " she said to herself. "Oh, shit. The professor's just talking about plain old sixty-nine."

Oreo's milkman, Milton, although not officially a tutor, was one of her favorite teachers. Milton had observed much along life's milk route and was eager to pass on his observations. As he came up the steps to leave his deposit, he would also deposit his thought for the day. Although others had doubtless made similar observations, it was from Milton the milkman that Oreo first heard (here cast in Milton's favorite syntactical form): You ever notice that all dentists have hairy arms and a large wristwatch? You ever notice that insurance men walk fast? You ever notice that African men and women all look like men, except Masai warriors, who look like women? You ever notice that you feel guilty when a bank clerk checks up on your balance? You ever notice that you feel guilty sitting in a movie theater waiting for them to turn the lights out and start the picture?

Milton the milkman had an udderful of theories, his Grade A theory a three-stage rumination upon the supposition that short toes, kinky hair, and impacted wisdom teeth were signs that their bearers were further along on the evolutionary scale than long-toed, straight-haired, erupted-wisdom-toothed people. He came up on the porch one day, sat down, and took off his shoes and socks. He believed in visual aids to get his ideas across to modern, media-oriented youth. "Look," he said, pointing to his feet. "See? Short toes. Now, what does this mean? This means that I am on my way to being your man of the future. You ever notice that some people have toes like fingers? Now, I ask you, do we go around grasping things with our feet any more? The answer is no. Prehensile toes went out in the year one. Therefore, anybody with long toes is like a throwback. Therefore, I, Milton, with my short toes, am practically your man of the future. Pretty soon, toes will disappear altogether and people won't be able to walk. But that will be okay, because by then everybody will be their own helicopter. They'll be able to take off from a standing start and propel themselves wherever they want to go with some kind of individualized motor mechanism.

"Now, kinky hair. Kinky hair—like that beautiful fuzzy cloud you have—is not really kinky. It doesn't zig and zag. Kinky hair is actually coily. That's right—coily. Each little hair is practically by way of being a perfect circle. Now, these millions of coils on your head are all jumbled up, coiling around each other. That's why it hurts you to comb your hair. You're pulling in one direction, the coils may be pulling in sixteen other directions. But—and this is the main thing—while the coils are doing that, they are also forming air pockets. Now, air pockets do several things. One, they keep your head warm in the winter. Two, they keep your head cool in the summer. And, three, they protect you from concussions by absorbing the shock of blows to the head. Therefore, kinky hair is certainly more useful than straight hair. It is obviously advanced hair. I mean, the evolutionary wheel had to take a couple of wrong turns before it came up with kinky hair.

"Now, impacted wisdom teeth. Everyone knows that wisdom teeth are disappearing altogether. We don't need all those teeth, what with your processed foods, your tenderized meats. Our jaws are trying to tell us something. Our gums are saying, 'Enough, already. Who needs this?' So to make the message a little clearer, the wisdom teeth say, 'I'll just stay here under the gums. Nobody needs me out there anyway. Why should I sweat it, working away and only catching an edge of something here, a piece of something there?' So to sum up," he said, putting his socks and shoes back on, "short toes, kinky hair, and wisdom teeth that won't come out — these are your three indicators as to your superior person. If you should meet anybody with all three, you're shaking hands with the future, because such a person is so far beyond us, he or she makes the rest of us look like cavemen."

As Milton went off the porch, Oreo patted her kinky hair, tapped her short toes, and—with supreme confidence—looked forward to the day when her wisdom teeth refused to erupt.

Another of Oreo's regular tutors was Douglas Floors (né Flowers), her history instructor. Floors was a man of many parts — paranoid, tap dancer, cost accountant. But the chief part was the nature hater. His history lessons were extravagantly interrupted by heartfelt asides on what he had to put up with from trees and grass. He once told Oreo that he had offered to look after a friend's pachysandra over the weekend, an offer that was hastily withdrawn when he learned that pachysandra was a plant and not an elephant seer whom no one believed. Now he cut short a discourse on the importance of ziggurats to the average Babylonian to say with a shudder, "Last night, the sunset was particularly ugly. Nasty oranges and purples, foul pinks and blues. On my way here, I saw a bird with fat cheeks—and a chest with the coloration of an autumn leaf." He added dolefully, "Which is all right in its place: on an autumn leaf. At least you expect that *kind* of ugliness from an autumn leaf."

Floors abominated the Bay of Fundy, detested the Marianas Trench, abhorred the aurora borealis, reviled the Sargasso Sea, was chilled by the Poles, North and South, and loathed any other manifestation of Mother Nature, commonplace or remarkable. It was from him that Oreo learned historical sidelights that have been suppressed by the international botanist conspiracy (code name: Botany 500): the unsightly foliage that nearly demoralized Sparta along its line of march just before the Battle of Amphipolis; the cumulative ill effects of cumulus clouds and photosynthesis on Richard III; the cypress infestation that was the last straw to relatives of bubonic plague victims fleeing Tuscany in 1347; the vindictiveness and moral turpitude of the puny (and Punic) shrubbery at Zama, the crucial factor in Hannibal's defeat at the hands of Scipio Africanus Major; the *real* story behind the Wars of the Roses.

Whenever Floors came to teach, Louise flung a drop cloth over the hedges in front of the house, pulled the shades on the window giving onto the back yard, hid the flower vases and the century plant, and took the Turner and Constable reproductions off the walls. She changed James's sun-pattern poncho and made sure the children wore nothing depicting flowers, trees, birds, clouds, mountains, rivers, or anything else that could be construed as part of nature's bounty. Floors would enter, take off his dark glasses, turn his chair so that he would be facing a wall, and begin. "There's a noisome Indian summer breeze blowing out there today. Such a breeze was blowing on that November day when Charles II lay on his deathbed—and greatly influenced his decision to die and start the War of the Spanish Succession."

An important incident in the legend of Oreo

Louise's brother Herbert was a great traveler. On his return from Morocco or Afghanistan or Greece or Chile, he would stop by to see his sister, check on James's immobilization, and give Oreo and Jimmie C. the presents he had brought with him from foreign shores. He was a huge man, a 1 on the color scale. He had a scar from the corner of his lip to the top of his right ear, a memento of an incident of his childhood outside the village of Gladstone, when, with a callow slip of the tongue, he called two playmates of somewhat higher color-scale value black sons of bitches. Whenever he came to the house, he would go directly to the large mirror in the dining room, pull a flask from his hip pocket, drink deeply, growl, wipe his mouth with satisfaction, and say, "I'm Big Nigger Butler." It was strange to hear this from a man for whom Hermann Göring could serve as *Doppelgänger*.

Herbert would fling off his coat and take out a little black book clotted with columns of three-digit numbers, written in heavy pencil. Under or over each digit in a three-figure unit was a dot or a dash or a circle or a slanted line or a cross. Herbert took Oreo on his knee and explained to her what these mysterious markings meant. It was an elaborate system for playing the numbers, a passion he shared with his sister Louise. His diacritical marks showed him which numbers had come out, when, their pattern of recurrence (did 561 prefer to come out in December, for example?), their correlation with world events (did numbers starting with 8 always presage the fall of a South American government, for instance?), and so on through a warren of statistical complexities that only Herbert could keep track of—Herbert who could correctly multiply any figure up to five digits by any other figure up to five digits in his head. But there was one difference between Herbert and Louise. Herbert had never hit a number. Oh, he had come close—once. He had played 782 straight on the day that Louise played 782 in the box and thereby hit for seven hundred dollars when 827 came out. Other than that, he rarely had even one digit in common with the number that hit. But he kept showing Oreo his book, telling her that one of these days, when she was old enough, he would have her trace his markings in ink. He secretly believed that his niece's palimpsest of his numerical adventures would magically change his luck. His perverse delay (for Oreo had had her eraser and ballpoint at the ready for years) was a good example of herculean self-tantalization.

On one visit, Herbert had just returned from Africa. He had flung off his coat—made of the skin of a lion he had killed in a Nairobi pet shop—and had gone to his accustomed spot in front of the mirror to do his Big Nigger Butler routine, when all of a sudden there was a commotion behind him. He did not turn around, for he could see what was happening in the mirror. He had tossed his lion coat on a chair directly behind him, its hood with the opened-jawed lion's head nuzzling his back. Oreo, thinking that the skin covered a live lion, had jumped up on the table behind her uncle and was stalking the coat. She came up behind it slowly, her hands behind her. When she was close enough, she pulled her jump rope from behind her back, whipped it around the head and mane, and double-dutched the coat to death—or so she thought. Her uncle, watching all this in the mirror, was impressed with her bravery. "She sure got womb, that little mother," he said. "I wouldn't want to mess with her when she gets older. She is a ball buster and a *half*." He told the entire neighborhood about the incident. So it was that the legend of Oreo began to grow before she had cut her second teeth.

An important letter

At about this time, Oreo received a letter from her mother that influenced her thinking a great deal. Helen's letter had its usual quota of asides, such as her paranoia about white dentists: "Suppose your dentist is white and suppose he just happens to harbor an unconscious hatred of black people and suppose he is in a bad mood anyway when you come in. Might he not just happen to bear down on the old drill a little harder, go a little deeper than he needs to? I am just asking and don't want you to be warped for life by this thought. Besides, you still have your perfect little milk teeth. But since I'm on dentists, I will tell you about Dr. Goodbody. Dr. Goodbody starts spraying Lavoris before you even make an appointment. His sprayer bears a striking resemblance to a flame thrower. But who can blame him for his finickyness, considering the effluvium, the untreated sewage, the *ick* that issues from some people's mouths? But Dr. Goodbody has never realized that a patient who is going to a dentist is like a housewife who cleans up before the maid comes. Such goings on with water picks and dental floss and mouthwash and toothpaste — to say nothing of sandpaper!''

This digression brought Helen logically to the main topic of her letter: the oppression of women. ''This is a subject I've given a lot of thought to, and I think I have the answer. I've tried to encompass in my theory all the sociological, mythological, religious, philosophical, muscular, economic, cultural, musical, physical, ethical, intellectual, metaphysical, anthropological, gynecological, historical, hormonal, environmental, judicial, legal, moral, ethnic, governmental, linguistic, psychological, schizophrenic, glottal, racial, poetic, dental [this was the logical link], artistic, military, and urinary considerations from prehistoric times to the present. I have been able to synthesize these considerations into one inescapable formulation: men can knock the shit out of women.''

Helen's letter went on to point out the implications of her formulation for the theory of the so-called black matriarchs: it tore the theory all to hell. In a later day, Helen might have gone on to add (with a slip of the pen owing to hunger): ''There's no male chauvinist pork like a black male chauvinist pork.'' Now she contented herself with pointing out how her own mother still deferred to her father even in his immobilization, keeping on the safe side in case he ever came out of it. As Louise often said, ''He ain' gon [pronounced, by Louise and others, as if it were a French word, never as ''gone''] hab no scuse to box *my* jaws.''

Helen's letter so impressed Oreo that it led her to do two things: adopt a motto and develop a system of self-defense. The motto was *Nemo me impune lacessit*—''No one attacks me with impunity." "Ain't no nigger gon tell me what to do. I'll give him such a *klop* in the *kishkas!*" she said, lapsing into the inflections of her white-skinned black grandmother and (through her mother) her dark-skinned white grandfather, as she often did under stress.

She called her system of self-defense the Way of the Interstitial Thrust, or WIT. WIT was based on an Oriental dedication to attacking the body's soft, vulnerable spaces or, *au fond,* to making such spaces, or interstices, where previously none had existed; where, for example, a second before there had been an expanse of smooth, nonabraded skin and sturdy, unbroken bone. To this end, Oreo developed a series of moves that made other methods of self-defense—jiu-jitsu, karate, kung-fu, savate, judo, aikido, mikado, kikuyu, kendo, hondo, and shlong—obsolete by incorporating and improving upon their most effective aspects. With such awesome moves (or, as Oreo termed them, *blōs*) as the *hed-lok, shu-kik, i-pik, hed-brāc, i-bop, ul-na-brāc, hed-blō, fut-strīk, han-krus, tum-blō, nek-brāc, bal-brāc, bak-strīk, but-kik,* the size or musculature of the opponent was virtually academic. Whether he was big or small, fat or thin, well-built or spavined, Oreo could, when she was in a state of extreme concentration known as *hwip-as,* engage any opponent up to three times her size and weight and whip his natural ass.

She was once inadvertently in the state of *hwip-as* when she was riding in her uncle's car. A man standing on a corner as the car passed had seen her and had made sucking noises to denote his approval of her appearance. Oreo did not consciously know she had heard these primitive sounds, but as she was getting out of the car, she was in such an advanced state of *hwip-as* that when she yanked at the ashtray, mistakenly thinking it was a door handle, she heedlessly created for her uncle the only three-door club coupe in America.

Half WIT

Oreo's tutors were on vacation. She needed something to do to occupy her fourteen-year-old mind for a few weeks, so she put an ad in the papers. Three days later, she received a phone call from what sounded like a young white man.

"May I speak to Miss Christine Clark?" he asked.

"This is Christine Clark."

"Are you the girl who advertised in the Situations Wanted column of the *Inquirer?*"

"Yes."

"My name is Dr. Jafferts. I'm the medical examiner for district five. I was wondering if I could interest you in a job?"

"I hope so."

"Your ad said you're a recent college graduate."

"Yes, it did say that."

"And your field was Chinese history?"

"Yes."

"I see," he said. "Well, let me tell you a little about the job we have in mind. In this job, you'd be negotiating government contracts."

"Chinese history doesn't exactly prepare — "

"That's all right," he said generously. "We would train you. This job doesn't come under civil service. You'd be working with another woman. The job involves some traveling within a hundred-mile radius of the city. Do you drive?"

"Yes."

"The job pays ninety-five to start and gas-mileage money. The hours are nine to three-thirty, five days a week. How does that sound?"

"Fine."

"Now, here's the catch. Would you submit to a medical examination for the job?"

"Certainly. Where's your office?"

"Well, I don't exactly have any particular office. I have to travel all over the district. I can give you the examination over the phone."

Aha, thought Oreo. "Over the phone?" she asked.

"Yes. You'd be surprised at how thorough a phone examination can be." He paused, then said, "Do you have a house or an apartment?"

"House," said Oreo.

"And where is that located?"

She gave him her address.

"Are you alone?"

Oreo decided to go along with him. "Why, yes."

"I just asked because some of the questions may seem highly personal. But this is a combination psychological and medical exam, so don't be alarmed."

"I promise," said Oreo.

"How old are you?"

"Eighteen," lied Oreo.

"Are you a virgin?"

Which answer is better for a *shmuck* like this? she wondered, and, having decided, said, "No."

"Would you mind telling me the color of your underclothes?"

Oreo covered her mouth to keep from giggling.

"I mean, are they white or different colors like pink, blue?"

"All white," said Oreo.

"Um-hmm. And what material are they? Silk, rayon, cotton?"

"Nylon."

"I see. Now, would you mind telling me all the words you know that mean sexual intercourse?"

With a wicked smile, Oreo said, "Certainly. *Procreation, cohabitation, coition, coitus.*"

"No, no!" He sounded terribly disappointed. Then, clearing

his throat, he said calmly, "I don't mean . . . scientific terms. I mean just any words that might come to mind or that you might hear on the streets, for instance."

"I'm sorry," Oreo said. "Those are the only ones I can think of right now. Could I come back to that question?"

"Of course, of course," he snapped. "Now, have you ever admired your body in a mirror?"

"Sure. Often."

"Have you ever been roused? Does music ever make you want to—?" He broke off, then he said, "I've finished the psychological examination. Now I want you to take off your clothes and give yourself the medical." After a few moments he said, "Are they off?"

"No," said Oreo, "I'm having trouble with my wedgies."

The doctor continued, oblivious to her anachronistic answer. "Rub along the inside of your thigh and tell me when you get wet."

Oreo put down the phone and went over to water her begonia, then she came back and coughed into the phone to let the doctor know she was there.

"Are you wet yet?" he said wistfully.

Oreo said, "You know, doctor, the trouble with masturbation is you come too fast. There's no one for you to give directions to. You know, like 'No, not like that, like this. No, yes, no, harder, softer, up, down. No, no, I'm losing it. Yes, yes, that's it, stay there, right there. No, no, not like that—the way you were doing it before. Yes, that's it.' And there's no one for you *not* to give directions to. You know what I mean, doctor?"

There was a moan at the other end of the line. "I'd like to come over and give you a complete examination," said the moaner hoarsely.

"Why don't you do that," said the moanee sweetly.

"I'll bring my tools with me," the doctor said, in one last effort at pretense.

"Tools?" said Oreo. "One will be enough. Oh, by the way, doctor, I've finally thought of some words. I don't know how they slipped my mind before." Oreo said a lot of words that begin with *p* and *c* and *t* and *x*, that rhyme with *bunt* and *pooky* and *noontang*.

The doctor let out a gasp as big as Masters and Johnson and said he could be at her place in an hour. Oreo told him that she would wait for him on her front porch and that she would be wearing a begonia leaf.

She went immediately to a house three doors down from her and told a neighbor, Betty Williams, that she wanted to play a trick on an acquaintance. Betty was the neighborhood nymphomaniac. For two cents she would fuck a plunger. In fact, the story of Betty and the plumber's friend was a West Philadelphia legend. Anyone who thought that the shibboleth *friend* referred to a person was known to be an outsider and was therefore the object of xenophobic ridicule and scorn. Betty agreed to help her young friend Oreo.

So it was that when Dr. Jafferts came panting down the street, already slavering, it was Betty who, wearing the begonia leaf, waylaid him, as it were, on Oreo's porch and led him to her house, where Oreo was in hiding.

After a few preliminaries involving the you-sounded-different-over-the-phone routine, the doctor—a young *shmegegge* who looked like the kind of person who doted on tapioca pudding, and *ergo propter hoc*, whose favorite Marx Brother was Gummo—was seated in a chair cruelly sited to give him a view up Betty's short skirt. Sitting on a high stool, Betty began a rhythmic opening and closing of her legs, revealing and concealing a tangle of pubic hair. The sweat stood out on the doctor's head after the first two open-close, open-close beats. After a while, he seemed in danger of drowning in his own juice.

But Oreo's plan was without mercy. Simultaneously with the

rhythms she was laying down from her stool, Betty began telling the doctor one of her favorite jokes. "It's about this man and woman who go down to Florida on their fifteenth wedding anniversary. They get up in their room, and the first thing they do is take off all their clothes."

The doctor licked his lips in anticipation, his eyes fixed on Betty's open-close, open-close.

Betty was beginning to overheat from hearing her own story, but she went on. "And the man says to the woman, says, 'Honey, we been married all these years now and we always do it the same way. Let's screw a *new* way this time. Now, you stand over in that corner, and I'll stand over here. Then we'll run toward each other and meet in the middle.' So they go to the different corners and start running toward each other. But they miss and run right past. The man is going so fast, he goes sailing out the open window. His room is on the tenth story, but he's lucky 'cause he falls in the swimming pool. But he's afraid to come out 'cause he don't have no clothes on. Everybody seems to be running to the hotel and nobody's paying him no mind, but he's still afraid to come out the pool buck naked. Then he sees this bellhop ready to go in the hotel, and he calls him over. He says, 'Say, bellhop, I want to get out the pool, but I can't 'cause I ain't got no clothes on.' The bellhop don't even look surprised. He says, 'That's all right, sir, nobody'll pay no 'ttention to you. You just come on out.' The man says, 'What do you mean nobody'll pay no 'ttention to me? I'm buck naked!' The bellhop says, 'I know, sir, but most of the people are up on the tenth floor trying to figure out a way to get a woman off a doorknob.' "

By this time both Betty and the doctor were raging beasts. As the doctor ran to the attack—or, rather, the collaboration—Oreo came out of hiding and gave him a quick *shu-kik* to the groin, then got his jaw in the classic *nek-brāc* position. With his

life but a *blō* away, he promised Oreo he would never again
annoy innocent young women by phone or in person with his
snortings and slaverings. With a half-force *bak-bop* she propelled him off Betty's porch and watched as he shmegeggely
fled the street.

She turned back just in time to hear Betty saying plaintively,
"But what about me?"

Oreo realized that it had been very brave and self-sacrificing
of Betty to participate in this little hoax. But her face brightened
when she saw what time it was. She gave Betty the good news.
"What about you? It's five-thirty. Your father will be home any
minute now. Do what you usually do in these circumstances.
Fuck *him.*"

5 Tokens Deposited

Will Farmer

James had been immobilized for fifteen years when Louise decided to take a boyfriend. By this time, she had added drinking to her cooking/eating hobbies and weighed in at a good two hundred pounds. She had a love-tap on her that could paralyze yeast for three days. Louise met her boyfriend, Will Farmer, at a pay party given by her club, the Rainbow Skinners. The Rainbow Skinners got together every Friday night to conduct the regular club business, which was to eat, drink, and play pitty-pat and Pokeno, and to conduct the special club business, which was to plan pay parties, which they gave to raise money to give other pay parties, and so on, unto several generations.

Whenever Louise brought Will home for dinner, she said, "Make yo'seff comf-*tub*ble, Frank . . . I mean, John . . . I say, *Will*. You jus' like one de fam'ly."

After he had eaten one of Louise's specialties, Will, who was in his eighties (this was a Platonic relationship—or maybe Hegelian), would creak into the living room to relax. Once there, he would settle into a chair opposite James and succumb to a myoclonic jerk off to sleep. With his downcurving nose pincering toward his chin like a chela and a cigar held fast between clenched gums, he resembled a pegged lobster. His body became as straight and stiff as a bed slat as he began an inevitable slide to the floor. Just before he clattered into James, Louise would wake him up, thereby preventing him from making a body-temperature cancel mark across her husband's half swastika. It was Louise's lot to be surrounded—or, rather, flanked—by rigid but unavailing masculine spare parts— James and Will each in his own quirky fashion an instance of the-part-for-the-whole, a synecdoche of manhood.

Helen in a hotel room, Winnetka, Illinois

She was listening to Vivaldi's *Concerto in D Minor for Guitar and Viola d'Amore*. Her head equation

$$V = \theta \exp \left[-\int_0^t \psi(\tau) \, d\tau \right]$$

meant that she thought it was time that she went home to visit her family and got Oreo started on her journey to learn the secret of her birth. The phone rang, interrupting the music and breaking off another equation at a crucial operation. It was a wrong number, a woman selling magazine subscriptions. Helen was annoyed, so she let the woman go through the whole *megillah*. Finally, she said, "You've convinced me that I can't beat your low, low prices. I think I'll take a three-year subscription to *Field and Stream*." The vendor was overjoyed (this was her first actual sale in 5,235 calls). Then Helen said, "That is, of course, if you have a braille edition." The magazine woman apologized wholeheartedly for her company's lack of foresight —a choice of words which Helen pointed out was particularly unfortunate for a person with her handicap to hear. With further apologies, muffled sobs, and long-distance groveling over her lack of tact, the woman hung up.

Someone was obviously circulating a defective telephone-sales list, for a few minutes later a dance studio called. Helen debated a moment over whether she should be a paraplegic or an amputee but decided that either would be tasteless and settled for spasticity. Again, apologies, sobs, and groveling. Helen was able to complete her equation:

$$C = H - MB^2$$

where C = catharsis, psf
      H = homesickness, cu ft
      M = meanness, mep
      B = Bell telephone, min

Jimmie C. and his friend

Jimmie C. and Fonzelle Scarsdale had been best friends ever since Oreo had beat Fonny up during her first practice session of WIT. Fonzelle showed Jimmie C. his report card. He was a straight-F student. He was not exceptionally stupid but had no time for studies, preferring to spend most of his free hours perfecting his walk ("I like to walk *heavy*, man," he had confided to Jimmie C.).

Jimmie C., distressed, said, "What is your mother going to say when she sees this? My heart norblats for you, my hands curbel."

"Hell, man, she'll just give me a party."

"A joyber? What kind of joyber?"

"A do-better-next-time party, jim. What else? But I'm hot, though. That yalla-nigger gym teacher give me a F in phiz ed. Now, you *know* I'm good in gym, jack. I'd like to bust that nigger up 'side his head."

"Who are you talking about? Mr. Ozaka? He's Japanese."

"They got you fooled too, huh? Them so-called Japs, Chinks, all them—they *all* niggers. Just trying to chicken out of all the heavy shit going down on us *black* niggers. But they niggers just the same. One of these days, Charlie Chalk gon peep their game, then he'll start treating them just the way he do us." He laughed at the prospect.

Fonzelle put his report card back in his wallet and pulled out a celluloid zigzag of identification cards. Each one showed his picture, but the names on the cards ranged from toothsome (Vasquez Delacorte, Miguel Salamanca) to bland (Ronald Gray, Dave Johnson). "In case I ever get picked up, the pigs will be confused, dig?" He compressed the pleats. "My cousin's a cop. I went with him when he had to testify in night court the other day. This foxy chick walks in. Man, she was really together. Legs so big and rounded off. I scrambled to write that address down. But the judge, he's keeping it all to hisself. I couldn't hardly hear, man. You know what they fined that chick? Ten dollars and costs! If it was some ol' nappy-head broad, some pepperhead, they woulda thrown her ass *under* the jail. Gee-me-Christmas, there's some shit going down, jim!"

Jimmie C. nodded in sympathy.

"Hey man," Fonzelle said, "I'm looking for a job."

"Doing what?"

"As a lover, man. That's what I'm best at. What's the opposite of red?"

"Bormel?" Jimmie C. offered.

"Yeah, blue. I get me a blue light and put it outside my door. Did I tell you about the last one I had. I told her, 'Three dollars! Are you kidding? Where I come from, *you* pay *me!*' She wasn't bad, either. Really squared me away. After I came out, I saw this faggot. I thought it was a chick at first. I said, 'What you mean you ain't no girl, girl?' I told Doris about that, and she cracked up. Doris is cool, jim. She may be a dyke, but she

one stone *fox*. Wouldn't mind some of that cat myself.'' He
giggled. ''Know what she told me the other day? She had to go
to the doctor, see? Had a infection in her cat. So the doctor
examines her, does his little number with the slides and things,
and says, 'Miss Jefferson, I don't understand this. You a virgin,
you still cherry and all, yet and still you got this infection in
your cat. And this ain't no *ordinary* infection. This kinda germ,
we usually find it in people's *mouth*. It's a—whatchacall—a
oral germ. Now, Miss Jefferson, how do you explain that?'
Doris says that without even thinking, she comes out and says,
'Well, doctor, I sat on a dirty teaspoon.' '' Fonzelle doubled
over, whooping and hollering.

Jimmie C. smiled gently, not wanting to offend his friend by
telling him he didn't know what the varnok he was talking
about.

''You got a telephone book?'' Fonzelle asked.

Jimmie C. handed it to him, and Fonzelle dialed a number.
''Hello, Alcoholic Anonymous? Please listen careful, now.
Scotch on the rocks, gin and tonic, screwdriver, bloody Mary,
muscatel, martini, sneaky Pete—'' He doubled up again.
''They hung up. I can usually get in about ten of them before
they see where I'm coming from.''

Jimmie C. was just about to tell him never to use his phone
again for such aglug purposes, when his mother, whom he had
not seen for almost a year, walked in.

''*Nu*, how's my baby?'' Helen said, embracing him.

Jimmie C. could not even sing, his small body was curbeling
so with joy. Such was his curbelation that he did not notice that
Fonzelle had said good-bye and was executing a heavy walk, its
choreography a combination of Motown and early Clara Ward,
out the door.

When Oreo saw her mother, she said, ''Later, *Mamanyu*,''
and went out into the back yard to cry.

When Louise saw her daughter, she said, "Well, I be John Brown! Look who's yere!" She kissed Helen, pulled her over to James, who grinned and seemed about to get up, and went straight to the kitchen to begin preparing a nice little homecoming meal.

La Carte du Dîner
d'Hélène

Allow 40 min for AMERICAN AND/OR JEWISH dishes.
(Choice of six in each course. No substitutions.)

Hors d'Oeuvre

halibut *imojo*

CHEESE AND CRACKERS

Leberknödel

dim sum

pâté maison

funghi marinati

PICKLED HERRING

sashimi

empanadas

vatrushki

Zubrowka

Aquavit

Pepsi

——— ———

Soupe

mtori

NEW ENGLAND CLAM CHOWDER

Hühner Suppe

stracciatella

MATZO-BALL SOUP

awase miso

yen-wo-t'ang

petite marmite

canja

rassolnik

Amontillado

Madeira

Poisson

samaki kavu

FRIED SMELTS

Forelle blau mit Kapern

hung-shao-yü

saumon poché à la Louise

scampi alla griglia

SMOKED SABLE

takara bune

pescado yucateco

osetrina zalivnaya

1961 Montrachet, Chassagne-Montrachet

Entrée

zilzil alecha

BRAISED SHORT RIBS OF BEEF

Kalbshaxen

fu-chu-jou-pien

côtes de veau en papillote

osso buco

STEAMED CALF'S FOOT

tori mushiyaki

matambre

shashlyk

1953 Château Pétrus, Pomerol

Rôt

frangainho piripiri

ROAST TURKEY WITH CORNBREAD

STUFFING

Wiener Gans

Pei-ching-k'ao-ya

faisan Souvaroff

pollo al diavolo

ROAST CHICKEN

GOLDA MEIR

yakitori

conejo en coco

kotmis satsivi

1947 Château Margaux, Médoc

Entremets

ovos moles de papaia

LEMON SHERBET

Gefüllte Melonen

shih-chin-kuo-pin

soufflé glacé Hélène

gelato torinese

TSIMMES

kusamochi

leche de coco

kisel

1959 Champagne, Veuve Clicquot

Relevé

mokoto

fritto misto

GLAZED HAM

SALAMI SURPRISE MOSHE DAYAN

Sardellenschnitzel

tatsuta age

hao-shih-niu-jou

feijoada

noisettes d'agneau Christine

basturma

1964 Chambertin, Gevrey-Chambertin

Salade

yegomen kitfo

insalata di pomodori

POTATO SALAD

COLESLAW MURRAY

Roter Rübenkren

horenso hitashi

liang-pan-huang-kua

ensalada de nopalitos

salade russe

rossolye

Dessert

cocada amarela

APPLE PIE WITH OREO CRUST

Sachertorte

hsing-jen-ping

*Mont Blanc au chocolat
du deux Jameses*

spumoni

HALVAH

kyogashi

manjar blanco

paskha

1953 Sauternes, Château Coutet, Barsac

Le thé, Constant Comment

Le café, Chock *full* o' Nuts

Cognac

Calvados

What happened while Louise was cooking

Five people in the neighborhood went insane from the bouquets that wafted to them from Louise's kitchen. The tongues of two men macerated in the overload from their salivary glands. Three men and a woman had to be chained up by their families when they began gnawing at a *quincaillerie* of substances that wiser heads have found to be inedible. These substances—which blind chance had put within the compass of snatchability of the unfortunate four—ranged from butterfly nuts to galoshes, with a catalog of intervening items that good taste precludes mention of here. In a section of West Philadelphia referred to as "down the Bottom," at some remove from the Clarks' neighborhood, a woman who had never laid eyes on Oreo's family was heard to remark, "That Louise cooking again. Helen must be home. I wish that woman would send out a warning when she gon do this." And she adjusted her husband's chains so that they would not rattle against the hot-water pipes and keep her awake all night.

Helen entertains

Helen told the family stories of her life on the road. She acted out all the parts, animate and inanimate (one of her best bits was a bowl of mashed potatoes being covered with gravy). The family favorite that night was the story she told about playing at a house party in the all-black suburb of Whitehall, so much in the news when low-income whites were making their first pitiful attempts to get in. The upper-middle-class blacks of Whitehall objected to the palefaces, not because they were poor ("The poor we have with us always," said town spokesman, the Reverend Cotton Smith-Jones, rector of St. John's Episcopal Church), but because they were white ("We just do not want whitey, with his honky ways, around us," said Reverend Smith-Jones to a chorus of genteel Episcopalian "Amens"). As

Smith-Jones pointed out, whitey was beyond help. Chuck did not groove on crime in the streets, the way black people did; he did not dig getting his head whipped, his house robbed, his wife raped, the way black people did; he was not really into getting his jollies over his youngsters' popping pills, tripping out, or shooting up, the way black people did. Such uptight, constipated people should not be allowed to mingle with decent, pleasure-loving black folk. That was the true story, but officially Whitehall had to be against the would-be intruders on the basis of poverty.

The town adopted a strict housing code, which was automatically rescinded for blacks and reinstated whenever whites appeared. (The code was shredded, its particles sprinkled into confiscated timed-release capsules, and is now part of the consciousness of millions of cold sufferers.) "Keep Whitehall black," the townspeople chanted in their characteristically rich baritones and basses. "If you're black, you're all right, jack; if you're white, get out of my sight," said others in aberrant Butterfly McQueen falsettos. These and other racist slogans were heard as the social, moral, economic, and political life of the town was threatened.

The white blue-collar workers who labored so faithfully at the Smith-Jones Afro Wig and Dashiki Co., Inc., were welcome to earn their daily bread in the town, but they were not welcome to bring their low-cholesterol foods, their derivative folk-rock music, and their sentimental craxploitation films to Whitehall. The poor, the white, and the disadvantaged could go jump.

The people of Whitehall set up floodlights to play over the outskirts of the neighboring, honky-loving black town, whose lawns (formerly reasonably manicured but now nervously bitten to the quick) bore sad witness to the instant herbaphobia that whites brought with them. Black Whitehall posted sentries and devised elaborate alarm/gotcha systems (the showpiece was a giant microwave oven with the door ajar). The Whitehall

PO-lice raised attack dogs on a special "preview" diet of saltines and the white meat of turkeys. Helen quoted Reverend
Smith-Jones as saying, in his down-home way, "If any chalks
should be rash enough to come in here, those dogs will jump
on them like white on rice."

"Pass me some *tsimmes*," said Helen, when she had finished
with Whitehall. She tasted it, blew her mother a kiss. "You
know who made a lousy *tsimmes*—Mrs. Zipstein."

At the mention of the wife of the man who had pickled him
into anti-Semitism, James stirred in his corner. He immediately
went back to concentrating on swallowing the Veuve Clicquot
Jimmie C. was feeding him, grinning as he reminisced about
Gladstone's village idiot.

"You ever yere from de daughter? Whatchacall?" said
Louise.

"Sadie. Sadie-Above-It-All, the Jewish princess. No, I wonder what ever happened to her."

Oreo watched with anticipation as her mother got up from her
seat to do some *shtiklech*. "Here's Mrs. Zipstein," Helen said.
She bent over, holding her back. As she walked, she pointed to
her feet. "Mrs. Zipstein has those lumpy black shoes that look
like they have potatoes inside—no, like she has a lot of *little*
feet stuck to her regular foot. She's walking, see? 'Oi, oi, oi,
doit and filt, filt and doit. God to gad id op. Oi, oi, oi.' "
Helen straightened up. Instantly she was Sadie being carried on
a pillow by Nubian slaves. 'Be careful with my gown, you
graubyon! You, on the right—don't *glitch* or you'll tear it!
This is no *shmatte*, you know. Cost a fortune.' " Helen/Sadie's
arms flapped helplessly. " 'Oh my God, the floor's dirty—
come quick, somebody, and clean it up. Quick or I'll turn
blue.' " Helen sat down. "Nobody enjoys digging in other
people's dirt, but Sadie can't even come near her *own*. She
could be sitting on the toilet and she'd say, 'I'm sorry, I just
can't do it. Somebody, come in and wipe!' They could cut her

salary to a dollar ninety-eight a week and her 'girl-who-comes-in-twice-a-week'—who's probably older than her mother—would be the last thing she'd give up. 'There's always a *shvartze* to do these nasty things, so I should worry?' Ah, but the guilt. 'I don't know what it is, Debbie, but I can't bring myself to stay at home when Beulah's there. I do my important shopping on those two days.' Beulah down there on her knees probably reminds her of her mother, Mrs. Clean. As for Mrs. Clean herself, maybe she's always making with the rubbing and scrubbing because there's nothing else for a religious Jewish woman to do." Helen was suddenly a rabbi. " 'Go to the *mikvah* and stop *nudzhing*, you dirty women, you. Don't defile our scholars with your monthlies and your sinful ways. It's enough, already, and stretching a point besides that we let you light the *shabbes* candle. So cook, so clean, so make amends.' " Helen paused. "So vot am I tokkink?" she said, laughing, and changed the subject. "Mother, do you remember when I was going with Freddie Cole, the football player?"

"I disremember de name."

"You'd remember if you saw him, a real hulk, a Baby Huey. Well, anyway, he says to me on the phone one day, 'Helen, I'm gon bring you something real special tonight—one perfect rose.' He must have seen that in a movie or something. Well, anyway, that night, he lumbers up the steps, his ham fist like a misshapen vase for the rosebud he's clutching." She paused to demonstrate. Her imitation of Freddie's bulk and gait was so exact that, in that instant, Louise remembered him. "He gives it to me, and I say, 'Oh, Freddie, it's lovely now, but it's going to be a real beauty when it opens.' He gives me this dumb look, grabs the rose, and says, 'Duh, I can fix that.' And with a rip, a tear, a shred, he breaks open the petals one by one and hands it back to me. *'Bulvan!'* I screamed, and threw him out."

Jimmie C. and Oreo laughed, James grinned in his corner, and Louise said, "Bull what?"

A bloom in the bloomers

Talk of roses and *mikvahs* reminded Oreo that it was time to change her sanitary napkin. She excused herself from the table.

Oreo's menarche had been at age eight. She had been minding her own business, experimenting to see whether her pet turtle would try to mate with an army helmet, half a walnut shell, or a swatch of linoleum (the "bottom-shell hypothesis"), when she felt a slight contraction in her lower abdomen. She was vague about the area—it happened so fast—but it was somewhere below the *pupik* and above the *mons veneris*. She went to the bathroom to check on a stickiness she felt—and saw the blood. *"Oi gevalt,"* she said, "what the fuck is this shit?"

She summoned Louise, who looked at Oreo's panties and handed her a Kotex. Louise did not believe in tampons, which were too newfangled for her. "Ain't but one thing spose to go up in dere," she told Oreo. She explained to Oreo the implications of this issue and that she could expect it for three to five days in every twenty-eight. Louise was only slightly surprised that Oreo had started so young. That was the way it was with Oreo. She was, however, astonished when she saw that the gouts of blood had formed an American Beauty rose in the crotch of Oreo's panties. Her own uterine lining had always reminded her of bits of raw liver, but Oreo's bloomer decoration looked as if it had been squeezed from a pastry bag.

"What do we call this?" Oreo asked.

"Well, you kin call it fallin' off de ruff or hab'm de rag on or de cuss. But it mos' ladylike to say, 'Grandma, I hab my purriod.' "

Oreo shook her head. She looked at the red of her blood, the white of the pad, the blue of the thread running down the middle, and said, "No, I'll call it flag day."

Louise nodded her head with satisfaction. "Dat right pat'rotic of you, chile." She left Oreo in the bathroom and went to the kitchen. For some reason, she was torn between fixing calf's liver Veneziana and baking a cake.

Oreo had never seen any reason to tell Louise or anyone else that her period came not every twenty-eight days, but on the following monthly schedule: on the thirtieth day in September, April, June, and November; on the thirty-first day in all the rest, except February, when it came on the twenty-eighth (and every fourth year on February 29). Flag day was for Oreo just that—one day. Twenty-four times on that day—once every sixty minutes—she would extrude one blood rose, like a womb-clock telling sanguinary hours. On those days, Oreo set her watch by herself and adjusted all the other timepieces in the house. Now she changed her pad and went back to have a private talk with her mother.

Helen and Oreo *shmooz*

Helen said, "Have you seen the TV commercial where the housewife is being stoned to death for using the wrong detergent, and this voice comes from out of a burning bush to egg the stone throwers on?"

"Yes," said Oreo.

"The bush is your father. Have you seen the one where the housewife gets a rash when a little man jumps out of her toilet bowl?"

"Yes."

"The bowl and the rash—your father. What about the one where the man is thinking of telling his wife she has dandruff, while the woman is thinking of a good way to break it to him about his b.o.?"

"The b.o. and the dandruff—my father," said Oreo.

"No, the woman." Helen explained that Oreo's father was now the king of the voice-over actors. He had found his niche after being in as many flop stage shows as Oreo now had years, sixteen and a half. Samuel's combined run in the shows was sixteen days and a half-curtain — one play had closed before the first-act curtain was completely up.

"Your father has recently remarried," Helen went on. "A Georgia peach, I hear."

"Any reason why he never visited me and Jimmie C. or bothered to drop us a line or even acknowledge our existence?" asked Oreo.

"Of course there's a reason."

"What?"

"He's a *shmuck*."

That made sense to Oreo.

"Also, he wants his father's *gelt*. Jacob isn't about to leave him any bread if all Sam can show for it is *shvartze* children. You expected different, *noch?*" Helen sighed. "In any case, baby, I came home this trip with a special purpose. It is time you undertook to learn the secret of your birth. I thought that you would not be ready until you were at least eighteen, but from what I have seen and heard, you are ready now. When your father and I were about to split up, he gave me this piece of paper, which I have carried with me on all my travels. He said that when I thought you were old enough to decipher the clues written here, he would know it was time for him to tell you what you have a right to know. It is not for me to tell you this secret. It is for Samuel alone. He's still in New York, but I don't have his address. If he's such a big deal, he should be easy enough to find." She handed Oreo the paper, which had turned brown from years of Helen's spilling coffee on it.

The handwriting was intelligible in spite of the coffee stains. The meaning of the first item on the list was not so clear. "It says here: 'Sword and sandals.' What about it? Buy the sword and sandals? Find the sword and sandals? *Stuff* the sword and sandals? What?"

"I can help you with that one," Helen said, "but all that other jazz is a whole 'nother thing. You're going to have to figure that out by yourself. Come with me." She went out into the back yard, Oreo following behind her.

Helen pointed to a huge rock in the northeast corner of the yard. "Can you lift that?"

Without a word, Oreo moved the boulder with one hand. It was Silly Putty that Jimmie C. had been saving for years.

"Tell me what's under it," Helen said.

"Nothing."

"Oh, yeah, I remember now. I decided that was a *tsedrayt* place to put them. They're in the house."

Oreo followed her back inside. Helen went upstairs to Oreo's room and straight to the third floorboard from the window. She started to bend over, then said, "Technically, you're supposed to do this." She showed Oreo a place where she could get her fingers under the board.

Oreo pried it up and took out what had been hidden underneath: a mezuzah on a thin chain and a pair of bed socks. "This he calls sword and sandals?"

"Hand them to me," Helen said. They sat on the bed to look at the uncacheables. The mezuzah and chain had turned green. "Cheapskate. He told me they were solid gold." Around the mezuzah was a piece of paper held in place by a rubber band. Helen rolled the rubber band off and handed the paper to Oreo.

Oreo read it aloud: " 'For the word of God is quick, and powerful, and sharper than any two-edged sword . . . (Hebrews 4:12).' "

"*Golem,*" said Helen, addressing Samuel, "that's New Testament!" She gave Oreo the bed socks, saying, "Reach in."

In the left bed sock was a ribbon of paper that read: "So you shouldn't catch a chill." Oreo too was moved to address her absentee father. "You're so thoughtful, Poppa," she said curling her lip. "If only I'm lucky enough to find you after all these years, I'll give you such a *zetz!*"

6 Ta-ta Troezen

Oreo's good-byes to her tutors

Milton the milkman came up on the porch and said to Oreo, "I hear you're leaving us to go find your father. Well, good luck to you. Funny thing about trips. You ever notice that if you meet somebody where they're not supposed to be, in a foreign country, say, or another city, you're happier to see them than if you bumped into them every now and then where they *were* supposed to be? I mean, take me, for instance. You see me almost every day and you're glad to see me, but we're just acquaintances, right? You couldn't call us friends. But if you saw me in Cincinnati, we'd act like we were long lost buddies. And if we met in France—why, there'd be no separating us. Then we'd meet again in Philly and we'd be back to being just acquaintances again, right? Now, before you go, I'd like to tell you my theory of divorce, based on the experience of a friend of mine. Now, this friend of mine—let's call him Stan—and his wife —let's call her Alice—had a big problem. She preferred a night bath *before* sex, he liked a morning shower *after* sex. What with one thing and another, one of them was always too clean or too dirty for the other one. So they rarely got together, so they got a divorce. Now, my theory is that the divorce rate could be reduced by ninety percent if, before marriage, couples would honestly discuss, one, the time of day they like to have sex and, two, the time of day they like to take baths and/or showers. A lot of heartache could be avoided later if they did this, because you can tell a lot about a person's character from these two things. Well, goodbye, kid. It's been a pleasure serving you all these years. Take care, and remember to drink at least a quart of milk a day."

"Good-bye, Milton."

Douglas Floors interrupted a crucial discussion of the Sino-Soviet War on Oreo's last day with him to inveigh against Central Park. "It is not quite so bad as Fairmount Park, of course, being smaller, but it is bad enough. The foul Sheep Meadow, the treacherous Great Lawn, and—I actually get a *frisson* every time I think of it—the Ramble, where benighted creatures actually go to watch *birds*." He shuddered behind his dark glasses and turned his chair more directly to the wall, the better to avoid seeing Louise's bare arm as she passed through the room. Her vaccination scar reminded him of a chrysanthemum. "I contribute to an enlightened East Coast group determined to pave all the parks. We'd like to start with Central. Our research indicates we have the best chance there. Of course, there are the lunatic conservation groups to contend with, but they will soon be neutralized by hay fever, poison ivy, ticks, and all the other little goodies their beloved Mother Nature inflicts on them whenever they go a-Maying." He snickered with nonnatural satisfaction.

"Remember," he said as he was leaving, "look out for rock outcroppings. Manhattan is full of schist."

And so are you, thought Oreo, misunderstanding him.

"Good-bye, Oreo."
"Good-bye, Doug."

Professor Lindau, after all his years of giving blood, was now taking. We went daily for a transfusion of the blood he had donated over the last decade, convinced by Milton the milkman that getting back his callow plasma, his jejune erythrocytes, his puerile leukocytes, his tender platelets would make him young again. Oreo believed that his conflations with his latest wedge were doing more for his rejuvenation than any old stale blood.

For her last assignment, the professor had given her a standard treatise in the field of economic agronomy upon which she was to model an essay on the same subject. She read the first and last words of the treatise, titled *Lying Fallow, or What You Should Know About Federal Subsidies*, and started and ended her essay with similar words. In *Lying Fallow,* the first word was *snow* and the last word was *potatoes.* In her book-length essay *(Secretaries of Agriculture I Have Known, or God: The First Economic Agronomist),* Oreo experimented with *monsoon* and *broccoli* as her first and last words, but decided they were too exotic, and, what is more, *monsoon* had too many syllables. Already she had strayed from the obvious pattern *Fallow'*s author had established with his forceful yet sensitive first and last words. After an evening with Roget, Oreo decided that her first word would be *rain* and her last word *rice.* She was more than willing to sacrifice syllables (her two to *Fallow'*s four) for alliteration. She quickly filled in the middle section of her essay, using the same technique. What she sacrificed in cogency, she gained in mechanicality (her serendipitous assembly-line gobbledygook against *Fallow'*s numbing agroeconomic clarity). Thus a typical sentence in *Fallow:* "Wheat farm B showed a declining profit-loss ratio during the harvest season," became in Oreo's manuscript: "Oat ranch wasp played the drooping excess-death proportion while a crop pepper." The professor was amused by Oreo's little farewell drollery, which ran to more than six hundred pages, single-spaced.

After the lesson, the professor excused himself and went to the bathroom. When he returned, he said, "Now that I have sifted out, I shall not go into a long wearing away. I shall merely give you a big comfort and take my leave." He hugged Oreo.

"Good-bye, professor."

"God be with ye, Oreo."

Oreo's good-byes to her family

The family farewells took three days because Louise needed the time to prepare a box lunch for her granddaughter to take on her journey perilous. The peroration of those good-byes went as follows.

Oreo said good-bye to her grandfather first, since that would take the shortest amount of time. "Good-bye, Grandfather," she said, kissing him on the cheek.

James, who had been grinning a second before, stopped grinning. There was a vacant stare on his face. This often happened and signaled the fact that he was giving his facial muscles a rest.

Oreo went next to Louise. "You look real nice, chile. Yo' white dress is spotless—you might eem say maculin." Louise dragged over Oreo's box lunch—more accurately, her duffel-bag lunch, since that was what it was in. They could not find a box big enough for all the food Louise had prepared.

Oreo strapped the lunch to her backpack frame. Since the food took up so much space, Oreo had to repack the other equipment she was taking on her journey. She soon grew tired of shifting it around, said, "Oh, the hell with it," and shoved it into the duffel bag next to the lunch. It was a toothbrush, but difficult to pack because its interproximal stimulator, or rubber tip, and its bristles faced in opposite directions. Oreo kissed Louise. "Good-bye, Grandmother."

Louise kissed her. " 'Bye, Oreo."

Jimmie C. made a long speech in cha-key-key-wah, telling Oreo how much he loved her and promising not to be a *yold.* Then he said, "I know you won't be gone for a spavol time, but"—and he sang this—"nevertheless and winnie-the-pooh, verily, I'm going to miss you." His voice had changed with age.. His sweet countertenor was now a sweet boy soprano.

She kissed him on both cheeks. "Good-bye, Jimmie C."

"Vladi, Oreo."

When Helen embraced Oreo, she did not say anything, but her head equation, brought on by Jimmie C.'s keening in the background, was a simple

$$L = P + GD$$

where L = leavetaking, mph
  P = pain, ppm
  G = *gevalts,* cwt
  D = *davening,* pf

"Good-bye, Oreo," Helen said when her equation was over. She was doubly sad, since she too would soon be leaving, to go on the road again.

"Good-bye, Mother."

Suddenly there was a sound like the primal rasp of a rusty hinge on a long unopened door—the pearly gates, perhaps. "Now, as I was saying . . . ," James croaked in his disused voice.

The whole family was stunned. They gaped at James in amazement. He was not aware of it now, but a few moments earlier all the good-byes had led him to believe that he was being abandoned. The shock of this fearful defection had quickened his broken blood vessel, which reached out across the vascular gap like a severed snake, probing the brain's topography for its other half. It made a slipknot around the break as a temporary measure until it could repair itself permanently. His anterograde amnesia disappeared. He stood up with a crisp popping and cracking of joints, the sound of Louise snapping gigantic green beans. His half swastika straightened into a ramrod.

His wife and daughter embraced him joyously, and he was reintroduced to his grandchildren for perhaps the umpty-third time.

"Well, I hate to greet and run . . . ," Oreo began. She had no shame.

When Oreo's impending journey was explained to him, a shudder ran through him at the mention of Samuel's name. But the slipknot in his brain heid fast. James was somewhat consoled when he was told that Samuel and Helen had been divorced for years. Helen promised to postpone going on her road trip for a few days in order to help Louise catch James up on all that he had missed during his years of amnesia. She had come to love the road, but once James was fully recovered and making money again, she could make shorter swings and come home more often.

Louise timidly approached her husband. "Do de name Will Farmer ring a gong?" she asked.

James thought a while, shook his head. "No, can't say that it does. Do I know him?"

"No, and I don' neither," she said, a glaze coming over her eyes as she lied in her teeth. "De name jus' come to me in a dream. I was dreaming 'bout one dem horny-back Baptist churches."

"You mean hard-shell," James said.

"Yeah, one dem. Anyway, a man was rollin' in de aisles, and de preacher say, 'You bet' come on out cho ack, Will Farmer.' Jus' thought you might recomember " ody by dat name."

James put a strain on his slipknot trying to figure out why he should know someone in Louise's dream, but he shook it off and went on to other things. "Helen, what do you think of this idea? I was thinking of making a special mailing to all the homes for used Jews and—"

"You mean old folks' homes?" asked Helen.

"Naturally. Well, I was thinking—"

Oreo interrupted to initiate a final round of good-byes, then slipped out the door as unobtrusively as she could, considering her backpack.

Betty the nymphomaniac tore herself away from her father long enough to wave good-bye from her bedroom window and shout, "Don't forget those dirty postcards you promised me!"

"Vladi, vladi," Jimmie C. called wistfully from the front porch until she was out of sight.

And Oreo was on her way.

PART TWO: MEANDERING

7 Periphetes

On the subway-elevated to Thirtieth Street Station

Oreo did what she always did on subways. She speculated or she compared. She speculated on how many people in, say, Denver, Colorado, were at that very moment making love. How many people in Cincinnati were having their teeth filled? As the El passed the Arena and the gilded dome of Provident Mutual's clock tower, in a mad rush to become a true subway with its plunge into the Fortieth Street stop, Oreo wondered how many people in Honolulu were scratching themselves. Was the number of people taking books out of the library in Duluth higher than one-tenth of one percent of the city's car owners? she mused. And what about the ratio of nose picking per thousand population in Portland, Oregon—or Portland, Maine, for that matter?

When she had tired of speculating, she went on to comparing. She looked up and down both sides of the car. On her first sweep, she concentrated on the size and shape of all the noses she could see. She awarded appropriate but valueless (imaginary) prizes to the possessors of the largest, smallest, and most unusual. A man wearing an astrakhan cap won the prize for the largest, with a nose big enough to accommodate nostrils that put Oreo in mind of adjacent plane hangars, fur-lined. His prize: free monthly vacuuming with a yet-to-be-invented nose Hoover. Modeling clay, the prize for the smallest nose, went to a red-headed woman with the nose of an ant. A hand passing from the redhead's formicine brow to her mouth would have to make no humanoid detours around cartilaginous prominences. Most unusual was the cross-eyed young man whose nose pointed to his left ear. Picasso *réchauffé*. His prize wasn't really his. It was a blindfold for others to wear in his presence.

Before she could go on to hands and shoes, Oreo got a seat. Sitting on the edge of the seat because of her backpack, she felt at the neck of her dress to make sure the mezuzah was still in place. She loosened the drawstring of her black handbag (the kind that looks like a horse's feed bag), pushed aside the bed socks her father had left her, and took out the coffee-stained list of clues.

1. Sword and sandals
2. Three legs
3. The great divide
4. Sow
5. Kicks
6. Pretzel
7. Fitting
8. Down by the river
9. Temple
10. Lucky number
11. Amazing
12. Sails

She crossed off the first item on the list. If number 2 was as farfetched as number 1 had been, ''Three legs'' could mean anything from a broken chair to Siamese twins. No matter. She was ready for any kind of shit, prepared to go where she was not wanted, to butt in where she had no business, to test her meddle all over the map. Oreo was one pushy chick.

Her bravery was beyond question. She had chosen, against the advice of older, more cautious adventurers, to eschew the easy canoe trip up the Delaware, piece-of-cake portage across the swamplands of New Jersey, and no-sweat glissade across the Hudson to Manhattan and to travel instead the far more problematic overland route via the Penn Central Railroad. What further ensign of Oreo's courage need be cited?

The subway concourse at Thirtieth Street

Oreo knew that there were several stiff trials ahead before she reached the official starting point of her overland journey, the Waiting Room of Thirtieth Street Station. The first and second trials came together: the Broken Escalator and the Leaky Pipes. Countless previous travelers had suffered broken ankles and/or Chinese water torture as they made their way between the subway and Thirtieth Street Station. With the advent of wide-heeled ugly shoes, which replaced hamstring-snapping spike heels, much of the danger had been taken out of the Broken Escalator's gaping treads. Much—in fact, all—of the movement had been taken out of the B.E. almost immediately after it began its rounds. Thus it had had a life of only two minutes and thirty seconds as a moving staircase before it expired to become the Broken Escalator of Philadelphia legend. Oreo had prepared for this leg of the journey by wearing sandals, which provided firm footing on the treads of the B.E. and also served as a showcase for her short-toed perfect feet.

The Leaky Pipes filled the traveler's need for irritation, humiliation, irrigation, and syncopation. According to the number of drops that fell on the traveler from the Leaky Pipes, he or she was irritated, humiliated, or irrigated. These degrees were largely a function of the Pipes' syncopation. With a simple one, *two*, three, *four*, a few even simpler souls would be caught by the drops of the offbeat. One who fell victim three or more times to this rhythm could safely be said to have passed beyond the bounds of irritation and into the slink of humiliation. The unlucky ones were those who got caught in a *one*, two, three, *four*, — , six, seven, eight. They would end up soaking wet by the time they got to the foot or the head (depending on their direction) of the Broken Escalator. Ninety percent of those caught by the *one*, two, three, *four*, — , six, seven, eight were white. They just couldn't get the hang of it. Black people were usually caught by the normal, unsyncopated, *one,* two, *one*, two—it was so simple, they couldn't believe it.

Oreo stood at the top of the B.E. and closed her eyes. She did not want to be distracted by looking at the drops. She just listened. She was in luck. The Pipes were in the one, *two,* three, *four* phase. She opened her eyes and observed that the drops *(two* and *four)* hit the same side of the B.E. on every other tread. It was a simple matter then to make her way down along the dry side, leaping over the treads on which the drops fell to avoid lateral splash. She did so hastily — and just in time too, for the Pipes switched into a different cycle just as her sandal hit the last tread, and one drop narrowly missed her exposed heel.

The third trial was suffering through the graffiti of Cool Clam, Kool Rock, Pinto, Timetable, Zoom Lens, and Corn Bread (the self-styled "King of the Walls," who crowned his *B* with a three-pronged diadem). It was not considered fair to squint and stumble along the passageway to the station. No, the fully open eye had to be offered up to such xenophobic, no-news lines as

DRACULA AND MANUFACTURERS HANOVER TRUST SUCK

the polymorphous-perversity of

BABE LOVES
BILL & MARY & LASSIE & SPAM

the airy, wuthering affirmation of

CHARLOTTE & EMILY LIVE!

the Platonic pique of

SOCRATES THINKS HE KNOWS ALL THE QUESTIONS

Oreo stared at these writings, a test of her strength. So intense was her concentration that at first she paid little notice to a tickle at her right shoulder. She felt it again and whirled to look into the eyes of a lame man she had passed near the Babe-Bill-Mary-Lassie-Spam graffito. One of the foil-wrapped packages from her duffel-bag lunch was in his hand. He had been picking her packet! She reached out to grab it but ducked when she saw the man's arm go around in a baseball swing. There was a *whoosh!* as molecules of air bumped against one another, taking the cut her head should have taken. Strike one. With the count 0-1, she noticed that the bat was a cane. She ducked again for strike two. "Well, aint this a blip!" Oreo said aloud, finally getting annoyed. She grabbed the cane and gave the man a mild *hed-blō*. She did not want to strike a lame old man with a full-force *hed-krac*. When the old pickpacket saw the look in her eye, he turned and ran down the passageway at Olympic speed. He was really hot*footing* it, honey! He was really picking them up and putting them down! Because of her backpack, Oreo did not catch him until he neared the end of the passageway. Felling him with a flying *fut-kik*, she pressed on his Adam's apple with his cane until he promised he would not try to get up until she gave him leave.

She asked him his alias and his m.o. Perry recounted how he had gone into a hardware store and asked for a copper rod. The proprietor brought it to him, saying they were having a special on copper rods that day and that he was entitled to a fifteen percent discount. Perry, caviling emptor, who had read in the papers that the discount was supposed to be twenty percent, took the rod and racked up the storekeeper's head with it. He paid not a copper but, rather, copped the copper before the coppers came and he had to cop a plea. He had taken the rod home, sheathed it in wood, crooked one end, and brazenly decorated the other end with a brass ferrule. With this cupreous cudgel and a fake limp, he had been lurking in the subway concourse, preying on unwary commuters, rampaging up and down the passageway.

"So why haven't I read about this in the papers?" Oreo asked. "We're only a stone's throw from the *Bulletin* building."

"Oh, I just started fifteen minutes ago. You were my first victim, not counting the hardware guy."

Oreo helped Perry up off the ground, advising him that better he should be home waiting for his social security check. She confiscated his cane and admonished him that the way of the cutpurse was hard and drear. He wasn't convinced. Then she said, "I can sum up your ability as a *gonif* in one word."

"What's that?"

"Feh!"

He was convinced.

Oreo in the Waiting Room of Thirtieth Street Station

The trials of Getting a Ticket, Checking Departure Time, Finding the Track, and Waiting for the Late Train are too typical to chronicle here. While Oreo was in the state of Waiting for the Late Train, she decided to cross "Three legs" off her list. If Perry's cane, now her walking stick, was not the third leg of the Sphinx's hoary riddle about old age, she did not care what it was. She also decided that since this was, after all, her quest (so far a matter of low emprise), she would cross all the other clues off her list whenever she felt justified in doing so. This was not logical, but tough syll. For instance, number 4 on the list was "Sow." Did this pig in a poke indeed refer to something piglike or to something seedlike? To a pork chop or to a Burpee catalog? If her father was going to give such dumb clues, she was going to prove she was her father's daughter. When necessary, she could outdumb any scrock this side of Jimmie C. The arrival of the Silver Gimp — two hours and twelve minutes late — interrupted her smug assessment of how dumb she could be if given half a chance.

Oreo on the train

She had passed through the Finding a Seat phase and was now in the state of Hoping to Have the Seat All to Myself. She took off her backpack and put it on the overhead rack. As each potential seatmate came down the aisle, Oreo gave a hacking cough or made her cheek go into a rapid tic or talked animatedly to herself or tried to look fat, then she laid her handbag and walking stick on the adjoining seat and put a this-isn't-mine expression on her face. But these were seasoned travelers. They knew what she was up to. Since most of them were in the pre-

Hoping to Have the Seat All to Myself phase, they passed on down the aisle, avoiding the eyes of the *shlemiels* who were Hoping to Have Someone Nice to Talk to All the Way to New York. As the train filled, the hardened travelers knew that it was pie-in-the-sky to hold out for a double seat, and each of them settled down to the bread-and-butter business of Hoping My Seatmate Will Keep His/Her Trap Shut and Let Me Read the Paper and the even more fervent Hoping No Mewling Brats Are Aboard.

One young blond had been traipsing up and down the aisles for five minutes. Oreo's first thought when she saw him was that he was almost as good-looking as she was, and she enjoyed watching the other passengers watch him. On this trip, the young man stopped in front of her with arms akimbo, resigned, and said, "All right, honey, I've checked, and next to me you're the prettiest thing on this train, so we might as well sit together. Give these Poor Pitiful Pearls something to look at."

Oreo smiled appreciatively at his *chutzpah* and moved her handbag and cane off the seat.

Before he sat down, he put a black case, about the size of a typewriter, on the overhead rack. He tried to move Oreo's backpack over, but it wouldn't budge. "Is this yours?" he asked.

Oreo nodded.

"What's in it—a piece of Jupiter?"

Oreo laughed. "No, my lunch. On Jupiter it would weigh more than twice as much—between skatey-eight and fifty-'leven pounds."

"Good, good. I see I can talk to you."

By the time the train pulled into North Philadelphia, Waverley Honor—"Can you *believe* that name?" he said. "In this case Honor is a place, not a code, thank God!"—knew eight things about Oreo. "Okay, that's enough about you. Now, go ahead, ask me what I do."

"What do you do, Waverley?" Oreo said dutifully.

"Are you ready for this?" He paused. "I'm a traveling executioner."

Oreo did the obligatory take.

"See that black case?" Waverley pointed to the overhead rack.

Oreo nodded. "It looks like a typewriter case."

"Guess what's in it."

"A small electric chair," Oreo said, playing straight.

"Good guess. No, a typewriter."

"Oh, shit," said Oreo.

Waverley placated her. "But it *was* a good guess. It's my Remington electric. Carry it with me on special jobs. It's a Quiet-Riter."

"So tell me, already, and cut the crap," said Oreo.

Waverley explained that he was a Kelly Girl, the fastest shift key in the East among office temporaries. Whenever a big corporation was having a major shake-up anywhere on the eastern seaboard, Waverley got the call to pack his Remington.

"Yes, but what exactly do you do?" asked Oreo.

"I thought you'd never ask." He moved closer to Oreo so that their conversation could not be overheard. "My last job was typical. I get the call from Kelly, right? They say, 'So-and-so Corporation needs you.' So-and-so Corporation shall be nameless, because, after all, a boy can't tell *everything* he knows." He paused for the laugh. "But believe me, honey, this is a biggie. I mean, you can't fart without their having something to do with it. Anyway, I show up at the building — one of those all-glass mothers. I flash my special pass at the guard. I wish I could use that identification card on all my jobs— absolutely *adorable* picture of me. Anyway, I take the back elevator to the fifty-second floor. The receptionist shows me to my cubicle. A man comes in a minute later with a locked briefcase. He opens it and explains the job. It's straight copy work.

What I am doing is typing the termination notices of four hundred top executives. Off with their heads! That's why I call myself the traveling executioner. I mean, honey, most of those guys had been with that company since 1910, and they don't know *what* the fuck is going to hit them in their next pay check." He raised his eyebrows, an intricate maneuver involving a series of infinitesimal ascensions until the brows reached a plateau that, above all, tokened a pause for a rhetorical question. "Can you believe that? Well, my *dear*, the work was *so* mechanical and *so* boring that I *insisted* on having a radio the second day. So while I was decapitating these mothers from Scarsdale and Stamford and Darien, I was digging Aretha and Tina Turner and James Brown. Talk about ironic! While Tina is doing her thing on 'I Want to Take You Higher,' I'm lowering the boom on these forty-five-thousand-dollar-a-year men. Made me feel just *terrible!* I really sympathize with upper-income people, honey. They're *my* kind of minority."

While Waverley went to get a drink of water, Oreo stared at the dirty cardboard on the back of the seat in front of her:

Thanks for riding Penn Central ▰ **Have a pleasant trip**

She looked out the window as the train passed a small station and saw another sign that, for an instant, made her think she was in a foreign country, until she realized that some letters were missing:

TRA

OCATION 5

As the train pulled into Trenton, Oreo got hungry. She hauled her backpack from the overhead rack and was about to start in, when she realized she was being selfish—besides, it wouldn't hurt to have a carload of travelers in her debt. Reserving only a few choice bundles, she enlisted Waverley's aid and distributed the rest to the other passengers. In a few minutes, groans and moans were heard amidst all the *fressing*.

Between bites, Waverley kept saying, "Oh my God, it's so good I'm coming in my pants."

The whole car broke into applause when Oreo went to get a cup of water. She bowed this way and that as she came back to her seat. She sat there for a while digesting Louise's Apollonian stuffed grape leaves, her revolutionary piroshki. She was trying to decide what shade of blue the sky was. It was the recycled blue of a pair of fifty-dollar French jeans (or jeannettes) that had been deliberately faded. She decided that from now on, she would call that shade jive blue. Douglas Floors would approve.

Waverley was looking over her shoulder. Suddenly he sat back and sighed. "You're the first nice person I've talked to in a long time. Can I drop my beads?"

"Sure, go ahead."

He confided that he was not only a traveling executioner, but also a *gay* traveling executioner.

"*Nu*, so vot else is new?" she said, doing one of her mother's voices.

He made a stage swishy gesture. "I'm beginning to think the whole world is." He then gave a list of movie stars, past and present, who were "that way"; it included everyone except Rin-Tin-Tin and John Wayne. "Even though the Duke's real name is Marion and he has that funny walk, we're pretty sure he's straight, but we're not all *that* definite about Rinty. Lassie, of course, is a drag queen from *way* back."

Waverley said that he had been very depressed since he and his last lover had split up. At first he had just sat around feeling sorry for himself, typing by day and jerking off by night.

"Then I decided, the hell with that. I did something I've never done before. I went out cruising in all the bars. Did all the things I've always wanted to do. I felt justified because I was tired of living like a vegetable."

"You wanted to live like a piece of meat," Oreo said.

Waverley nodded appreciatively. "Oh, you are evil, *e-vil!* Anyway, I had all kinds of guys. In the third week, I had my first Oriental."

"Is it true what they say about Oriental men?"

"What?"

"That their balls are like this"—she placed one fist on top of the other—"instead of side by side?"

Another nod, another "Evil, *e-vil!*" He said he would top that by starting a rumor that Castilian fags had a double lisp. Then he opened his wallet. "Let me show you some pictures." He smiled as he looked at the first one. "These are two of my best friends, Phyllis and Billie."

Oreo nodded. "Phyllis looks like Ava Gardner."

"That's Billie, with an *i-e*. Phyllis is the one who looks like a truck driver. But that just goes to show you looks are deceiving. Phyllis doesn't drive trucks. She fixes them. My mother got hold of this one—she's always popping in on me, snooping around, but that's another story. Anyway, when she saw this, I had to tell her Phyll was Billie's *boy*friend. But if you look close, you can see her bra strap through the tee shirt. I showed it to Phyll's ex-husband. I thought he would wet his drawers, he laughed so hard. He's gay, too. A real swish, honey. He's Filipino and they were going to send him back to the islands. He wanted to stay here and he and Phyll were good buddies, so she married him." He shook his head, remembering. "You should have seen her at the wedding. She let her hair grow long and looked pretty good, for her. Joe, that's the guy she married, had to buy her a girdle and stockings and show her how to walk in heels. When she walked, it was a complete panic.'' He stood up and did a hoarse, deep-voiced cowhand on stilts. '' 'By God, when I get out of these damn things, I'll never put them on again.' This was years ago, when girls used to wear dresses to work. But old Phyll would always wear her overalls. Of course, she *was* a mechanic. If her bosses knew she was a girl, they weren't saying. She was a damn *good* mechanic.''

"She looks tough," said Oreo. "Does she give Billie a hard way to go?"

Waverley looked genuinely shocked. "Of *course* not. *Billie's* the butch. Phyll's the sweetest girl you'd ever want to meet. She taught me how to knit. Gives cooking lessons to anyone who asks her. She didn't *have* to marry Joe. And then there was the baby—"

"The baby?"

"Sure. Joe said he always wanted one, so Phyll said okay. She made the right decision too. Joe's the best mother a baby could want. But that Billie—she'd break your balls as soon as look at you.''

"Or twist your tits," Oreo said.

"What?"

"Never mind—a failure of empathy."

Waverley went on with his adventures. All his talk of cocks he had known and loved reminded Oreo that she had forgotten to pack the gift she had for her father. It was a plaster of Paris mold of Jimmie C.'s uncircumcised penis. Helen had refused to let the hospital take a hem in her son's decoration, saying that she considered it mutilation and that when he was old enough, she would let him decide whether he wanted to have it done. He had not decided because Helen had not put the question to him. Helen had not brought it out in the open because she still did not consider Jimmie C. old enough to decide. Jimmie C.

brought it out in the open only to go to the bathroom and to conform to Oreo's special request—no, threat—for a mold. He conformed to her special request because he loved his sister and because she threatened to tell him one of the "suppose" lines that she had been saving up to make him faint. He, in turn, had a special request, which he sang with a hauntingly sweet melodic line: "Nevertheless and winnie-the-pooh, whatever you do, don't paint it green." For one fiendish moment, Oreo had contemplated doing just that, but she contented herself with deciding which of two questions she would put to Samuel when she gave him the mold: "How do you like that *putz?*" or "How do you like *that, putz?*" She had been leaning toward the second, but now all that was moot, since she had forgotten the *putz* in question.

As the train approached the next stop, Waverley said, "Well, this is it. Today Newark, tomorrow Rahway. Could *you* stand such excitement?" They exchanged addresses, and he pulled his black case down from the overhead rack. "Ooo, do I have to pee—the first bar I come to gets the gold," he said piss elegantly.

"Any pot in the storm," said Oreo. She had no shame. She watched Honor bound for a tearoom.

8 Sinis

Oreo in a phone booth at Penn Station

She opened the Manhattan directory. There were twenty-six Samuel Schwartzes and twenty-two S. Schwartzes. She made a list of likely Schwartzes, leaving out businesses and other obvious wrong leads. She picked her first try at random.

Oreo checked her backpack in a locker and bought a booklet of New York maps. The maps told her she should take the IRT subway, then switch to the number 5 bus.

Oreo on the subway

Oreo wondered about the relative funk quotient after three-quarters of play of the New York Jets as compared with the New York Knicks. Was football basically smellier than basketball? On the one hand, basketball uniforms did not have sleeves and the players therefore got a chance to air their pits during the game. Football players, on the other hand, were padded and wrapped. No chance for pit airing there. But—and it was a considerable but—they played outdoors. There were no proximate brick-and-mortar barriers to funk dissipation. Another consideration: although football involved intense periodic effort, it was so specialized that every mother's son got a chance to rest between bits. Oreo doubted whether dedicated linebackers dared risk their concentration by taking time out to apply spray, cream, or roll-on deodorant during their rest periods. Basketball, with its continual stampede up and down the court—and with its big stars playing virtually the full forty-eight minutes—seemed to offer little chance for deodorant application, even in the face (or pit) of desire or necessity. And what of hockey? Did ice absorb funk? The parameters were tricky.

Football: a subway reverie

Picture this, sports fans. It is the Super Bowl. A woman in full football gear (custom-made) runs onto the field. (Some spectators at first think that the shoulder pads of a demented 120-pound lad have slipped to the front.) This poor woman loves football with a doomed and touching passion. Every man who has longed for the field as he sat rooted to the stands was at least informed with *possibility,* however faint. If he were but fifty pounds heavier, but five seconds fleeter . . . But this is a woman. Imagine what astrodomes of nature and nurture she has had to friedan in order to test that artificial turf. She has reached the line of scrimmage. She ducks under a ham-haunched center and scoops up the ball. She starts to run a down-and-out pattern. What happens next? This is the *Super* Bowl, folks. *Bon appétit!* They Eat Her. Yes, fans, one crackback block and opposing players join in the gorge. They tear that cheeky female apart, devour her, uniform and all. Watch as a tattered leftover (part of the lower dexter curve of the number 8, the hip of that most feminine number, the number she wore in all her fantasy games) escapes and skitters across the field toward the tumescence-red first-down marker, one of the many totems of the male klan that kuklux the field. (The marker is a circle with a center pee/sperm-hole bullet above a vertex-down isosceles triangle, representing the penis in cross section above a Lindau wedge, or vagina—the missionary position.) Back home at setside, male viewers lick their lips and burp. Nielsen women feel a *frisson* of fear, shame, and guilt. The President's eyes glaze over. And the game resumes with a ferocity and joy unequaled in the history of sports. The next day, the newspapers insist that a high-school student (male) ran onto the field and was escorted off. Everyone, especially the players (who all have a touch of salmonella), agrees that that is what happened. The text of the President's ecstatic telephone calls to both coaches and each and every player is released to the public. He has proclaimed football henceforth and forevermore the national sport (and diet).

Oreo on the number 5 bus

Within a few minutes after she got on, Oreo realized she was riding the famed crazy ladies' bus. She had heard about it in Philadelphia. She was in luck. There were two *meshuggenes* aboard. One was tall, sharp-boned, and sharp-tongued. Her dark-blue dress with white polka dots snagged on her like a rag on a splinter, tail ends of sentences shredded from her mouth. ". . . away from me! . . . shit hell alone!" she raged as she pushed her way to the back, where she stood blocking the aisle. To Oreo, she looked like a Penelope.

The other was a short, gray-haired woman sitting near the front of the bus. She showed one broken middle tooth when she smiled (a curable smile). There was an unremitting smell of aluminum chlorhydroxide about her. Oreo guessed that the woman always washed and dressed as if she were going for a thorough physical after which she would be run over by a car and strangers would see her underwear. If true, she was as normal as the rest of the people on the bus, and there was no hope —except, of course, for the smile. She wore a crisp dress of green, white, and blue stripes and had elastic bands on her wrists. Her shoes were white, with a small bas-relief floral design in pale green and pink on the toe. A Sophie, perhaps? The conversation piece of her outfit was her shopping bag. It was kraft with five thin red wave-design lines across the top. On it floated a message printed neatly in red crayon, beginning on the top wave:

WHO IS USING ME AS SOME KIND OF A SCREEN AND EVERYONE THAT IS OPPRESSED I HAVE TO LOOK AT BECAUSE PEOPLE WANT THEIR AILMENTS ON THE SCREEN. I CAN'T TALK TO ANYONE BUT IT'S HEARD. MY ONLY BROTHER IS 71 YEARS OF AGE AND VERY SICK AND IF I VISIT AND TALK ON THE PHONE THE CONVERSATION IS HEARD. ISN'T THAT INFRINGING ON MY PRIVACY??? I'M NEAR 64 YEARS OF AGE AND IT'S VERY NERVE RACKING. NO ONE EVER EXPLAINED TO ME WHAT IT IS.

She seemed generally in good spirits, but occasionally she would clutch her wrists and cry, "Ow, ow," or look as if she were about to weep. But the cry of pain, the mask of sorrow were momentary. An instant later, she was smiling again. She had a well-developed social consciousness. She talked to the air space in front of her about poor people, Vietnam, and unemployment.

Between Sophie and Penelope the bus passengers did not

know where not to look. Some tried surreptitious eyeball rolls from side to side, most stared straight ahead and pretended the two women were not there. Penelope was too involved with extending her sovereignty to be aware of the effect she was having on the socially conscious Sophie, who was amused by Penelope's preoccupation with manifest destiny, particularly whenever Pen delivered herself of a choice piece of verbal territorial incursion. Sophie had obviously diagnosed Penelope's trouble as fallen arches. Several times Sophie obliquely addressed her with the same words. "I didn't work today," she would say to the air space. "I just rode around the city. You can have my seat."

". . . out of here!" said Penelope. ". . . off me!"

At which, Sophie would cut short a giggle to renew her comments on society's unfortunates. "The hoi polloi," she said. (Oh, Oreo thought, sympathetically noting the repetition of the article, she just stammered in two languages.) "All that education, and what good is it? Now they can't find jobs." She clucked in sympathy. "I don't give to churches, but if I have a spare dollar, I give to veterans' organizations." She read aloud a headline across the aisle about a bank robbery, then said, "They weren't educated, but they had their omens and their voodoo. They had the right answers. They knew, they knew. Tea leaves. Believe me, I hit four seventy-eight for a couple hundred dollars. They knew, they knew. Ben Franklin said, 'Early to bed, early to rise.' They don't even know how to say that today."

As the bus passed Sixty-second and Broadway, someone said approvingly, "Look at that. The Jewish Guild for the Blind doesn't have to wash its windows—nobody has to see out."

The man to Oreo's left was reading the front page of the *Daily News*. When he flipped the paper to scan the back sports page, Sophie read the front-page banner headline aloud. Oreo remembered that the headline had been set up like this:

Porno Panel:
_____

END ALL BANS
ON ADULT SMUT

To Oreo, this headline was a comment on itself. Sophie seemed reluctant to add anything to her reading of the banner head. It was not one of her subjects. More to her taste was the headline over a story about two starved, skull-fractured children whose mother was under observation at Bellevue:

FIND BODIES
OF 2 TOTS;
TEST MOM

Oreo had read this story over the shoulder of the woman to her right. Porno panel or no porno panel, Oreo considered the use of "Tots" and "Mom," in the circumstances, particularly obscene, the space limitations of tabloids notwithstanding.

"Poor woman," began Sophie. But before she was well into her desultory views on battered children, mental illness, and exorbitant hospital rates, she had to break off to watch Penelope spear her way through the crowd and get off by the back door.

". . . out of here! . . . off me!" said Penelope. Oreo watched as she posted herself in front of the post office (Ansonia station), then abandoned her post just in time to board a bus that had been tailgating the number 5 for several blocks.

The people at the back of the bus were noticeably relieved at Penelope's departure. They talked among themselves, survivors after rescue. The people at the front of the bus stared enviously toward the rear. They still had Sophie. But with Penelope gone, Sophie quieted down. She stopped reading headlines and was content with clutching her wrists several times for a few modulated "Ow's" and tapping lightly on her shopping bag.

As the bus skirted a park—which Oreo's booklet told her was Riverside—Sophie got up to leave. She went to the back door, and with a sedate "Out, please," she was gone.

All was quiet for a few more blocks. Then an elderly gentleman with one bad eye got up to leave. Oreo was sure it was Mr. Sammler. Her hunch was confirmed when he was followed off the bus by a dapper young man in a camel's hair coat.

A few blocks later, Oreo herself got off the bus. She walked to West End Avenue, found the address she had written down, and told the doorman she wanted to see Schwartz.

"Schwartz? In four-B?" asked the doorman.

"Is that the only Schwartz in the building?"

"Yeah."

Then, of course, dummy, thought Oreo. "Say Christine is on her way up."

The doorman buzzed 4-B and gave his message.

"Send her up," said a deep voice over the intercom as Oreo got into the elevator.

A few minutes later, Oreo was back downstairs. The Schwartz in 4-B was too young to be her father. Besides, she was Chinese.

Oreo on Broadway

She stopped when she came to a bar. She went in, walked straight to the back, went to the ladies' room, peed, and walked out. She was always disconcerted when she had to do this— walk into a place where she was considered a minor. Fortunately, because of her constant bullshit, she was often disguised as an adult. On the occasions when she was challenged and had to admit that she was a minor, Oreo was deeply embarrassed. She did not scruple going into a bar and not ordering anything. She drank only fine wines and Pepsi on the rocks. What is more, she was basically tight. She did not mind relieving herself when all around her knew that that was all she was going to do. Any pot in the storm—the chestnut she had trotted out for Waverley—was her motto for these occasions. She had other, even worse puns for other occasions. But to call Oreo a minor was, slowly and caerphilly, to drive a shaft into the pits of her cheeseparing soul. She did not consider herself a minor at or of or in anything.

Oreo on Broadway again

She was hungry. Now she was sorry that she had given Louise's fine food to a bunch of pig-eyed strangers. And Waverley Honor had eaten like a mother, the faggot. Oreo was getting testy. She had a lot of money with her, but she did not want to spend it if she could help it. Cheap. Hunger finally forced her to buy a Blimpie, a vicious imitation of a hoagie. Her refined palate, trained and coddled *chez* Louise, still had blotches and patches that brooked nothing but junk foods. Thus she could within hours savor her grandmother's thrifty, piping haggis and the rotten potato salad from Murray's delicatessen; Louise's holey, many-tongued fondue and the galosh pizza from Rosa's Trattoria; a *blanc de blancs* champagne and a blankety-blank Pepsi, which she now washed the Blimpie down with. Her testiness was disappearing.

Oreo goes to the park

She decided to take a walk through the park the bus had passed and make up her mind about what she was going to do next. She used her walking stick as a piton for climbing rocks and hillocks in the park. It was not necessary, considering the modesty of Riverside's ups and downs, but it made Oreo feel more like an adventurer.

When she stopped to rest, she looked up the addresses on her list in her book of maps. There were several S. or Samuel Schwartzes in the immediate neighborhood. She could make a few quick runs to check them out, using the park as an R and R base.

That evening

Oreo was exhausted. None of the S.'s or Sams belonged to her, but they had been diverting. There was the Sam on Eighty-ninth Street who wanted to adopt her; the Samuel on Columbus Avenue who saw voices ("Stick your fingers in your nose," Oreo advised him, "and they'll go away"); the S. on Cathedral Parkway who refused to say what the S. stood for (when Oreo guessed Snicklefritz on her second try, he turned blue, and she had to call an ambulance); the S. on Seventy-fifth Street who turned out to be a Shirley who had changed the name to an initial in the directory listing because of obscene phone calls ("My wife was very put off, psychologically and actually speaking, by heavy breathers who asked for me," he explained). There was the Samuel on Broadway who, along with his wife, was in jail awaiting trial for the murder of his son Melvin. Mr. and Mrs. Schwartz had learned of their son's plot to smother them in their beds and throw himself on the mercy of the court as an orphan, so they got him first. A neighbor told Oreo what the accused couple had said as they were dragged away: "Imagine the *chutzpah* on that kid—to think of a plot like that!" Sympathy in the building was running heavily in favor of the alleged murderers. Melvin had been known on the block as Smart Ass.

Because of these and other Schwartzes, Oreo had decided to call it a day. She had gone crazy at a delicatessen on Broadway called Zabar's and had bought a lot of goodies to eat, the gourmet in her temporarily winning out over the stingy person. To compensate for her lack of control around good food, she was going to save money by sleeping overnight in the park instead of checking into a hotel. She had found that Riverside Park's major drawback as a campsite was that it was long and narrow. It was flanked on the west by the Hudson River and the West Side Highway. Because of its narrowness, it had been difficult for Oreo to find a secluded spot, away from children, dogs, bicycle riders, tennis players, joggers, lovers. The place she had chosen for her picnic dinner she thought would be ideal for her overnight bivouac. It was hidden by trees and a huge rock, was near a water fountain and a park john, and was, for the moment, clear of people. She shoved her orange and white Zabar's shopping bag under a natural shelf in the rock and went to the john.

As she sat there, she noticed a hole about the size of a half dollar in the door that would provide a midget's-eye view of the toilet. Sure enough, a few moments later a midget's eye appeared at the hole. Oreo could recognize one anywhere. The midget giggled, and Oreo picked up an empty cigarette pack that someone had dropped on the floor and slammed it against the hole.

"It's giving me Marlboros," said a high-pitched voice.

Oreo got tired of stretching from the toilet seat to the door and dropped the pack. The hole was clear for a few moments. Then the eye came back. A few seconds later, wiggling fingers replaced the eye. Oreo grabbed the fingers and twisted them with a gentle but persuasive torque. The fingers were withdrawn from the hole hastily. "Yah, yah, that didn't hurt," said the voice.

"It will the next time," Oreo warned. She finished quickly and moved silently to the door. When she yanked it open and looked down, she was disappointed in herself. It wasn't a midget, just a normal-sized redheaded shifty-eyed kid of about eight.

"It's a gypsy!" the boy howled when he saw Oreo, and he ran off.

What kind of dumb kid thinks I'm a gypsy? Oreo thought. A Canadian dumb kid, she found out a few minutes later, when he came back with his parents. Oreo smiled. The boy's parents were midgets. She hadn't lost her eye for spotting midget blood after all.

"I'm Moe," the man said.

"And I'm Flo," said the woman.

"And we're here to say hello," they said together.

Oreo was about to introduce herself, but she thought that more than three rhymes in one chorus would be too Cole Porter. Instead, she leaned down and said, "And what's your name, little boy?"

"Look into your crystal ball, gypsy."

Scrock, thought Oreo.

His parents apologized for his bad manners. "Joe's his name," said his father.

"And we came," said his mother, who obviously leaned toward internal rhymes, "heigh-ho-the-derry-o . . ."

". . . from Ontario."

Moe and Flo Doe explained, in maddening doggerel, that they sold dog whistles and had been traveling all over so that Joe, who would inherit the business, would really get to know his territory—North America.

"Yep, we came from way out yonda," said Moe.

"On a Honda," Oreo put in before Flo could open her mouth.

"Yes, yes, yes. How'd you guess?" Moe said, grabbing the whole couplet for himself and thus revealing a selfish streak that Flo would doubtless have to contend with in their later, choliambic years as they went scazoning toward life's dead end.

How many caesuras would a rhymester as undisciplined as Moe not hesitate to rush into? Oreo wondered. How many catalectics make acatalectic, spondees amphimacerize in his mad rush to complete rhymes all by himself, without the help and support of the musette he loved? True, Oreo had been guilty of infringement when she snatched—nay, usurped—Flo's Honda line, but she had just met the midget woman and could hardly be accused of disloyalty.

The twice-deprived Flo raised a determined chin and said, "Why pay the rent? Pitch a tent," leaving Moe with his mouth open.

Oreo saw that Flo could take care of herself and stopped worrying about her. The couple explained that although three Does could ride with comfort on one motor scooter, they always traveled with two, so that either Flo or Moe was riding with Joe while either Flo or Moe rode the scooter with the family camping gear. They saved on hotel bills by camping, usually illegally, in parks and any other wide spots in the road they could find.

Oreo admired their thrift. She went back to her rock, a stone's throw away, and took out her buffet of noshes. Since the odds were that the Does could not eat much (a nanonosh), she offered to share her food with them. They declined with a klutzy quatrain (prose version: they were looking forward to the menu they had planned and wanted to get their camp set up before they prepared their evening meal). Oreo sat on her rock ledge and watched them. While she munched on smoked sable, chopped liver, and scallioned cream cheese, the munchkins pitched a hop-o'-my-thumb tent, then scurried to and fro with their dollhouse equipment.

Flo motioned Oreo over to ask that she watch the charcoal fire they had just started in the grill while she and Moe went to the bathroom. They didn't want little Joe poking at it.

"Whatever you do . . . ," said Moe.

"I beg of you . . . ," said Flo.

". . . don't let the flame go out . . ."

". . . scout."

Moe had obviously learned his lesson. He had left long pauses for Flo's lines.

Oreo turned to the fire as they walked off. Groovy, she thought, a sacred flame to tend. She noticed that the Does' charcoal briquettes were about the size of Chiclets.

"It's starting to go out," Joe complained. He was staring at the flames with pyromaniacal intensity.

"Oh, shut up. It is not."

"Boy, will they be mad when they come back and see that you let the fire go out. It has to be a certain heat for what we're cooking."

Oreo looked at the fire. It *was* dying down. She had never tended a charcoal grill before. She couldn't let the flame go out and scrock up her sacred trust. A failed fire tender? Never! Now, what had Flo done to get the fire going? Oreo had seen her pour some stuff from a red can over the black Chiclets. Oreo took the can and gave the dying flames a generous dousing. With a phoenix tune, the flames sprang back to life and shot up the side of the can, just in front of Oreo's hand. *Whoosh, whoosh!* flapped the wings of the phoenix as the flames soared several feet straight up from the nozzle of the can. With unseemly haste, Oreo set the can shakily on the ground. It teetered and finally fell, sending a weed of flame scuttering through the dry grass. Oreo started for the can, hesitated, started again, and finally dashed forward to right it on a flat rock. Flames thrummed merrily from the nozzle.

Oreo backed off to survey the situation. *"Oi vei,* you mothers," she said to the scampering flames. She turned quickly. Joe was a safe distance away behind a tree, his shifty eyes wide with excitement and glee. He was *laughing* at Oreo. Oreo ran first to the weed of flame and danced on it. Her sandal caught fire. She slipped it off her heel and flung it away. It hit a scabby sycamore and fell into some grass beckoning from a fork of the tree. The grass caught fire. Joe was in a pyrophilous frenzy over Oreo's concatenating combustions. As she hopped about putting them out one by one, she knew that she was avoiding the main problem. She could hear the murmurs of the unsuspecting recreators—who might soon be piecemeal all over the foliage because Oreo was chicken shit!

She was stamping out the last small fire when she forced herself to face the red can with its high-powered *Whoosh, whoosh!* She calculated her chances. "If it hasn't exploded yet, it probably won't explode. On the other hand, *since* it hasn't exploded yet, it's probably ready to explode. If *I* blow, who knows how wide an area might go if *it* should blow? On the other hand, it certainly would be dumb if I were to go over there and do the heroine bit, save everybody in the park, and get blown up myself. I mean, I don't even *know* these people."

In the time it took to read all that, Oreo had run over to the Does' camping equipment, picked up a wee potholder in the shape of a wee mitt, shoved it on her index and middle fingers, flung herself at the can, and cut off its thrum *in flagrante*. Oreo smiled. Chicken shit my Aunt Minnie!

Joe looked disgusted. The only flames he had going for him now were the ones on the charcoal grill, the original sacred flame. He ran over to the grill hungrily.

Just then, Flo and Moe came back. They thanked Oreo for keeping the fire going.

"Heh, heh," Joe snickered.

"Before we sup . . . ," said Flo.

". . . please fill this cup," Moe told Joe. He was stretching a point to make the rhyme. The "cup" was a bucket.

"It's what we need—don't you feel?" he said to his wife.

"Oh, yes, indeed—to make our meal."

"We almost needed some water for this whole place," Joe said, smiling nastily at Oreo. He went off swinging his bucket and whistling a medley of gypsy tunes.

Oreo asked the couple what they were fixing that required the special temperature that Joe had mentioned. But of course: braised dog biscuits. The Does said that dog biscuits were the perfect food for small campers. They had all the vitamins and minerals for the adult midget minimum daily requirement, they were lightweight, easy to pack and carry, and they were tasty. Braising over a hot charcoal fire brought out their subtle flavor.

Oreo made a mental note to tell Louise. But why this preoccupation with dogs? she wondered. Dog whistles, dog biscuits.

"You see things from their point of view . . . ," said Flo.

". . . down amidst all this do-do," said Moe, lifting his leg high as he walked over the grass.

That night

On her afternoon walk, Oreo had discovered the Seventy-ninth Street Boat Basin, where private yachts, speedboats, and houseboats were moored. She thought it would look pretty at night and was headed there when she heard music. Somewhere near the boat basin a rock group was working out. As she walked along the esplanade toward the boats, the music seemed to come from above her. Several people were going up the steps that led from the esplanade to an undomed rotunda, the upper perimeter of which served as a traffic circle for cars entering or leaving the West Side Highway at Seventy-ninth Street. The rotunda itself was a pedestrian underpass of the highway exit; its archways encircled a large central fountain. Earlier that day, Oreo had watched children and dogs playing in the fountain under black and white signs that read:

NO PERSONS
ANIMALS
PERMITTED
IN WATER

That afternoon, strollers had sauntered coolly through the frescade of overlapping shadows cast by the archways. Now, for some reason, no one was allowed access to the rotunda from the esplanade.

Oreo and several other people backtracked through the park and went to the upper perimeter of the rotunda, darting through the circling traffic to get to the narrow ledge that formed the base of the waist-high upper wall. They looked down on a rothschild of rich people (dancing), round tables (sprouting beach umbrellas), and rock groups (playing at opposite arcs of the stone circle).

None of the onlookers seemed to know what was going on, so Oreo crossed the traffic circle, ducked under the chain draped across the steps leading to the rotunda, and joined the party. No one questioned her as she wandered around tasting canapés and reading place cards. A few movie and television personalities walked by and pretended to know her when she pretended to know them.

She was about to leave when a boy of about eighteen—tall, thin, and supercilious in his black tie and white dinner jacket, with a nose as pointy and put-upon as an ice cream cone—asked her to dance. They were essentially dancing by themselves, one occasionally glancing at the other to see whether the other saw what a good dancer the glancer was.

Finally Oreo said, "I've been to so many benefits lately, I can't keep track."

"Tay-Sachs."

"Christine Clark."

"No, dear, that's the name of the disease this little party's in aid of."

"Never heard of it," said Oreo.

"Of course not. It's virtually exclusive to Jews—Ashkenazim."

"*Nu,* I'm half Jewish."

"Half a loaf is better than none."

"And sickle-cell anemia to you."

"Never heard of it," he said.

"Of course not. It's virtually exclusive to blacks—gesundheit."

"Some people have all the luck."

"Well, mine has obviously run out—I met you. But half a wit is better than none."

They stopped dancing and got down to the real business of seeing who could top whom. It went on for about fifteen minutes, his tit for her tat, and vice-verbal, until they both got tired and conceded the match was a draw.

Oreo never discovered her opponent's name, but she was happy for the chance she'd had to flex her snot-nosed-kid muscles. She headed back to the campsite, comforted by the knowledge that the Jewish half of her had kept her from getting sickle-cell anemia and the black half had warded off Tay-Sachs disease.

Back at the campsite

Oreo said good night to the Does, fifty baby steps away, and snuggled under her rock ledge on newspapers she had chosen for the purpose. She had picked ad pages with a high percentage of white space, not only because their good-taste quotient was likely to be high, but also because it would cut down on the amount of newsprint that could come off on her dress.

She slept fitfully, awakened during the wee hours by the cat-purrs that the Does affected for snores, the thuds and howls of muggers and muggees, the simpering of police in drag. Some time later, Oreo heard what must have been the reputedly beauteous band of female rapists who, according to the under-side of Oreo's bottom sheet, had been terrorizing Riverside Park for three weeks. At about 4 A.M. they dragged yet another victim into some nearby bushes ("If you can't get it up, we take it off"). Before the ravishingly ravishing ravishers ravished him, the man offered several limp excuses. It was all Oreo could do to keep from cracking up over his piteous protests that he was too afraid that he would not be able to get a hard-on to get a hard-on, that he wasn't usually like this, and could he come back on Tuesday instead. "Now, let's not run off half-cocked," said the obvious leader of the band. The man offered to substitute sucking for fucking. The leader castigated him. "Hell, no! My *dog* could do that. Besides, we're not in this for pleasure. We're out to teach you fathering mother-jumpers a lesson. Now, which is it—up or off?" Oreo turned over and went back to sleep.

The next morning

Oreo washed, brushed her teeth, and fluffed out her afro in the park john, then ate the delicatessen leftovers. Moe and Flo were still sleeping. Three minikin feet were sticking through the flap of their teeny tent. Oreo assumed that the other foot was inside Joe's feet were nowhere to be seen. He must be off playing somewhere, she guessed.

Oreo picked up her walking stick and went for a stroll to wake herself up and prepare for the new day. She had been walking for only a few minutes, when she heard yelps and whimpering in the bushes to her right. She thought at first that it might be the rape victim of the night before, but these noises

were less animalistic than his had been. She crept silently in the
direction of the sounds of distress. She parted the bushes. Her
irises contracted in disbelief. There was little Joe Doe, laughing
and playing happily with a dog. He had an eccentric sense of
humor. The human-sounding yelps and whimpers came from a
sad-faced Chihuahua. Joe had tied the dog to two sprung sap-
lings and was about to chop the retaining rope with his boy
scout ax. Oreo rushed over and grabbed the ax from him. She
hated to see the little brat having fun. She untied the grateful
Chihuahua, who went nickering away on spidery legs, making a
detour around—or, rather, through—the two halves of the
corpse of a Pekingese. Oreo *thought* it was a Pekingese. It was
either that or oat smut. Without a word, Oreo grabbed Joe by
the wrist and dragged him after her.

"Where are we going, gypsy?"

Oreo did not answer.

"I hate dogs. And dog whistles. And dog biscuits."

Oreo did not answer.

"Why do I have to have midgets for parents? Even if they
were regular-size short people, it would be okay. But, no, they
have to go and be midgets — and *short* midgets at that! I'm only
eight and already I'm taller than they are. It's not fair!"

Oreo did not answer.

"They make me sick with their rhymes. I have to have *some*
fun!"

Oreo did not answer. She kept dragging Joe behind her until
she found what she had been looking for, a playground full of
kids. Oreo rounded up ten of them. She explained what she
wanted them to do. She offered them a nickel apiece if they did
a good job. They held out for a dime. She hesitated, then agreed.

When they were ready, Oreo found a good seat on a swing
and watched. The ten children split up into two groups, five on
each side. The kids started their game with relish, screaming

and yelling for blood. The game was tug-of-war. The "rope" was Joe's body.

In a few seconds, Joe began to yelp and whimper the way the Chihuahua had. "I'll do anything you ask!" he yelled to Oreo.

Oreo tried to stop the game. The kids wanted to go on. Oreo hadn't gotten her money's worth yet, they said. Joe had been faking, they said. They hadn't gotten to the best part, the tearing asunder, they said. They gave Joe one more yank for the pot before Oreo rescued him. Each side claimed victory. Oreo examined Joe's arms with her keen eyes. One limb was an eighth of an inch longer than it had been, one only a sixteenth. Oreo, wincing at the expense, gave an extra dime to the winning side.

"Big deal—two cents apiece," the winners grumbled as they went off. The losers gazed longingly at Joe's short arm. In a few minutes, all the children were playing hopscotch, jumping rope, sliding the slides, sawing and seeing on the seesaw, a tableau of innocence.

Oreo took Joe aside. "Now you know how it feels. You promise you'll never do that to a dog again?"

"What about cats?"

"No cats."

"Squirrels?"

Oreo hesitated. She held no big brief for squirrels. They were sort of scrocky-looking. Finally she said, "No, absolutely not. No living things whatsoever."

Joe was downcast.

"And about your parents—you should be grateful they're not giants like my mother and father."

Joe was fascinated. "Really?"

"When Moe and Flo spank you, what does it feel like?"

"Butterfly kisses," Joe admitted.

"Imagine what it feels like to get a *potch* from a giant. One shot and you've had it. My last spanking was when I was six. I still have the marks.''

"Let me see?'' Joe asked gleefully.

"You see my skin? I used to be white. This is a bruise.''

Joe's eyes popped. "You gotta be kidding.''

"Would I lie to you?''

"Yeah.''

"So what. Be nice or I'll kill you.''

By the time they got back to the campsite, Oreo had convinced Joe that his parents were seed pearls beyond price and that if he tortured any more animals she would find him and throw him to the children. Oreo's catalog of the abuses he would suffer at the hands of underage Torquemadas made him hysterical. She had to calm him down before Moe and Flo saw him.

Oreo was happy. It had been a productive morning. She had evened the score with Joe for his medley of gypsy tunes—especially "Zigeuner'' and "Golden Earrings''—thereby upholding her motto: *Nemo me impune lacessit.* And she was able to cross "The great divide'' off her list.

9 Phaea

Boxes — Corrugated & Fibre
Boxes — Metal
Boxes — Paper
Boxes — Specialty & Fancy
Boxes — Wooden

Oreo had looked under all these headings in the yellow pages before she found a Jacob Schwartz who made boxes. She was glad Jacob—if this was the right Jacob—had not called his company the Reliance Box Co. or Best Boxes, Inc., or New York Box, Ltd. She knew beforehand that even if Jacob's name was listed, she would not find it until last, after she had looked under all the other headings. This always happened to her. She tried some *kopdrayenish* on kismet by not going in order. She skipped from ''Corrugated'' to ''Wooden'' to ''Paper'' to ''Metal.'' It did not work. That was exactly what kismet—a smart cookie—expected her to do. Jacob was under the last heading: ''Specialty & Fancy.'' A small box told about his boxes:

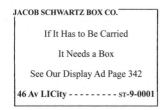

JACOB SCHWARTZ BOX CO.

If It Has to Be Carried

It Needs a Box

See Our Display Ad Page 342

46 Av LICity - - - - - - - - - ST-9-0001

Oreo liked Jacob's motto almost as much as she liked that of Chaim Epstein & Daughter, Inc.: "A Box Is a Box Is a Box But—Don't Mention—We're *Menshen*."

On the subway to Long Island City

Oreo looked at shoes and tried to guess what their wearers were like before she glanced up for confirmation. She guessed wrong on a pair of calf-hugging white boots. They were on a wall-eyed teenager with a lordotic slouch—obviously a failed drum majorette—and not on a Hadassah lady with a blue rinse, a type among whom such boots had been *de rigueur* for several seasons. She got the vacationing prostitute in the Grecian sandals (orange) that laced up to her zorch (exposed); the eleven-year-old tomboy with high-topped Pro-Keds; the black queen with liberation pumps by Gucci (red for the blood of black people, black for their race, and green for the money Gucci was making from this style); the barefoot heroin addict who had painted his feet shoe black; the waif in waif shoes; the wingéd bedroom slippers of a ninety-year-old employee of the Hermes Messenger Service.

Other than this diversion and seeing types of boxes that she hadn't known existed (a box for leftover french fries; a fake jewel box for real jewelry inside a real jewel box for fake jewelry; a box that could be used as an extra room for the growing family, a maid's room, or a guest room—a stock item popular with building contractors all over the country), Oreo's trip was wasted. Jacob was in Miami at the Fontainebleau ("Fountain Blue," said his French secretary, perfecting her American accent).

Oreo had learned her lesson: don't go when you can call. She called Equity. She called AFTRA. She called SAG. They all told her the same thing, more or less.

The less part:

Did she want the Sam Schwartz who had to change his name because there was already a Sam Schwartz on their roster or the other Sam Schwartz?

The other Sam Schwartz.

That would be Sam Schwartz, right?

Right. Would Equity-AFTRA-SAG give out his number, please?

Sorry. Can't divulge that information. Call his agent.

Would Equity-AFTRA-SAG give out his agent's number?

Sorry. Don't have that information.

What about the Sam Schwartz that changed his name?

That would be Scott Scott.

Kept his initials, eh?

What?

Nothing. And, of course, Equity-AFTRA-SAG can't give out his number either, right?

The more part:

"Is it a job?" the woman on the line said, lowering her voice.

"Yes," Oreo lied. "Mike Nichols is talking about a two-picture deal."

"Okay, here's the number. Tell him Sally at the SAG office put you in touch with him. Don't forget, *Sally.*"

"Right. Sally. SAG. I'll tell him."

En route to Scott Scott's

Oreo had let his number ring one hundred and eighteen times before she decided to go to the Village on the chance that he might show up. She liked the flatted fifth on the afterbeat of the ring and could have listened to it all day, but finally she had torn herself away.

Oreo was standing on the corner of Eighth Street and the Avenue of the Americas. The traffic standard gave a mechanical belch and turned green. "Where is Sixth Avenue?" she asked a man standing next to her.

"You're looking at it," the man said.

"It says 'Avenue of the Americas.' "

"I don't care *what* it says. It's *Sixth* Avenue." The man crossed the street, looking back angrily at Oreo.

Oreo had noticed that New Yorkers called things whatever they wanted to call them. Thus Houston Street was not the "Hews-ton" of Texas, but "House-ton"; the so-called squares named Sheridan, Duffy, Abingdon, Jackson, Cooper, and Father Demo were closer to being triangles; hopskotch was called, in some potheaded precincts of Gotham, potsy; and New Yorkers stood "on," not "in," line.

Oreo made two side trips — one to sniff the cheeses in a store called Cheese Village, another to sniff the books in a library called Jefferson Market. The library reminded her of a castle, with its spiral staircase, traceried windows, and low archways into the paradoxically bright dungeon of the reference room.

At Scott Scott's

Oreo knocked. There was no answer. She was about to turn away, when a woman carrying an armload of groceries came up to the door. She was about thirty-five, with the harried look of a septiplegic cephalopod.

"Are you looking for someone?" the woman asked, eyeing Oreo's walking stick.

"Does Scott Scott live here?"

"Do you have the time?" The woman was trying to hold up the groceries, get her key out, and bite her nails at the same time.

"It's about three o'clock."

"Scott should be home any minute now. You can come in and wait for him if you like."

Oreo was shown into a tiny apartment cluttered with statuettes, globes, certificates—and now with groceries, which the woman had dropped. "They're Scott's acting awards," the woman said, gesturing around the room with her elbows and chin. "I'm Mrs. Scott."

Oreo had had enough fun watching Mrs. Scott juggle the groceries; it was time to help her. She rounded up stray beef patties as she trailed Mrs. Scott into a kitchen that was just big enough to let one slice of bread pop out of the toaster before it could actually be called crowded.

"I must get Scott's tea ready. He likes his tea as soon as he comes in." She found an old bag of Earl Grey behind the toaster.

Oreo backed out of the kitchen to wait for Scott. She saw Mrs. Scott drop the same teaspoon seven times. Then the woman pulled herself together and dropped a cup for a change. Fortunately, it was empty, and its fall was cushioned by the groceries, which Mrs. Scott had dropped again. An orange rolled by Oreo's foot. She picked it up and ate it quickly—she thought she might go mad if it rolled by her one more time. It was what General Mills must go through when Betty Crocker was in mittelschmerz.

Oreo looked around the apartment. Under the clutter, she could see that the Scotts had at least one piece of furniture that they were protecting. It was an expensive plastic couch, which the Scotts had had the bad taste to cover with cheap upholstery, so that neither family nor visitors could get the look or feel of its fundamental, its rich plasticness. Oreo, ever alert, had spied the plastic through a worn spot in the upholstery. She was upset. To spend all that money on plastic and not show it!

A few minutes later, the door opened and a French-accented voice said, "I am arrived."

Mrs. Scott came bursting out of the kitchen, tripping over a bunch of bananas. "Scott's here!" she said as if it were a miracle.

To Oreo, it was something less. The mature man, possibly her father, whom she had been expecting turned out to be an eleven-year-old actor. He had the dark, knowing eyes of a street urchin, and his black hair, a jaunty morion, peaked front and back. All his movements were quick and sure. What his mother dropped on the one hand, he could surely catch, offhandedly, on the other hand—while doing three other things, yawning.

Breaking a vase as she pointed to her son, Mrs. Scott introduced the boy. He put his school books next to what Oreo now saw was a Play-Doh configuration of three Oscars, a Grammy, and an Emmy.

"Hi, Scott," said Oreo.

The boy threw his arms wide. "What is this that this is that you are so formal? I wish that you me call of my prename."

"Okay. Hi, Scott."

"Well!" said Scott, nodding and rubbing his hands with apache aplomb. "Well, well, well, that goes." He laid his finger aside his nose. "Then, so, in that case, thereupon! How you call you, young girl?"

"I call myself Christine Clark."

"Well, well, well, that goes. Since what hour wait you for me?"

"Since three hours less ten minutes," said Oreo.

"What a damage!" He turned to his mother. "I have need of the tea," he said, speaking the speech trippingly on the tongue as his mother went trippingly into the kitchen.

While Mrs. Scott was klutzing around, Oreo explained that she obviously had the wrong Scott Scott. The Scott Scott she wanted, né Samuel Schwartz, had changed his name for stage purposes.

Scott nodded vigorously. "You have reason. *Me,* this Scott here—this is me."

"But your mother's last name is Scott too."

Scott shrugged. "This is true. You have reason."

Mrs. Scott came back in, squishing a tomato underfoot — that is, in her case, underfeet. She explained that she had changed her name for two reasons: one, she hated her husband for not deserting her because she hated him, thereby putting her to the trouble of deserting him; and, two, she knew her son would be famous someday, and she wanted part of that action. When people spoke of Scott Scott, they would be speaking of her too, since her real first name was also Scott. She and her son had taken her maiden names. Parenthetically, she said that she had assumed Oreo was one of her son's chums from Professional Children's School. He had many older friends, she said.

"Which reminds me," Oreo said, "Sally at the SAG office asked me to say hello for her."

"Ah, yes, Sally—my old. She is—how you say?—a veritable pedophile." He shrugged again. "But that is the war."

"That woman!" said Mrs. Scott with a shudder. She took the dripping teabag from Scott's cup and plunked it into Oreo's cup of hot water. "I hope you don't mind," she apologized.

"Not at all. I like weak tea. My grandmother calls it 'water bewitched.' "

Scott clapped his hands. "This is magnificent! That phrase there—this is the word just." He turned to his mother. "Mama, my cabbage flower, have we of the outside of works to offer this visitor charming?"

While his mother stumbled into the kitchen, Scott excused himself to go to the room of bath. Amidst klunks, bangs, and thuds, Mrs. Scott chatted with Oreo. Oreo marveled at young Scott's accent. She told his mother that his inflection was so musically Gallic, she had had to remind herself that he was speaking English and not French. Mrs. Scott said that Scott came home with a different accent each day. Fortunately, she knew many languages and could follow him most of the time; but for two days the week before, because of her ignorance of Shluh and Kingwana syntax, Scott might as well have been speaking Shluh and Kingwana.

When Scott came back (one step and he loomed before them), Oreo told him that the other Sam Schwartz—the one who was still Sam Schwartz—must be her father.

Scott stroked his chin, then snapped his fingers. "There is!" He put his hand gently on Oreo's shoulder. "Then, so, in that case, thereupon, the path of your father, it has crossed the mine many of times. The ten-eighth April, I think, that day there, your father, he was the voice of a bubble of soap, and I the fall of the snows of yesteryear," he said, perhaps quoting Villon. He paced the floor (two and one-thirty-second paces) and turned sharply. "Have you the knowledge of the mathematics?" he asked pointedly.

"*Oui*—I mean, yes," said Oreo.

Scott removed his school books from the Play-Doh sculpture garden, saying that if Oreo would help him with his math problems, he would give her some leads to her father's whereabouts.

Scott Scott's math problems and
Oreo's fake answers (the real answers are found
only in the teacher's edition of this book)

Q. Gloria spent a certain amount for a new dress, a pair of shoes, and a purse. If the combined cost of the purse and shoes was $150 more than the cost of the dress, and the combined cost of the dress and purse was $127 less than twice the cost of the shoes, what is Gloria's real name?

A. In round figures, Shirley.

Q. An aspiring starlet rode a train that traveled at 70 miles per hour from Kenosha, Wisconsin, to the terminal in Los Angeles. She took a limousine that traveled at 20 miles per hour to Watts, escaping in a motor launch that traveled at 14 knots to Knott's Berry Farm. The entire trip of 2,289 miles required how many *coups d'états* if the starlet spent seven times as long on the motor launch as she did in the limousine?

A. Not counting Carmen Miranda, 3; counting Twentieth Century-Fox and General Maxwell D. Taylor, 547 at one blow of state.

Q. Jim has gone to school six times as long as Harry, and in 4 years he will have gone to school twice as long. What grade of motor oil does Jim use?

A. The question assumes a knowledge of calculus, thermodynamics, and jacks. It is not fair, and I refuse to answer it.

Q. A girl can clean her room in 46 minutes, and her roommate can do the job in 22 minutes. How long will it take them to figure out that they are wasting their time because the house has been condemned?

A. Two shakes of Charles Lamb's tale.

Q. To lay in a straight walk from his house to his gate, a man used 92 feet of foundation into which he poured 40 cubic feet of concrete to make a slab 8 inches thick. Name his disease and its seriousness, or dimensions.

A. Schizophrenia. A 2-inch diagonal split.

Q. A sales representative was allowed 17 cents per mile for the use of his car, a 1928 Auburn, and $4 a day for general expenses (another auburn). One month, he submitted expenses totaling $8,332, which he was reimbursed, to cover the cost of these two items. If the mileage charge was $46.82 less than his daily allowance, what name did this salesman sign to the ha-ha-I-got-away note he sent from Nicaragua?

A. A Distant Drummer.

Q. A babysitter charged 72 cents per hour before midnight and $1.10 per hour after midnight. During a certain month, the babysitter earned $12.60 and the number of hours worked before midnight lacked 2 hours of being six times the number of hours work after midnight. How many of you assumed the babysitter was female, and how many of you were correct in that assumption?

A. Three, two, and seventeen, especially Nicholas Chauvin.

Q. Tim and Tom were brothers who had a housepainting business. If Tim could paint 2 cubic feet per minute in decorator colors while Tom was painting his face blue and holding the ladder for Tim, what did the neighbors call the brothers after Tim's operation?

A. The Oddball and the Evenball.

Scott was delighted with Oreo's skillful mathematical manipulations. It was very curious, he said, that he himself had no aptitude for such things, yet he could recognize the right answer when he saw it. He complimented Oreo on her "to know-to do," which he could see she had much of. His mother tried to help him as much as she could, but she was involved in her own creative work. She did not come by her clumsiness naturally, he explained, but had developed it, through years of diligence and application, into an art form. For a person with her creative bent, she had been born with a handicap that would have made a lesser woman give up in despair or change her *métier:* grace. It had taken years of practice to overcome her inborn agility, dexterity, deftness, and finesse and develop to a point of such consummate cloddishness, such eye-popping lack of coordination that she could not see out of both eyes at the same time.

She had not reached the summit of achievement to which she aspired, however, Scott confided. No, that day was still many vandalized vases, squashed tomatoes (a *mechuleh* medley), and lightly fantastic trippings away. That day would be reached only when his mother had perfected her art to such a point that she would be able to make breathing and blinking totally voluntary actions. Then and only then would she be ready to star in a play she had written for them both, *Clumsy Claudette at the UN*, in which she played the title role of warmongering *bulbenik* and he played the world's greatest pacifist translator. The marquee would read: SCOTT SCOTT AND SCOTT SCOTT IN SCOTT SCOTT'S CLUMSY CLAUDETTE AT THE UN. They had agreed that although she would give up the stage after the run of the play, she would continue to share in any fame that accrued to his Scott Scott as though it were her own. It was to him equal, since he was convinced that the play, a marvelous melding of their unique talents, would probably run for their lifetime or until one of them was eighty-five, whichever was later.

As his mother exploded from the kitchen with the tray of hors d'oeuvres, Scott rushed over to her. "Permit me. The outside of works — *me,* I them will carry." He took the tray from her. "Rest you on that chair-long there."

Mrs. Scott must have been tired. She tripped only twice on her way to the couch. Scott brought the tray over — a farrago of spills and misses, which Oreo tasted only out of an experimental sense of politeness.

"You said you might have some information about my father?" said Oreo, picking up a plain cracker whose spread was a blob on the underside of the tray.

"Ah, yes, one moment, if it you pleases." Scott tore a sheet of paper from his three-ringed looseleaf notebook and wrote something with a flourish. "There is!" he said, handing it to Oreo. He explained that she might be able to find her father at either of two sound studios uptown, one on the East Side, the other in Harlem.

Oreo thanked the Scotts for their hospitality and got up to leave.

"So long. It was nice meeting you," said Mrs. Scott. She waved good-bye, knocking over a stool, which set up a vibration, which made a cup fall off a hook on the kitchen wall and crash to the floor, where she could trip over the shards later.

"To the to see again," said Scott. He opened the door for Oreo.

"To God," said Oreo, swinging her walking stick in salute.

Oreo on Second Avenue in the seventies

No one at the In-the-Groove Sound Studios had seen Samuel Schwartz for several weeks. As Oreo walked up the street, she saw a pig run squealing out of a doorway, a bacon's dozen of pursuers pork-barreling after it. Oreo started running too. As she neared the building from which the pig had made its exit, she saw that it was a pork butcher's. In its attempt at escape, the pig had made a shambles of the shambles. Oreo continued in the pig pursuit. The porker darted across the street. Oreo flung her walking stick at its legs. The cane did a double whirl, tripping up the pig. A taxi turning into Second Avenue screeched on its brakes, but not in time. The cab sideswiped the pig, which tottered a few feet, then fell dead in front of Temple Shaaray Tefila, directly across from the pork store.

Unwittingly, Oreo was the indirect cause of the pig's death, but as she reflected on its porcine demise, she realized that she could take out her list again. That hashed rasher of bacon defiling the temple sidewalk—that surely was "Sow." Yes, that must be so.

10 *Sciron*

Oreo and Mr. Soundman

Mr. Soundman, Inc., was in a renovated brownstone on Lenox Avenue. Oreo could hear the strange permutations of words speeded up and slowed down, rushed backward and whisked forward, the barbaric yawp of words cut off in mid-syllable (the choked consonants, the disavowed vowels), burdened with excessive volume, affecting elusive portent. Words were all over the floor. Words and time. What word was that there in the corner, curled up like a fetus? And this umbilicus of sound, what caesarean intervention had ripped it untimely from its mother root? Sound boomed off the walls, rocketing around the hallways as it charged out of an open door marked CONTROL ROOM B.

Reep-warf-shuh, reep-warf-shuh, reep-warf-shuh, repeated some backward sounds as Oreo stuck her head in the door. An engineer in a desk chair wheeled among three machines—two tape decks and a master-control console—his ropy arms whipping about like licorice twists. Two pencils stuck out at forty-five-degree angles from his hedgelike natural, pruned to topiary perfection and so bulbous that, along with his dark, chitinous skin and his sunglasses with huge brown convex lenses, he had the look of an undersized mock-up of a movie monster—the grasshopper that spritzed on Las Vegas.

The soundman noticed Oreo on one of his whirls and motioned her into a chair. He stopped the two tape machines. Then he deftly unreeled a three-foot length of tape from one end of a reel, pulled it back and forth between the sound heads (*Raugh-vooff-skunge, raugh-vooff-skunge,* it went as it sawed between the heads), found the spot he wanted, and made a quick slice with a razor. The piece fell to the floor amidst the curly riot of words previously dispatched. How many *reep-warf-shuhs* and *raugh-vooff-skunges* that piece represented, Oreo couldn't guess. The engineer then laid a loose end of the tape still on the reel in a groove at the front of his machine, stripped in a piece of white leader from another reel with Scotch tape and a razor, whirled the gray reels of his tape deck a few times, then stopped. He walked out of the control room, motioning Oreo to follow him.

They walked down the hall to a small office. So far neither of them had said a word. The engineer pointed to a chair next to a desk piled with a stack of oddly shaped cardboards. Oreo sat down. Since the man didn't say anything but merely looked at her expectantly — or, rather, his glasses were turned toward her —she said, "I'm Christine Clark. Is Slim Jackson around?"

The man pointed to himself, then shuffled through the pile of cardboards next to him on the desk. He held one up. It was shaped like a cartoon balloon, and the message read: YOU'RE LOOKING AT HIM.

"Can't you talk?" Oreo asked. He shook his head. After establishing that Slim was neither antisocial nor laryngitic but mute, Oreo asked permission to look through his balloons so that she would know the range of answers he was prepared to give. She found the usual:

FORGET IT, CLYDE

RUN IT DOWN FOR ME

RIGHT ON

YOU GOTTA BE KIDDING

LATER FOR THAT

GROOVY

TOUGH TITTY

I CAN DIG IT

WATCH YOUR MOUTH

DIFFERENT STROKES FOR DIFFERENT FOLKS

She saw that he had translated the typical cartoon asterisk-spiral-star-exclamation point-scribble as a straightforward FUCK YOU, YOU MUTHA. He had a pile of blank balloons and a stack of balloons with drawings: a cocktail glass with an olive followed by a question mark; a Star of David followed by a question mark; an egg-shaped cartoon character with a surprised look on its face (the "That's funny—you don't look Jewish" follow-up to the Star of David? Oreo wondered); an inverted pyramid of three dots and an upcurving line; the three dots again with a downcurving line; a clenched fist with the middle finger raised in the "up yours" position. These last Oreo thought redundant, since Slim could easily pantomime them or use an available word balloon. True, the drawings gave him shades of translation that might be lost in the original gesture. Besides, his blank cards indicated that he was not unaware of the limitations of form balloons. Oreo conceded her argument with herself to herself. Yes, both the words and the drawings had a place.

"I was told I might be able to find Sam Schwartz here," Oreo said.

Slim pulled one of his pencil antennas out of his hair, printed something on a balloon, and held it up: TRY NEXT DOOR TO-NIGHT.

"What's next door?"

He wrote and crossed out, wrote and crossed out. Then held up his cardboard voice: A W̸H̸ A C̸A̸T̸ A HOUSE OF JOY.

"Oh, a whorehouse," said Oreo.

Slim looked at her appraisingly. He shuffled through his standard balloons and pulled out a cartoon of a bibbed man with his tongue hanging out, knife and fork at the ready over a turkey drumstick.

"Likes women with big legs?" Oreo guessed.

Slim looked disappointed. He shook his head as he printed and held up: LIKES DARK MEAT.

So, dear old Dad is already two-timing his second wife. "Do you know where I could find him now? Do you have his address?"

Slim shook his head. I DON'T TRY TO KEEP TRACK OF WHITEY, he ballooned. She started to get up, but Slim held up his hand. SAY SOMETHING, another balloon demanded.

"Like what?"

He shrugged.

"Jack Sprat could eat no fat. His wife could eat no lean."

Slim rotated his wrists, his hands indicating "keep going."

Oreo switched to something more appropriate for a soundman. "Though I speak with the tongues of men and of angels and have not charity, I am become as a sounding brass or a tinkling cymbal."

Slim held up his hand. COULD YOU RECORD A FEW LINES FOR ME? he printed.

Oreo shrugged. "I guess so."

He beckoned her as he went out of the office and back into Control Room B. He did his Shiva routine with the reels of tape on his machines, taking some off, putting some on, twirling his dials. He had her go through a door into the soundproof studio He disappeared for a few minutes and came back carrying some sheets of paper and a stack of his balloons. He put the papers down on the table in front of her, adjusted her mike, then went back into the control room. She watched him through the glass partition. He held up a balloon that said: GIVE ME A LEVEL, PLEASE. He pointed to the script he had left with her.

In a loud voice, she read what was written at the top of the sheet. "Mr. Soundman, Incorporated. Account Number 3051478."

Slim held one finger to his lips. Oreo read the same thing in a normal voice. Slim made the "okay" sign with thumb and index finger and gestured for her to continue reading.

Oreo cleared her throat and read. "In these busy days of rush, rush, rush, it's nice to have friends you can depend on when you need them. We at Tante Ruchel's Kosher Kitchens want you to know you can depend on us. I was saying to my *tante* just the other day — and my *tante* is your *tante* — I said to her, 'What won't you think of next?' And she told me. I want to share with you the wisdom of this marvelous woman. You know her by her prizewinning *tchulent*, you've marveled over her *kasha varnishkes*, and thrilled to her *kugel*. Now she has outdone even herself. Now Tante Ruchel brings you a product that will revolutionize your holiday dinners. So sit down, pull up a chair, and be the first to hear over the miracle of the air-waves about a miracle of a product—"

Slim waved her to a stop. YOU'RE POPPING YOUR P'S.

Oreo quickly looked over what she had read. She saw a "prizewinning," a couple of "products," and a "pull." She said these aloud tentatively. They all popped. She could not figure out how to get her mouth around a *p* without a little explosion of air. Behind the glass, Slim moved his lips in what Oreo assumed was a non-*p*-popping demonstration. Of course *his p*'s didn't pop. Besides, it seemed to her he was mouthing *m*'s, not *p*'s. She'd sound pretty silly talking about "mroducts," "mull," and "mrizewinning." She tried again, imitating Slim's lip movements. After a little practice, she noticed that even to her ears there were fewer rags of breath catching at the grille as she pushed the pesky words past the microphone, which Slim had placed slightly to her left.

She did another take. This time the *p*'s were popless, but Slim ballooned: A LITTLE MORE JEWISH, PLEASE.

Oreo tried to think of how her mother would do this. She pretended she *was* Tante Ruchel's niece, as the copy said. She got to the punchline again. ". . . be the first to hear over the miracle of the airwaves about a miracle of a product: Tante Ruchel's Frozen Passover TV Seder." Oreo laughed to herself. If her grandfather had thought of this, he could have sold a million of them as fast as Louise could cook them.

She consulted Slim about two apparent typographical errors in the next paragraph and was assured that the client did indeed want the copy read as the soundman instructed.

YAHWEH, he explained.

Oreo shrugged and continued. "Passover is a celebration of freedom, gee-dash-dee's gift to our people. So why spend precious holiday time shopping and preparing? The ell-dash-are-dee has seen fit to provide you with Tante Ruchel, a real *bren*. Let her do it for you. When it's time for Seder, you'll be able to sit back, calm and cool, and say, 'It's such a *mechaieh* to have Tante Ruchel for a friend.' Have you ever been so *farchadat* on the holiday that when your youngest starts in with the *Fier Kashehs*, you say, 'Don't ask so many questions?' Pesach is such an important holiday—a happy *yontiff*, as we say—you wouldn't want to forget anything and slight the traditions of our people. Don't worry, Tante Ruchel has thought of everything. No one will be able to point the accusing finger at you and say, 'See, she forgot the parsley.' Parsley-shmarsley—have we got a meal for you! First of all, Tante Ruchel's Frozen Passover TV Seder comes in special foil trays—kosherized for the occasion. Use them once and throw them away. No worry come next Pesach about did your Uncle Louie forget and mix up the special china for Passover week with the everyday. Tante Ruchel would not make a move without our own *mashgiach* by her side to see that everything is strictly strictly. In fact, our *mashgiach* is so strict, he's known in the FAM—the Federation of American Mashgiachs—as Murray the *yenta*. And it goes without saying that each and every lamb is led to the slaughter by our own *shochet,* who, if he didn't work for us, would be a world-famous surgeon. For that reason, we call him Dr. Jacobs. It's only his due.''

Oreo paused to say that she needed some water. Slim stopped his tape and went out of the control room. He came back to the studio a few seconds later with a paper cup of water. He winked, patted Oreo on the shoulder, and went back to start his machine again.

Oreo cleared her throat and went on. ''By now, you're all ears. 'What is Tante Ruchel serving for Passover?' you query. I'm glad you asked. This Seder meal was tested in our kosher kitchens for an entire year until we came up with just the right amount of everything—so you should feel nice and full but not so stuffed you could *plotz*. Each individual tray has eight sections—get the symbolism?—and in each section a gem of a dish. To start, Tante Ruchel has improved on her famous matzo-ball soup. She found an old family recipe in a trunk in the attic just the other day. It's the same delicious soup Tante

Ruchel has always made—but with one new secret ingredient that makes it divine, an ingredient that if we told you, you'd say, 'Of course.' But we can't tell you, dear customers, because our competitors have ears also. Suffice it to say that such delicious broth, such secret-ingredient matzo balls you have never in your life tasted. You could strap a pair of Tante Ruchel's matzos to your shoulders and fly—that's how light they are. As Tante Ruchel was joking just the other day when she taste-tested her latest batch of matzos, 'Let's try and work out a deal with Pan Am.'

"In the next section, you have your chopped chicken liver, with an extra portion of *shmaltz* so that you can mix it to your own taste. Next to that is Tante Ruchel's justly famous *gefilte* fish. Next to that is our *chrain,* with an extra wallop especially for Passover. Next to that is a hard-boiled egg, already halved for your convenience. The main course, occupying a double section all its own, is baby lamb shank—roasted to perfection and garnished with generous sprigs of parsley. See, Tante Ruchel didn't forget. A packet of kosher salt comes with every frozen Seder. 'What's for dessert?' you ask. For dessert we have, of course, *charoseth,* but it's Tante Ruchel's own special blend of apples, nuts, and cinnamon—a taste treat you'll never forget. Tante Ruchel has even thought of wine. Where state laws permit, you'll find a two-ounce container of holiday wine in the eighth and final tray section. Be sure to remove the container before you pop the Seder into the oven. Yes, believe it or not, that's all you have to do to serve your family a delicious, traditional Passover meal. Just pop Tante Ruchel's Frozen Passover TV Seder into a three fifty oven, relax for thirty minutes, and your family will think you slaved over a hot stove for days. Remember our motto: 'A holiday for your family should be a holiday for you also. Let Tante Ruchel worry.' Look for Tante Ruchel's Frozen Passover TV Seders in your grocer's freezer.

Why wait for Passover? Try one today. Who's to say no?''

Slim had her redo a couple of sections here and there, which he called ''wild'' lines, but he seemed pleased.

''How did you know I could do it?'' Oreo asked.

NICE VOICE, SLIGHT JEWISH ACCENT, he ballooned.

''What Jewish accent?'' Oreo protested.

Slim pointed to his ear—the ''Golden Conch'' he had termed it earlier in the session. REMINDS ME OF SAM SCHWARTZ, he printed.

''I've never met the man,'' Oreo said wryly.

Slim shrugged a ''So what can I tell you?'' and pointed again to his ear.

They went back to Slim's office, where he had Oreo sign a release saying she had been paid for doing the commercial and had no further claims on Mr. Soundman, Inc. Then he gave Oreo ten dollars.

''How much would a pro get for doing that?'' she asked.

A LOT MORE, his balloon admitted.

''Well?''

Slim handed her another ten dollars and held up his REMINDS ME OF SAM SCHWARTZ cardboard again.

Oreo shrugged a ''So what can I tell you?'' and shook his hand.

Oreo outside Mr. Soundman, Inc.

She stood in the doorway and saw a curious procession coming down the street. A black pimp and ten prostitutes, five white, five black, in alternating colors, wended toward her in a ragged V, a checkerboard wedge of wedges. The pimp's walk reminded Oreo of Fonzelle, her brother's friend. But Fonzelle's was a heavy choreography, this one lighter, more fluid. It was as though the pimp were swimming down the street, a swan breasting the current for his cygnets. The cob would take two stroking steps, glide to a stop, flutter his arms ostentatiously to his hips, turn to see that he was still followed at a respectful distance, and continue downstream. His clothes seemed to grow out of him, hugging his lithe, sigmoid torso more snugly than a suit of lights a torero's sinuosity. He was fledged in a suit of pearlescent pink velvet, a soft dawn-gray shirt, a blushing-rose string tie. His long-billed velvet cap raked this way and that as he skewed about to check on the progress of his brood. The rake's progress, Oreo thought, and laughed to herself. Occasionally he paused to buff his nails, perking his chest with anseriform hauteur. When he stopped, the women stopped; when he moved on, they followed. Oreo decided to name him after an adulterer and, as a student of British history, dubbed him Parnell.

The first woman behind the pimp carried a high stool and a white parasol. She was obviously his bottom woman, since she had been entrusted with his throne. She was white. The next eight pens in the bevy carried only their purses and a pent-up expression. The last woman in line, black, carried a shoeshine box with a built-in footrest. His next-to-bottom woman, Oreo surmised. Only the favorites got to do all the extra work. Oreo's assessment of their relative rank was supported by the fact that all the women except the first and last were wearing similar crotch-high red dresses, while the bottom women wore pink ones that matched Parnell's suit, enabling the dullest observer to distinguish the stars from the chorus line at a glance.

The group passed Mr. Soundman and came to a halt in front of the next stoop. Parnell casually turned to face the street and crossed his arms. He uncrossed them long enough to snap his fingers, then crossed them again. The white bottom woman placed the stool under his bottom, the parasol over his head, and the pimp sat, one rose-booted foot on the middle rung of the stool, the other straight in front of him. He snapped his fingers again. The black bottom woman approached him, carrying the shoeshine box as though it were a chalice. She lifted his foot from the ground and placed it on the footrest.

The two bottom women then stepped to either side of him. He snapped his fingers again. The two queens nodded to their eight ladies-in-waiting. The first of the eight took a deep breath, knelt before her liege lord, and began shining his shoes. After about five minutes of creaming, buffing, and polishing, the pimp snapped his fingers.

It's a wonder the friction from all that finger-snapping doesn't set his phalanges on fire, Oreo was thinking, when she saw that the pimp was repaying his bootblack—or, rather, bootrose— with a boot in the behind. Oreo was alone in her surprise. The two queens were impassive, the ladies-in-waiting stolid. The shoe polisher herself apparently regarded the boot as her customary tip. She merely rubbed her rear and hurried up the steps of the building in front of which all this took place. She disappeared inside.

Oreo did not persist in her surprise when she saw that this ritual was to be repeated through all the women in line: the polishing of the boot, the booting by the boot, the hotfooting it into the building. By the time the last woman had snapped her rag at the rose-colored boots, the sun was virtually recoiling from the surface of the leather. Sunbeams gratefully ricocheted away whenever Parnell wiggled his toes. Another finger-snap and the two queens helped him off his stool, which one retrieved while the other fetched the shoeshine box. As the two women turned to go up the steps, the pimp gave them both a resounding whack on the bottom, this time with his hand, further proof that they held a special place in his balls.

He stood on the sidewalk, one hand on his hip, gazing with shielded eyes at his coruscating boots. All his women were inside, but he seemed to relish just standing there on the sidewalk.

Oreo estimated that half the block was watching from windows and doorways just as she was. Finally, she could stand it no longer. She reached into her handbag and put some loose change in the middle of one of the ten-dollar bills Slim had paid her. She crushed the bill lightly around the coins and bounced down the steps, humming to herself and swinging her cane. She walked briskly past Parnell, smiling a free and open smile.

She was a step beyond him before he spoke. "Hello, big stuff," he said softly, "where you going with your bad self?"

Oreo didn't answer.

"Not speaking, huh? Dicty, ain't you, Miss Siditty? Okay, hello, *small* stuff," he said in a put-down voice.

Oreo turned, looked at his crotch, pointedly assessing the cob's cobs, and said, "Hello, *no* stuff."

"Ouch!" he said. "You got me that time, baby." He smiled and glided toward her.

Oreo smiled back and dropped the money. The coins tinkled all over the sidewalk, but the pimp did not make a move toward them. His eyes glommed on to the ten-dollar bill. Oreo pretended to be preoccupied with gathering all her coins. She turned away from Parnell. In that split second, he bent over to pick up the bill. In the second half of that split second, Oreo turned back to see a lovely close-up of his rear. She drew back her walking stick like a pool cue and (decisions, decisions) leaned toward ball-breaking or buggery. Oh, hell, she decided, I don't want to get pimp shit all over his nice cane. She switched her grip and instead gave him a grand-slam clout across the ass. If his howl meant anything, it meant that he was now the only person on the block with four cheeks to sit on. Parnell staggered and fell into the gutter. As Oreo ran down the street, she saw three things happen. One, a sanitation truck came into the street. *Flush!* Two, all up and down the street, witnesses to the flushing, at the extreme edge of hysterical laughter, clung to their windowsills (Parnell's suit was ruined, but the water merely beaded on his boots and ran back into the gutter). Three, Parnell's women appeared at the door, a look of revelation on their faces.

11 Cercyon

Oreo catching her breath around the corner

She smiled her cookie smile every time she thought of Parnell's
sodden rise from the gutter. His arms extended like wings away
from his soiled and dripping suit, his fingers spoked out from
his palms at a web-splitting stretch. Oreo hoped that the look of
revelation on the faces of the prostitutes meant that they had
discovered Parnell was vulnerable. If one stranger could whip
his ass, why not ten friends?

Oreo knew she would have to be careful as she roamed
around the neighborhood waiting for her father to show up at
the whorehouse. Parnell did not look like the kind who would
take to humiliation like a swan to lakes. As soon as he changed
his clothes, he would probably be out looking for her — a drag,
since she had to hang around to try to catch Samuel before he
started catting.

Oreo was hungry. She ducked into a luncheonette, sat in a
booth in the back, and ordered a hot-sausage sandwich, a
Shabazz bean pie, and a Pepsi.

The woman behind the counter, obviously the owner, was huge, a giant high-yellow Buddha. To the tune of "St. Louis Woman," she sang, "I hate to see my only son go down, I hate to see my only son go down." She repeated these lines thirty-seven times. The repetition was driving Oreo mad—she wanted to hear the rest of the parody.

The woman beckoned to her when the sausage was ready. Oreo carried the food to the booth herself. No one else was in the place. The woman did not seem inclined to talk, had merely grunted, to show she had heard, when Oreo ordered, and now went back to her copy of *Vogue*. Oreo did a double take. *Vogue?* She had misjudged the woman. *Harper's Bazaar*, yes; *Vogue*, no, she would have sworn. Oreo now saw that she had missed the gaining-circulation squint of the eyes, the condé nast flare of the nostrils. Oreo was disappointed in herself. It was like mixing up the Brontës. After all, Branwell's staggering style was not Anne's.

The whole episode was an affront to Oreo's judgment, and she resolved to be less quick to snap in future. For example, what of the only son the woman was so musically concerned for? Oreo could not refrain from wondering, Is he real or imaginary? She was at first inclined to think real. A woman with the proprietor's solidity gave one the impression of practicality, a reflex grasp of — no, a stranglehold on — everyday life. Such a woman, with her banana fingers, might well despair of the sexual proclivities of any son who was not a Kodiak bear and hence, to forestall such despair, would train up her child in the way he should go, which would be in any direction but down. Any blow jobs connected with any son of this mother would be to, not fro. Another point: the reader of *Vogue* was ofttimes a traditionalist. A traditionalist would wear at all times—waking and sleeping, resting or laying waste the countryside—a wedding ring. Oreo looked again at the banana fingers of the left hand. No band of gold bruised the bunch. This, of course, was not conclusive proof. It would be hard to find a ring that could contain those plantains. What is more, a store owner might think it politic to keep valuables that were not for sale out of sight of thieves. But Oreo felt that if this woman had a ring, she would wear it—and let thieves come if they dared. No, she was not married; she had no relatives, not even a sonlike nephew to sing about. Nephews who worked for her would toil around the clock and think twice before complaining about the low wages—and there was no nephew in sight. Q.E.D. The copy of *Vogue* was again the crucial clue. It took imagination to persist in reading a magazine whose cover date was January, 1928. Yes, the only son of the song was—*mirabile cantabile* (which in Oreo's pidgin Latin meant "wonderful to sing")— imaginary.

Oreo finished her bean pie, took a last swig of Pepsi, and paid the check. She said good evening to the proprietor, who grunted, licked her finger, and turned a page of her magazine. This Sakyamuni was now sitting on one of her counter stools, her apron hammocked across her knees. If she sat like that much longer, impassive and idol-like, she would present a cruel temptation to deranged incense burners in the neighborhood.

Oreo pushed open the screen door. She raised her chin to sniff the dark, peppery air outside the luncheonette, when suddenly her left arm made a distinct L behind her back. Her walking stick was jerked from her right hand. She turned her head. Out of the corner of her eye, she could see Parnell. "Oh shit," she said softly.

"Um-hm," Parnell gloated. "Got you by the *short* hairs this time, baby."

"Can we talk this over?" Oreo asked.

"Oh, we gon talk it over, all right—and *then* some." Parnell was marching her down the street with her arm still behind her back, making no attempt to hide the fact that he was coercing her. People looked on with perhaps a shade less curiosity than they would have lent to a change of traffic light.

One man greeted Parnell with "What's the haps, my man? See you got a new worker for the vineyard. She *saying* something too. Choice cut, man, choice," he said, looking Oreo up and down. She looked him up and down in retaliation, but he didn't notice as he swung down the street.

Oreo wondered whether to use WIT on Parnell right on the street, but she decided to wait and see what kind of game he would try to run. She told him there was no need to twist her arm. "I'm not going anywhere. I'll go along with your program."

"You better believe it. I got something special in store for you, baby. You really gon dig it. That is, it gon dig *you*." He chuckled to himself at his turn of phrase.

They turned into Parnell's block. He relaxed his grip, out of fatigue. She could see now that he was wearing a suit of identical cut and style to the fine pink feathers he had strutted earlier. This one was midnight blue, more appropriate for evening. His boots too were blue-black and scintillated like a vein of anthracite struck by a miner's Cyclopean lamp.

The hustler hustled Oreo up the front steps. Inside, the first floor was dark. All she could see was a light under a door at the end of a narrow hallway. They went up the stairs to the second floor. Parnell opened the door into a large square room with a huge wrestling mat in the center. On chairs around the periphery of the room were one little, two little, three little prostitutes, four little, five little, six little prostitutes, seven little, eight little, nine little prostitutes—where was the tenth? Oreo wondered. The black bottom woman was missing. The nine young women looked as if they were about to greet Oreo as a sorority sister. They started to make a place for her along the wall.

"This is the bitch that ruined my baby-ass-pink suit—and put my ass in a sling," announced Parnell. He tenderly touched his behind.

Oreo translated their collective murmur as "Oh-oh, too bad for you, honey." Behind their masks of loyalty, Oreo thought she detected a tentative snicker at Parnell.

"Now she gon get *hers* this evening," Parnell said. "Just in case any you bitches begin to *begin* to think you can run some shit on me, I'm gon show you what happens to little girls whose mamas didn't teach 'em no manners."

All this time, Oreo had been flexing her arm, ready to fling Parnell to the floor as soon as things got a bit sticky. But she was curious. She still had not peeped his hole card.

"Now, y'all have heard rumors to the effect that I'm keeping some kinda way-out instrument of torture in that spare room." He cocked his head toward a door at the opposite end of the room, cater-cornered from where he and Oreo were standing. "I want to tell you in front that this is one *heavy* torture, chicks. I ain't had to use it on any you yet. Y'all been good little girls, humping your hineys off for li'l ol' me. But this bitch"—he gave Oreo an extra arm twist, which she added to her revenge list—"this bitch is something else. It gon be my pleasure to see her split wide open."

Oreo was getting a little worried now—she might actually have to hurt Parnell. If push came to shove, how many of these women would fight for Parnell once she made her move and started pushing and shoving him all over this room? Would she have to rack them all up? And what the fuck was this instrument of torture?

Parnell snapped his fingers, and all heads snapped his way. He pointed to the woman farthest from him. "Knock three times on that door, then step aside." The woman looked puzzled but did as she was told. Nothing happened. "Knock again —harder," said Parnell. The woman had no sooner lifted her knuckles after the third knock than the door burst open. She did not step aside soon enough and was knocked down as something —Oreo at first thought it was a small white horse—rushed out and bore down on them. Oreo looked again. It was a man, virtually on all fours, caparisoned in a black loincloth.

He cantered over to Parnell and nuzzled his hand. Parnell patted him, and the man straightened up as far as he could, to a slight stoop. He was deeply muscled. His withers twitched as though covered with flies. His dark forelock covered his eyes like a shade as he pawed the ground, impatiently waiting for Parnell to tell him what to do.

"This is Kirk," Parnell said, stroking the man's back. "Kirk is from out of town, folks. Say hello to the bitches, Kirk."

Kirk raised his upper lip and nickered, showing teeth long and strong, with a decided overbite.

"Thattaboy," said Parnell. "We got your first American playmate for you, Kirk. Young and juicy. You like that don't you, Kirk?"

Kirk pawed the ground twice. Oreo assumed that meant "yes" and that "no" would be indicated by one hoof-strike.

"Strip for the ladies," Parnell said, pantomiming to make sure he understood.

After a moment of incomprehension, Kirk did as he was directed. A gasp went up from the nine prostitutes. Parnell looked, and looked again, with a "What hath God wrought?" expression of envy on his face. Kirk's equipment unfurled like a paper favor blown by Gabriel at the last party in the history of the world. His demanding "digit" made undiscriminating Uncle-Sam-wants-you gestures around the room.

Oreo was impressed. Male genitals had always reminded her of oysters, gizzards, and turkey wattles at best, a bunch of seedless grapes at worst. On the other hand, most marmoreal baskets (e.g., the David's) resembled the head of a mandrill (a

serendipitous pun). An inveterate crotch-watcher, she had once
made a list of sports figures whom she classified under the headings "Capons" and "Cockerels." The capons (mostly big-
game hunters, bowlers) were men whose horns could be described by any of the following (or similar) terms: *pecker, dick,
cock, thing, peter, prick, dangle, shmendrick, putz, shmuck.*
The cockerels (gymnasts, swimmers) sported any of the following: *shlong, dong, rod, tool, lumber.* Neutral words *(member,
penis)* were applicable in cases where the looseness or padding
of the standard uniform made definitive assessment impossible
(baseball, basketball, football, hockey, and tennis players). But
Kirk's stallion was a horse of another collar, of such dimensions
that he could have used a zeppelin for a condom.

"Are you planning what I think you're planning?" Oreo
asked cautiously.

"Um-hm," smirked Parnell.

"No-o-o!" the checkerboard Greek chorus chorused plaintively. Parnell silenced them with a glance.

"Does the fact that I'm a virgin get to you?" Oreo asked.

Parnell smiled as at a baby's funeral. "Just makes it all the
juicier." He gave her the look of the expert. "Besides, you
prob'ly lying. At your age, looking like you do? No *way.*"

Oreo saw that it was senseless to try the usual bullshit. She
made a straightforward proposition. "Three things: I get the
right of inspection for general cleanliness; there is to be no
rimming—just straight-on fucking; and I get to go to the bathroom before we start."

"I don't know where you get this what-you-will-do,
what-you-won't-do shit. You better watch your mouth 'fore I
bust you right now, bitch. But none them *requests* don't make
me no nevermind. My man here's gon do you in, chick. And I
do mean *do*, and I do mean *in*. So make your play—you ain't
gon get away, dig?" Kirk was getting restless. Parnell stroked

his back. "Just a little while now, Kirk. You let the little lady look at you now like a good boy."

"I hate to be a nag, but I don't want to touch it. Could somebody else do it for me?"

Parnell laughed. "You a funny bitch. You don't want to touch it, but it shit-sure gon touch you in more ways than one. But have your fun now. I'm gon be getting my jollies in a few minutes." He snapped his fingers. Without turning his head, he said, "Cecelia, turn this guy out for the girl, will you?"

In a second, one of the women appeared at his side. She reached down and expertly pulled back Kirk's foreskin. Oreo looked. Kirk had cornered the market on smegma. "You gotta be kidding," Oreo said. "He could open a cheese store under there."

Even Parnell's eyebrows shot up in distaste. "Take him to the crapper and wash him, Cecelia." He turned to Kirk. "Go with the nice lady, Kirk, but don't hurt her. She not for you. This one's for you," he said, fondly patting Oreo's afro.

Oreo was furious. She had been monumentally forbearing so far, out of curiosity—letting Parnell twist her arm, call her "bitch," and in general dump on her—but now she had had it. She hated anyone to touch her soft, cottony hair without permission. She was having a shit fit, gradually working herself up into a state of *hwip-as*. Parnell would be the sorriest pimp in Harlem when she got through with him. But she would first take on Kirk and get *that* over with. "May I go to the bathroom while Cecelia's taking care of Kirk?" she asked docilely.

"That's better. Now, if you'da come on that way from the git-go — you and me, we coulda got along. Always got room in my stable for a hot-chocolate filly like you. But first you gotta take your medicine for being a bad girl this afternoon." He snapped his fingers. "Go with her, Lil."

A *zaftig* black girl of about Oreo's age took her down the

corridor to the bathroom. As they were passing a small room opposite the bathroom, Oreo heard a man's resonant voice say something she couldn't make out and then a woman laugh. "Where's the woman I saw this afternoon carrying the shoeshine box?" Oreo asked.

"In there, turning a trick with one of her regular johns," said Lil, indicating the room of the voices.

Oreo realized that this was the first word she had heard any of the prostitutes speak in solo. She also realized that the regular john across from the john might well be her father. Wouldn't that be a blip? thought Oreo. She did not know which was more incredible—the possible coincidence or how badly she had to pee.

She went into the bathroom while Lil waited outside the door. In a few minutes, she had stripped except for her mezuzah, sandals, and brassiere (which she had always thought should be called a mammiere, since she had never seen anyone try to protect her arm with one). She left the mezuzah on for irony's sake, the sandals for comic effect, and the bra (or ma) because she was going to be taking advantage enough of Kirk without adding unrequited lust to his handicaps, an unavoidable state of mind, she felt, once he got hind sight of her perfect twin roes (Song of Solomon 4:5), to say nothing of Parnell's reaction and—who knew?—a couple of the girls' besides. Oreo reached into her handbag and pulled out a protective device she carried with her at all times. She wedged it into her wedge. She was ready.

Oreo goes to the mat

Parnell kept straightening the wrestling mat with the toe of his boot—on the theory, Oreo guessed, that anything he did with his hands he was *really doing*, but whatever he did with his foot was beneath notice and therefore no one could accuse him of performing useful labor. Parnell took Kirk to his corner and whispered in his ear, rubbing his back and giving his behind the athlete's homosexual underhand slap/feel of encouragement. The women shifted impatiently in their chairs, every once in a while casting at Oreo what she took to be Aristotle's glances of pity and fear leavened by De Sade's anticipation of unmentionable acts.

As agreed upon by both parties—Oreo with a nod, Kirk with two floor-pawings—Parnell snapped his fingers three times as the signal to begin. Oreo stood quietly where she was, in the center of the mat. Kirk came out of his corner with his nose wide open. As he advanced, his stallion did an impressive caracole right, a no-slouch caracole left, then majestically reared its head. He threw the unresisting Oreo to the floor, stretched her legs wide in the ready-set position of a nutcracker, took aim, tried to jam his pole into her vault and—much to his and everyone else's surprise—met with a barrier that propelled him backward and sent him bounding off the nearest wall.

The look of astonishment on Kirk's face as he gave the dullard's flat-eyed stare to his bruised cock and muscles would warm her heart's cockles for all the time she was alive, alive-o. The puzzlement of Parnell, the hoaxing of the whores—oh, Oreo could do nothing but smile her cookie smile.

The barrier Kirk had come upon (but not come upon) when he tried to pull a 401 (breaking and entering) was a false hymen made of elasticium, a newly discovered trivalent metal whose outstanding characteristic was enormous resiliency. Elasticium's discovery had been made possible by a grant from Citizens Against the Rape of Mommies (CAROM), an organization whose membership was limited to those who had had at least one child (or were in the seventh to ninth month of pregnancy) before being attacked (usually by their husbands, an independent survey revealed). CAROM's work was a clear case of mother succor (and thus an aid to rhymesters). Vindictiveness would soon lead CAROM's leadership to share false hymens with the world ("Maidenheads® are available in your choice of Cherry pink, Vestal Virgin white, or Black Widow black"), but Oreo had been able to get hold of a prototype because of her acquaintanceship with its inventor, Caresse Booteby.

À propos de bottes, Parnell helped Kirk off the floor with the toe of his boot and sent him back to the mat, as if to say, "I don't know what happened, but it shit-sure ain't gon happen again." It did. Kirk lowered his boom and *boing*-ed off Oreo's indehiscent cherry as if it were a tiny trampoline—which indeed, in effect, it was.

By now, the nine prostitutes were having a finger-popping time, whooping and hollering with uncontrolled delight. Parnell was hoarse from screaming at them to quiet down, polyped from screeching yet another set of futile instructions to the thwarted Kirk about the solution to Oreo's architecture. Poor Kirk's sexual charette availed him nothing. His back was lacerated from racketing against walls and furniture (once he had hit the black bottom woman's empty chair and had bounced on the floor like a dribbled basketball). After each encounter, totally confused and uncomprehending, he fanned the head of his angry-red penis, occasionally patting it in consolation for its failure. The battering his quondam battering ram was taking was making Oreo feel sorry for him. He was lathered with sweat from his efforts, his great heart about to burst. Oh, the heartbreak of satyriasis.

Oreo got up, tired of playing this game. "He's exhausted, fagged out—*oysgamitched!* It takes a better man than him to break *my* cherry," she taunted. "Why don't you send this gelding back where he came from?"

She knew that her words would enrage Parnell—the choler of a master whose pet has been maligned. Parnell rushed at her. This was the part she had been waiting for. Ducking his pimply right cross, she dealt him the humiliation special—a quick *fō-han-blō,* a lightning *bak-han-blō.* He dropped to the floor, more out of surprise than compulsion. The *blōs* had been meant to sting, not fell. The women made no move to help Parnell. They were immobilized, as if permanently, a frieze on an Attic temple.

Parnell shook his head in disbelief. "I'm not jiving now. Woman, I am gon break your natural ass."

"No shit?" said Oreo as he started to get up. "Don't talk so much with your mouth," she advised, quoting one of her grandmother's favorite lines, and she gave him a pendulum *tō-blō* to the lower jaw to make sure he would not. The slight crepitation she heard she at first feared was Parnell's mandible mealing. When she saw what had made the sound, she was even more horrified by what she had done: she had broken one of her sandal straps. "Oh, drat and double phoo," said Oreo. She dealt Parnell an *el-bō-krac* to the ear out of frustration. They were her favorite sandals.

So far Parnell had not touched her. He groped toward her like a man in a dream's slow motion running after a silent, insidious double-time train, a train he must catch before the something that is gaining on him engulfs him. She eluded his grasp. She was making her domination of Parnell into a contest the integrity of whose outcome she would consider compromised if the oil from the whorls of one of his fingers was seasoned with the salt of her light film of sweat. Her mezuzah flew, her bra osmosed moisture, her sandal flapped, lofting zephyrs of air that cooled her Maidenhead as she went through her repertoire of WIT: sarcastic *blōs* from *hed* to *tō,* the irony of a *fut* in the mouth, facetious wise-*kracs, kik*-y repartee, *strīk*-ing satire— in short, the persiflaging of Parnell.

When she had amused herself sufficiently, she straddled the prostrate pimp, arched his neck backward in a modified *hed-lok,* and addressed herself to the nine prostitutes. "How many of you would like to step on Parnell's boots?" she asked. "Who?" they chorused.

She had forgotten that she had made up the name Parnell and now did not want to know his true name. "Him," she said, ducking her head and maintaining leverage on Parnell's chin.

The frieze unstuck. Five women came forward, leaving metopes among the glyphs — a majority decision in the absence of the working whore, who still had not reappeared. Oreo blindfolded Parnell with the scarf of one of the five so that he could not see which of his bootblacks were scuffers, which (by abstention) still buffers. She turned him around with a semi-*ul-na-brāc.* As she did so, she looked around for Kirk. He was standing in a corner asleep, his legs crossed, his hands cupping a gathering of gonads, a tear runnel glistening on one cheek of his hanging head. "Poor thing," Oreo doubleentendred.

All the gristle had gone out of Parnell too. He seemed depressed. His proud, swanlike carriage was gone. In its place was a manifestly terminal droop. Swan's down, Oreo punned to herself. He stood quietly until the first of the five laid a dulling toe on his blue-black boots, then a tremor went through him.

Of the two women Oreo knew by name, Cecelia was a buffer, Lil a scuffer. If loyalty to Parnell had to be judged by this b-s choice, then Oreo had better use Lil as her intermediary for her final task in this house.

After the laying on of feet, Oreo called Lil over.

12 Procrustes, Cephissus, Apollo Delphinius

Oreo at Kropotkin's Shoe Store

While the manager, a Sidney, was on the phone, Oreo idly twirled her walking stick. Her dress was wrinkled from sleeping on the floor of Mr. Soundman, Inc. She had left Parnell's triumphant but weary. When she saw the slightly open window of the studio, she knew she could go no further that night. She pried the sash up with her cane and ducked in. (She left Slim Jackson a didactic balloon about carelessness.) Before she dropped off to sleep, she briefly considered how Parnell's *ménage à douze* might be affected by her little visit. She did not really care too much—except that it was the place where she had finally learned her father's address. As she had judged, Lil had been willing to help her. While Samuel was otherwise engaged, Lil had skillfully pilfered his ID.

Now that Oreo knew where Samuel was, she was in no hurry to get there. First things first. She needed new sandals. Hence her appearance, in the early bright, at the first shoe store she had found open — Kropotkin's. She tuned in to the young manager on the phone.

"Yeah, yeah, I know, I know. This is a terrible location. It's depressing, especially on a rainy day. The people up here want fashion, but they don't want to pay for it, what can I tell you? You should see my store. It's immaculate. You could eat off the floor. All my stores are like that. I tell you one thing, I'm glad for the experience. . . . Yeah, yeah, but now I know how to do all that stuff. I just want him to take me with him is all. I'm ready for bigger and better. I'm telling you, one store on Thirty-fourth Street would be better than two here. We did three thousand here last week, and we're happy to do it. I'm used to doing forty-three, maybe forty-six hundred. . . . So when are you getting your promotion? . . . Oh, I hear things, you know. I hear that maybe they're going to move Herbie Manstein and put you in his place. . . . No, I'm not kidding you. I'm not guaranteeing that's what's going to happen, but that's what I hear, anyway. . . . Yeah, for a small store I'm not doing so bad, but now I'm ready for bigger and better."

He turned to look as a worried-looking woman who had been waiting for some time tapped impatiently on the glass of the glove counter. "Listen, I have to go. The natives are restless. But have you heard the one about the eight A's? You know the old joke about the five A's, yeah? . . . Well, this one is the eight A's. Take a guess, go on. . . . No, that's pretty good. I'll have to remember that one, but that isn't it. It's an alcoholic who belongs to the automobile club and—get this—has narrow feet." His laugh was like elm blight—very Dutch.

He finally got off the phone and went to the counter.

"Please, *schnell*," said the woman.

"Yeah, *mach schnell*." He looked over his shoulder at Oreo, then said to the woman, "You mean you're in a hurry, right? You should say, 'I am in a hurry,' " he prompted in a slow, you-are-a-dummy voice.

The woman nodded as if to say, "I'll agree to anything as long as you hurry up and wait on me." She pointed to a pair of black kid gloves under the glass.

Sidney shook his head. "Those are not for you. You want my advice? Try a slightly larger glove." He took a pair of dark-blue woolen gloves from the case. He helped the woman put the left glove on. To Oreo, the fingers looked too long, like the woolly blue ape's. "See," Sidney said, "you'll be able to wiggle your fingers around in them. You don't want a glove too tight."

The woman shook her head, but she was desperate. She paid for the gloves and walked out.

"Do you have these in seven and a half?" Oreo asked, waving a pair of sandals that would do until she could get back to Philadelphia and buy a new pair of her special style (two simple crosspieces representing Chestnut and Market streets, which don't cross).

The manager took two pairs of sandals from a shelf behind the cash register and came over. "You want my advice? It doesn't matter to me. I don't care which pair you take. But if you take my advice, you'll take the pair that fits tighter."

"Why, do they stretch?"

"Yeah, it's Greek leather—stretches a lot. Now, American leather, that's another story." He didn't say what the other story was. He pointed to the sole. "You see this number here?"

Oreo looked at a 37. "That's a European size," she said.

He was obviously surprised that she knew. "Yeah, but see in here, it says seven and a half. We mark it ourselves. But take my advice—try the seven."

"Okay."

He knelt to help Oreo try one on. It was too small. Her big toe jammed against the strap, which had the give of an iron bar.

"Push, push," Sidney insisted. "It'll go, it'll go." He shoved the sandal further onto her foot.

"Stop, stop, you're humping my hallux," said Oreo, drawing back her foot. "What are you—*meshugge?*"

"Look, who's the expert here?"

"I'll take the seven and a half," Oreo said firmly.

He shrugged. "No skin off my nose."

"No skin off my toes," Oreo said. She changed into the new sandals and put the old ones in a box to throw away in the nearest wastebasket. She winced at the prospect of throwing away one perfectly good sandal.

When she paid Sidney, she said, "You know why business is bad? You give people the wrong sizes."

"Please, no lectures," he said, holding up his hand. "From you I don't need it, *oytser.*"

She was tempted to denounce him in cha-key-key-wah. "You know what I wish on you?" she said, imitating his inflections. "Part one, may you have a long bed and a short bed, and on the long bed may you have shortness of breath, and on the short bed may you long for the day when I release you from the following curse, which is part two: three weeks of every four you shouldn't make three thousand, you shouldn't make two thousand, you shouldn't make even one thousand. You should make, give or take a little here and there, *bubkes!* And the fourth week of every four, you should have the worst business of the month!"

She left in a huff, a snit, and high dudgeon, which many people believe to be automobiles but are actually states of mind. She heard Sidney mumble, "The trouble with the *shvartzes* today is they are beginning to learn about insurance."

Oreo at Woolworth's

She bought a zebra-print paper dress, which she intended to wear only until she could get herself cleaned up. She bought a black headband and a white headband. She ordered a hamburger and a black-and-white milk shake. She changed the hamburger to a grilled cheese; since she would soon see her father, she wanted to be in a state of kosher grace.

Oreo at the laundromat

She had changed into her paper dress in a bar. Now she was being hypnotized by her good dress's revolutions in the dryer. On the next bench, a Chinese woman waiting for her take-out laundry nodded her head in time to the music score she was reading. Every once in a while, she would laugh (scrutably enough, thought Oreo, who knew the score) at one of Mozart's lesser-known jokes, her lower lids pouching up under her epicanthic folds. Oreo, getting dizzy from watching her clothes, looked with little interest around the laundromat. The circular seas of the washing machines, the round Saharas of the dryers lulled her with their cyclic surge and thrum.

Then she saw something that perked up her curiosity. The side door opened, a man stepped in, dropped to his knees, and looked around as though choosing a path. It was to be toward the table where the customers folded their dry towels and linens, Oreo observed. A woman stood there now, the center of a sheet chinned to her chest, her arms rhythmically opening and closing as the sheet halved and thickened, halved and thickened. She did not notice as the crawler moved under the table, passing the table's legs and hers at a slow but steady creep. He did not slacken or increase his pace when he came out on the other side but merely kept going. He completed his traverse and went out the front door and down the street, still crawling. He attracted no more notice in the laundromat than would a large dog, for which he was mistaken by a man who shouted after him, "No dogs allowed—can't you read!" As if a dog would have brought his dirty clothes to such an inconvenient location.

Oreo's dryer stopped. She took out her dress and examined it. "Pristine, Christine," she said approvingly to herself. After a slight struggle, she released the dryer drum from her bra's metallic grasp.

Now what Oreo needed was the purifying waters of a tub or shower. She was grungy from her encounters with Kirk and Parnell, her night on the floor of Mr. Soundman, the dirty stares she had gotten from Sidney as she left Kropotkin's. She walked along St. Nicholas Avenue looking for a hotel, but she saw something better for her purposes.

Oreo at the sauna

It was run by Jordan Rivers. "Deep Rivers" he called himself, according to the eight-by-ten glossy of himself in the window. It was the first such photograph Oreo had ever seen where those dimensions referred to feet, not inches. This was less out of egotism than necessity, Oreo guessed. Judging by his photograph, Rivers was almost seven feet tall. He was as slender and black as a Dinka, his skin tone the more striking because of his apparel—what seemed to be a billowing white choir robe.

She went in. Much to her disappointment, Rivers did not appear. Only an attendant was on duty. After a few minutes of prying, Oreo learned that she had been right about the choir robe. Rivers had been an itinerant gospel singer for many years. He had sung so many choruses about washing sins away that, taking the gospels as gospel, he began to follow the letter and not the spirit of the spirituals. He left most of the work of running the business to his employees, devoting himself almost full time to purification. Dividing his lustral day in half, he sweltered in a sauna the first four hours, soaked in a tub another four. "He looks like Moby Prune," the attendant informed Oreo. Jordan Rivers was not his real name, and he had taken his nickname, "Deep," from one of his favorite spirituals. No one knew his real name. Whenever he lost favor with his employees, they called him "Muddy Waters" for spite. Oreo saw that Rivers carried his convictions about the redemptive powers of bath water to the extent of labeling the entrance to his domain SINNERS and the exit SAINTS.

Oreo in the sauna

Her eyeballs were hot globes of tapioca. She breathed in flues of fire without flame, exhaled dragon blasts, stirring up sultry harmattans in her private sudatorium. The wax in her ears was turning to honey. Liquid threads were in conflux at her belly button (an "inny"), which held a pondlet of sweat. Pores of unknown provenance opened and emptied, sending deltas of dross toward her navel's shore. When she judged she had nothing more to give, she stepped into a cold shower, which felt warm because of her sauna heat. When the chill deepened finally, she made the water hot, soaping and resoaping herself, finishing her ablutions with a vigorous shampoo. She combed out her afro to its fullest circumference, put on her dress, her new sandals, and her mezuzah (it felt cool in her clevice—a word Jimmie C. used to mean a cross between *cleavage* and *crevice*). Last, she chose her black headband because of the solemnity of the occasion. Her skin pinged with cleanliness. She felt godlike. Perhaps Jordan Rivers was on to something.

Oreo on 125th Street

She walked along swinging her cane. Workmen were changing the marquee of the Apollo, temple of soul.

NOW APPEARING

THE DOLPHINS

EXTRA ADDED ATTRAC

As Oreo passed the theater, the man at the top of the ladder dropped his *T*. "Jesus H. Christ!" he exclaimed, obviously obsessed with letters. He pointed to Oreo. "Is that a fox or is that a fox!"

The man holding the ladder said, "Absofuckinglutely," and began making fox-calling noises. "Where you going, sister? 'Cause whither thou goest, I will *definitely* go—you can believe that!"

Oreo was in no mood to spoil her good mood. She merely hooked her walking stick under the fallen *T* and flung it as far as she could over the marquee. It landed on a rooftop, but the men, heads thrown back in wonder, seemed to be awaiting its return as if it were a boomerang.

Oreo continued down the street, her cane resting on her shoulder like a club.

13 Medea, Aegeus

Oreo on the subway

She was too preoccupied to observe noses, mouths, and shoes and award prizes. She did overhear someone say impatiently, "No, no, Mondrian's the lines, the boxes. Modigliani's the long necks."

And: "She a Jew's poker. Take care the sinnygogue fo' 'em on Sat'd'ys."

This last gave her an idea whose ramifications she considered during the ride. Distractedly, she doodled on her clue list. Her basic doodles were silhouettes of men facing left and five-lobed leaves. Her subconscious view of her father as mystery man? A pointless, quinquefoliolate gesture to the Star of David? No. Silhouettes and leaves were what she drew best. Next to her profiles and palmates, she made a line of scythelike question marks. Next to that, she sketched an aerial view of a cloverleaf highway, her gunmetal-gray divisions making a cloisonné of the ground. Then with offhand but decisive sweeps, she crossed "Kicks," "Pretzel," "Fitting," "Down by the river," and

"Temple" off her list. How else to interpret the adventures involving Parnell, Kirk (he certainly had twisted himself every which way), Sidney of Kropotkin's Shoes (she was perhaps stretching a point on this one), Jordan Rivers' sauna, and the Apollo?

She did not notice that the subway had come to her stop until it was almost too late. She jumped to her feet and barely had time to get her trailing walking stick through the door before it closed. (Some of you who have noticed that Oreo has been shlepping a long stick will interpret said stick as a penis substitute. Wrong, Sibyl, it's a long stick.)

Oreo around the corner from her father's apartment building

It was, she realized, quite close to the very first place in which she had looked for her father when she arrived in New York— the street of the Chinese-lady Schwartz.

Oreo on her father's street

Left-right, left-right, left-right went her heart. *Thump/tap-thump, thump/tap-thump, thump/tap-thump* went her feet and cane.

Oreo in the foyer of her father's lobby

She looked down the ladder of names next to the line of black buttons. She pressed the button next to the slot marked 2-C. A strip of black plastic with white incised lettering announced: S. SCHWARTZ. A woman's voice squawked over the intercom. Oreo did not understand what she said. She assumed it was "Who is it?" or some other similar question. Oreo, with perfect diction and the precise British accent of Abba Eban, made up a sentence in grammatical gibberish. It sounded good even to her. A few seconds later, the buzzer buzzed, releasing the lock on the lobby door.

Oreo in the elevator

A short vertical leap, a settling jounce, a lighted 2, a suck-slide. Oreo stepped into the hallway. It had an acrid odor.

Oreo at her father's door

The odor was stronger. A tall, broad-browed woman appeared at the door. Oreo could not decide whether she looked more like Judith Anderson or the Statue of Liberty. After a few moments, she judged that the resemblance to the spike-headed Mother of Exiles was closer, the more so because the woman had one arm aloft, her fingers circling air. Just enough room for an invisible torch, thought Oreo. The woman seemed disinclined to lower it. Incipient catatonia or a painful underarm boil, Oreo diagnosed.

The woman's deep-set eyes narrowed at the sight of Oreo. "Yes, what is it?"

"Mr. Jenkins sent me." Oreo had noticed the superintendent's name on one of the first-floor mailboxes. "May I come in, Mrs. Schwartz?"

The woman opened the door a little wider. "I hope it is about fixing the intercom. I could not understand a word you said," she complained in a precise but heavily accented voice.

A Georgia Jew if Oreo had ever heard one. But the Georgia of Mingrelia and Tiflis, not Atlanta and (coincidence) Warm Springs. (A Mdivani, perhaps?) And she doubted whether peaches were native to the Caucasus. Her mother's information was only a few thousand miles off. "It's about proposed maid service for the building," Oreo said, adapting the Jew's poker idea she had gotten on the subway.

The woman narrowed her eyes at Oreo again. "I suppose it is all right. Come in, I cannot stand in the doorway all day."

As Oreo stepped in, her nostrils were assailed by a piercing bite that was no longer an odor but a physical attack—as though a cat were snared in her nares. Her eyes watered. "What *is* that?" she gasped.

The woman looked at her coolly. "Just something I am . . . dabbling with. You will get used to it." She said it as though she were used to dismissing other people's pain.

As the clawing sensation diminished, Oreo sniffed around. There was a distinct odor of cyanide in the room—coming from a dish of bitter almonds. One side of the large, L-shaped living room was a chemist's dream—chockablock with flasks, vials, retorts, Bunsen burners, a spectrum of chemical jams and jellies. If a chemist could dream, so could a cabalist. The opposite wall was hung with floor-to-ceiling charts—palmistry, astrology, phrenology; in a corner stood another, smaller chart, dense with numbers. A round table in front of the palmistry chart held tarot cards, tea leaves, and a crystal ball. This chick is *ready,* jim! Oreo marveled. She pictured the woman striding back and forth across the room (or did she fly?) fulfilling her own prophecies through her skill with mortar and pestle—with one hand, as it were, tied above her back.

A gentian petal of flame enclosed the saffron budding of one of five Bunsen burners. Above the floral combustion, a noxious exhalation—an effervescing retort, source of Oreo's nasal irritation. The nidor only added to her discomfort over not being able to state her business straightforwardly. Her father's new wife was obviously alone in the apartment. She had to stall until she could find out whether Samuel was expected. "Interesting place you have here," she began, trying to look undismayed at the array of cockamamie *objets d'arts noirs* she spied under the round table when she sat down. She could see only the top layer of the two-foot-high box. It was sectioned off into animal, vegetable, and mineral agencies: silver spikes and silver bullets; herbs that she could not readily identify; and, in what could be called the meat section, a shrunken head, a monkey's paw, and what looked like a small jar of chicken entrails.

"We call it home," the woman said flatly.

"Home is where the heart is," Oreo said agreeably. She cast a furtive eye at the box under the round table. She thought she saw a telltale cordate shadow in the nether regions of the meat section.

"Perhaps you would be good enough to explain why you have come?"

Oreo launched into a jive story grounded in years of specialized research (her collection of New Yorkiana was the envy of the New-York Historical Society). She told Mrs. Schwartz that the landlord, who owned several high-rent apartment buildings on the Upper West Side, had decided to take matters into his own hands concerning the city's foremost problem: roaches. Oreo held her breath in case she had made a drastic error and had mentioned the roach problem in one of the three buildings in New York that did not have them.

Mrs. Schwartz gave not an eye-narrow, not a lash-flutter. Oreo was reassured that she had not blown her cover through a blattid blunder. She went on with her bullshit. The landlord, she said, was concerned for the health and safety of his tenants, certainly. He was even more concerned that New Yorkers not be subject to social embarrassment when out-of-towners came to visit, went to the kitchen to get a drink of water, turned on the light, and started a career of *cucarachas* on their nightly sprint at the crack of a hundred-watt bulb ("Maude, you'll never believe what I saw in there. I always said your brother George was filthy. How can people *live* like that?"). Therefore the landlord proposed, for only a token rent increase—more a gesture of tenant solidarity than a true rent raise—to supplement the monthly visits by the Upper West Side Exterminating Company with weekly maid service for those who did not already employ professional cleaning women. The work of presently employed cleaning women would have to be thoroughly checked, of course, to see that their services met union standards. Yes, the building would now come under the guidelines set by Local 7431 of the International Dusters, Moppers, Washers, and Waxers, recently organized by the Teamsters. (The union logo was a clogged dust mop — so clogged, in fact, that it looked like a canine footpad.) Tenants who, out of sentiment, insisted on employing ninety-year-old cleaning women, who might chew but could not be said to be *up to* snuff, senior citizens (second class) who could no longer see where to dust and, in effect, merely moved the dirt from one place to another —such tenants might be required to pay a monthly fee for as long as their sentiment or their cleaning women (whichever died first) kept them in violation of IDMWW standards. Tenants who retained old family retainers but also employed union cleaning women and cleaning men (no sexual discrimination would be tolerated) and thereby reached union standards would not be fined, of course. Tenants who refused any service whatsoever—who in effect told the IDMWW to go suck on its mop —and whose apartments were judged health hazards by both the IDMWW shop steward and a majority of the tenant cleanliness committee would face eviction. The rent commission might have to decide the merits of individual cases.

Oreo was just warming to her subject when Mrs. Schwartz said, "But I *must* have roaches. I use them in my . . . work."

Oreo put on a concerned look. "I don't mean to tell you how to run your business, but would it be possible to breed them in captivity? That way, the rest of the apartment could be roach-free and you would still have sufficient numbers for your . . . work—and under controlled conditions."

The woman looked at Oreo sharply. "Excellent idea, excellent," she said slowly. Without lowering her arm, she nodded her torch hand several times. "I have other, more serious objections, Miss . . . ?"

"Christie," Oreo said quickly. "But just call me Anna." What would a foreigner know, anyway?

"I will get to my objections in a moment, but first I have a favor to ask of you, Miss . . . Christie."

There was a definite smirk on her face, Oreo decided. Either that or she had a facial tic without a toc, on top of her catatonia/boil. Oreo waited.

"Would you allow me to read your palm? I know you must have many more tenants to see today, but I assure you it will not take long. I see something in your face that interests me."

Oreo readily agreed.

They moved to the round table. Mrs. Schwartz shoved the animal-vegetable-mineral box against the wall so that they could both get their feet under the table. It was just as well. Oreo did not want to touch the ishy thing with a bare toe and inadvertently put a jambalaya jinx on her perfect feet. She liked her hexes straight, simple, homogeneous.

Mrs. Schwartz studied Oreo's palm silently for several minutes, her eyes rapidly scanning the mounts and lines. With a long-nailed finger she traced Oreo's rascettes. A chill pimpled along Oreo's right leg and around her hairline, as it always did when she was profoundly shaken by something—good or bad. Her body registered the same sensation for Buxtehude well played as for singing telegrams well sung, only her brain distinguishing between what she called "thrilly chills" and "chilly chills." Put on a sweater, her brain told her now.

When the woman dropped her hand as though it were a hot sea urchin, Oreo laid it to envy. She had had her palm read before and had been told that her Mounts of Jupiter, Venus,

Apollo, and Lower Mars were transcendent, her lines of Mercury and Life enviable, those of the Sun, Head, and Heart virtually a crime against the rest of humanity. In short, she had a fabulous, a mythic hand—the quintessential chiromantic reading (though some might cavil at a rather too well-developed Plain of Mars).

"Anything wrong?" Oreo asked.

The woman seemed to be agonizing over a grave decision. When, presumably, she had made up her mind, she was friendlier than she had been since Oreo's arrival. "You must stay and have some lunch with me, my dear. Can you do that?"

"I'd love to," Oreo lied. How was she going to fix lunch with one hand in the air? "Is there anything you'd like to tell me about the reading? Anything special?"

The woman dismissed this possibility with a peremptory flick of the left hand. "No, no, the usual, I am afraid. You will marry a basketball player at twenty-one, have three children— two boys and a girl—and live happily ever after."

Oreo knew all this was a stone *lie*. With *her* hand? Amaze the Amazons, perhaps—but live happily ever after with some jive guard and three crumb snatchers? Foul!

While Oreo was fuming, the door opened and two little boys, about six and seven, came in. Their identical cream-colored shirts and navy-blue caps, ties, and short pants suggested a school uniform or a mother with a twin fetish. They had latchkeys on chains around their necks and were carrying small plaid suitcases. The boys stood in front of the door, which they had not closed completely, rubbing what looked like black track shoes against the pitiful calves of their spindly legs and wrinkling their navy-blue knee socks, which they then hiked while keeping their eyes on Mrs. Schwartz and Oreo. They looked like frightened voles. Their large gold-brown lemur eyes seemed to be searching out escape routes.

"Close the door," said Mrs. Schwartz. "If I have told you once, I have told you thirty-two and five-eighths times."

The little things that give a foreigner away, thought Oreo. She probably says "Vanzetti and Sacco" too.

Reluctantly, the older of the two did as he was told. He jiggled the knob a few times as if to make sure he was not locked in.

"Come here and meet our visitor," Mrs. Schwartz commanded.

The children edged forward, eyes looming.

"Marvin, Edgar, say hello to Miss Christie."

"Anna," Oreo said.

"No—children should show respect for their elders," Mrs. Schwartz insisted.

The children aspirated almost inaudible hellos. Oreo gave them the expected pat on their caps, but they did not expect it and shied away.

"Go put your toys away," Mrs. Schwartz directed.

"So that's what's in those suitcases," said Oreo.

The woman looked at her strangely. "The suitcase *is* the toy, Miss Christie."

"Of course," Oreo quickly amended.

"It is what they *like* to play with," she said defensively.

"Certainly," said Oreo. What would those little voles have in their suitcase toys? Roadmap toys, spare-clothing toys, K-ration toys, Dr. Scholl's toys?

"And take off those silly track shoes. They are ruining the floor," Mrs. Schwartz said as the boys clattered into their room.

For the first time, Oreo noticed that the parquet swath from the front door to the children's room did bear a certain resemblance to Cobb's Creek Golf Links. Either that or the floor had never recovered from a bad case of a pox on this house.

"They don't look much like you," Oreo said, trying to hide the fact that it was a compliment to Mrs. Schwartz.

The woman obviously divined the flattery. She inclined her head in acknowledgment. "They are adopted. My own children . . . died. I felt the loss keenly and adopted these children . . . after."

She confided to Oreo that her first husband had been somewhat frivolous. His woolly-headed schemes had gotten him fleeced on several occasions. But their children had been dear to them both, their loss almost unbearable. To assuage her pain, she adopted the first children who came along—much to her regret. She was very disappointed in them. They were afraid of slime mold. ("They remind me of a certain animal I used to see when I was a child," she said. "I don't know the English word for it." Oreo smiled and said, "Vole.") Now all she wanted was children of her own loins. One of the things she was experimenting with was a pill that put the pleasure back into parturition. Mrs. Schwartz gestured to her equipment—occult and natural. "In this age of scientific miracles, man should no longer have to undergo the pain of childbirth," she said determinedly. She shook her head as though to clear it of further illogic. "But why am I boring you with my life story? I must fix that lunch I promised you."

She gave Oreo a magazine to read—to keep her away from the flasks and vials, Oreo guessed. No matter. Oreo was soon engrossed in "Burp: The Course of Smiling Among Groups of Israeli Infants in the First Eighteen Months of Life," the cover story in *Pitfalls of Gynecology*.

Mrs. Schwartz came back a few minutes later, not lighting her way with her invisible torch and balancing a tray of shrimp, saltines, lemon wedges, and water cress. As she was sliding the tray onto the coffee table in front of the couch, a man walked in. Oreo knew immediately that he was her father.

He was not exactly ugly (a litotes). He was in his early forties, had curly, almost kinky hair (which Oreo knew had been gray since his late teens), noble-savage nose and cheekbones, long cheek creases that would become dimples when he smiled, and the smug, God-favored lips of a covenant David (2 Samuel 7):

If he had seen Oreo, he made no sign. He went straight into a room opposite the children's.

Mrs. Schwartz excused herself and followed him. In a few moments, Oreo heard low, angry voices coming from the room. The children opened their bedroom door a crack, showing four eyes with a frightened lemur-shine, then closed it hastily. She tried to make out what the voices were saying, but all she could distinguish was the cadence of accusation and recrimination. "Where were you all night?" she imagined Mrs. Schwartz saying. "None of your beeswax," her father would answer. "I won't have you lusting after the harlots of Harlem," she would counter. "Who can *shtup* a woman who has one arm in the air all the time?" he would say. "It makes me think you're trying to tell me something."

Oreo did not touch the shrimp, although her mouth was watering. Might as well win some brownie points for politeness, she calculated.

A minute later, the door to the *chambre de combat* burst open and the Schwartzes came out. "I will not have that man coming here and frightening the children," said Mrs. Schwartz.

"So take the kids for a run in the park, the way you always do," Samuel said sarcastically.

"Someone from the landlord is here," Mrs. Schwartz said with a warning edge on her voice.

Oreo was ready. She took the mezuzah from her clĕvice and let it drop outside her dress. She gestured with it rather obviously as she said, "I would like to discuss the plan with your husband, Mrs. Schwartz. Mr. Jenkins wants to make sure the members of each family unit are in agreement.''

Samuel's eyes unfocused at the sight of the waggling mezuzah. He could have been doing a take for a hypnosis scene in a B movie. Trouper that he was, he recovered himself immediately. "Take Marvin and Edgar out. Dominic will be here any minute. I'll see Miss . . .''

"Christie, Anna," Oreo said. Her father smiled what she interpreted as a chip-off-the-old-block recognition smile. Probably thinking of his lousy clues, she would bet.

"Yes, I'll see Miss Christie out, Mildred.''

Without another word, Mrs. Schwartz turned on her heel and knocked on the door of the boys' room. Inclining her head, she motioned them out. They scurried past her, clutching their little suitcases. *Clack–r-i-i-p, clack–r-i-i-p* went their track shoes as they passed the par 3 section of the parquet. Mrs. Schwartz walked behind them. At the door she gave Samuel a look Oreo couldn't define, then said, "Don't forget to have your lunch, Miss Christie.''

When the door closed, Oreo stared at her father for several seconds without saying anything.

"So," he said finally.

"So," she said.

"You have my eyes.''

"I was going to say the same thing to you," said Oreo.

He absentmindedly picked up a shrimp. He brought it to within sniffing distance and stopped short. He threw it down violently. "I told her to get rid of this *trayf*. It's spoiled!''

The doorbell rang. "Who is it!" Samuel shouted.

"Dominic," answered a soft but penetrating voice.

"It's open.''

A man built like a highboy came in. He moved as if on castors. He looked at Oreo. He looked at Samuel. "You get away with murder," he said, snorting. "Bringing them right here to your house."

Samuel gave him a quick shake of the head and a look that said, "Shah!" Samuel turned to Oreo. "Excuse me a minute, Chris— Miss Christie."

He took Dominic into the short end of the living room's L. There was murmured conversation for a few minutes, and when her father returned, he said, "I have a big favor to ask of you, kid. I know we just met, and believe me I'd like nothing better than to have a real heart-to-heart right now. And I promise you, we'll have one—as soon as you get back from an errand I want you to run for me. That is, *if* you want to do it." He patted her hand and gave her an actor's look of fake sincerity or sincere fakery—she did not know which.

"What is it?" she said dryly.

While Dominic lurked in the base of the L, Samuel ran down a story that Oreo knew he was making up as he went along. In his story, Dominic was a play-school director whose little charges, seven boys and seven girls, had voted unanimously that before the day was out, they absolutely had to have, would turn blue if they did not get, a bulldog they had seen on an outing with Dominic as they strolled past a downtown pet shop window. Since — wonder of wonders — the pet shop owner just happened to be one of Samuel's very best friends, Dominic had come to him on bended knee (or oiled castors) to beg him to get a good (that is, low) price for the pedigreed dog from Minotti, said pet shop owner. Dominic could not go himself because he had a silver plate in his head (this was later confirmed when Samuel bade him remove his partial bridge — lower left molars —and, lo, it was made of silver), but he had brought with him the contributions of the parents of the fourteen children and the nickels and dimes of the children themselves. Now, since

Samuel would be very busy in the next few hours, it would be awfully sweet and considerate of Christine if she would act as his agent and buy and bring back the bulldog.

Oreo listened to this crock impassively. She now knew that she had come by her line of bullshit honestly. She told her father that she would do it. Samuel held up an envelope, which, he said, contained money and a note informing Minotti that the bearer was acting for the pet man's good friend Schwartz. When he had had time to write such a note, Oreo did not know. And why didn't he just phone Minotti and tell him she was coming? Tapped wires?

Samuel wrote the name and address of the pet shop on the envelope and sealed it. "Be very careful with this money," he said.

Oreo noticed as she took the envelope that the "nickels and dimes" of the tykes had evidently been exchanged for paper money. She was pissed off. "Isn't there anything you want to tell me before I go?" she said somewhat snappishly.

"Oh, that," Samuel said. He gave her a sly grin. "How'd you like my clues? Pretty good, eh?" He pointed to a small shelf of books near where Dominic was casting a square shadow. "The final clue to the answer is in one of those books. When you get back, I'll see if you can guess which one."

Oreo was thoroughly disgusted. "Another riddle, yet!" she said, sucking her teeth.

Samuel laughed. "You sound just like your mother." He put his arm around her shoulder, the better to hustle her out the door. "I'll be waiting, kid, so speed it up. I'll watch for you at the window. Wave to me if everything's okay."

"Why shouldn't everything be okay?" Oreo asked. "It's just a dog, right?"

Samuel didn't answer but smiled his fake or sincere smile.

Oreo picked up her walking stick, which she had leaned against a phonograph console by the front door. Samuel saw her to the elevator.

Out on the street, she turned and looked up to the second floor. Her father was at the window. He waved at her, then ducked back inside. Oreo turned and walked down the street, the tail of her black headband flying in the wind.

14 Minos, Pasipḥaë, Ariaḋne

Oreo at the pet shop

A grainy, high-contrast black-and-white photograph stippled the entire back wall. The dark mass covering the lower portion of the photograph, two-thirds of the picture area, was a rolling hillside, from which jutted, in profile, a file of bone-white tombstones, like the vertebrae of an unearthed prehistoric monster. It did not feel much like a pet shop. There were a few cages of scrawny animals, and two ink-blot Dalmatian puppies rorschached on the *New York Post* in the window, beneath cursive lettering that read: *Minotti's Pets*. But the place lacked an aura of true "pet-shop-ness." After a few moments, Oreo realized what was missing: musk. But how much scent could a few dogs, a monkey, a myna, and an empty fish tank muster? There *was* an odor in the air, dark brown and salty. What was it? Ah, yes, soy sauce. Oreo looked around. There were no cats in any of the cages. Perhaps Minotti's was a front for a Chinese restaurant. Sinophobic slurs aside, it was obvious that the Minottis were preparing dinner.

A short man of about sixty came out of the back room wiping his hands on a towel, which he tucked into his pants against his stove-bellied pot. He peered at Oreo over his bifocals.

"Mr. Minotti?"

He nodded. Oreo handed him the envelope. He opened it, looked inside. "Bovina!" he called to the closed swing door of the back room. There was no answer. He walked to the door, pushed it open, and called out again. With the door open, Oreo could hear the faint sound of a guitar.

"What are you yelling?" a woman's voice said impatiently.

Minotti stepped into the back room. "Put this away," Oreo heard him say. "And see if Adriana is ready." He came back into the shop.

Neither Oreo nor Minotti said anything while they waited. Oreo monkeyed with the monkey, waggling her fingers at him and making human faces. Minotti continued to peer at her over his glasses and wipe his hands on the towel. While Oreo was considering a reply to the myna's sly "Were you there when they crucified my Lord?" she heard something metallic roll past her foot and go under the monkey cage.

"*Stupido!* I dropped my ring!" Minotti exclaimed.

While he was trying to see under his pot, Oreo passed the crook of her cane under the monkey cage and hooked out three things: a dust mouse, the ring, and a Danish krone. She shoved the dust mouse back under the cage, where, she fancied, it could nibble dust cheese. She gave the ring and the coin to Minotti.

"*Ecco!* My lucky piece. She's lost now three weeks." He closed his fingers on a kiss, then released the *bacio* with a quick opening and extension of his fingers, a trap unsprung. "*Grazie, signorina, grazie.*"

"*Prego.*"

They went back to monkeying and peering. Oreo wondered

where the puppy was. Surely Dominic could not have mistaken a Dalmatian for a bulldog? She did not wonder long. A woman she assumed to be Mrs. Minotti came through the swing door nuzzling and cooing at a sturdy bulldog pup.

"Stop spoiling the dog," Minotti said. "You act foolish sometimes, Bovina."

The woman shrugged to Oreo and put the dog on the floor. He frolicked around her a few times, playfully minatory, then jumped against her leg to show he wanted to be picked up again. Bulldogs had always reminded Oreo of grumpy cowboys because of their horseshoe jaws and bowlegs. This one was more like an awkward child, anxious to please. He was the first knock-kneed, smiling bulldog she had ever seen. His coat showed signs of inordinate fondling—it looked as if it came from a thrift shop. "What's his name?" she asked.

"Toro—what else?" Mrs. Minotti said proudly. She picked the dog up again. "He's my precious *bambino*, eh?" The dog shoved his muzzle against her ear.

Minotti made a derisive comment about his wife and the dog with an expressive twist of the wrist.

"*La gelosia*," said Mrs. Minotti.

Minotti shook his head in exasperation. "Go see if Adriana is ready."

"I'm ready."

The voice was that of a young woman a few years older than Oreo. She had a black shawl of hair and wore a faded blue shirt and jeans. A guitar was slung over one shoulder, and in her right hand she was holding a dog collar studded with rhinestones. She took the dog from Mrs. Minotti and put the collar around his neck.

"*Il mio bambino, il mio bambino*," murmured Mrs. Minotti.

"Oh, Mother, for God's sake, Toro will be back as soon as this is delivered."

Her mother and father both gasped and put their fingers to their lips as if to seal hers.

The young woman laughed. "Yeah, I know. It's supposed to be a deep, dark secret," she teased. "How silly." She turned to Oreo. "I'm Adriana, by the way."

"Christine," said Oreo.

"How are you going back?"

"Subway. I got a little turned around coming down here. Lost my maps. I'm new in town," Oreo explained.

"I'm going that way—to the corner, anyway. I'll show you how to get where you're going."

"Thanks," said Oreo.

"You'll need a carrier. This is an active little bugger."

"Adriana," her father protested, with a pleading look.

"Okay, okay," she said. "I'll watch my language. Be right back." She left and came back in a few minutes with a black carrying case for the dog.

Mrs. Minotti gave Toro one more kiss and put him into the case. He whined for a few moments, then was quiet.

"Can you manage this and your cane too?" Adriana asked Oreo.

"I think so." Oreo picked up the case. "It's not heavy."

"Okay, we're off." Adriana kissed her mother and father "See you in a few hours—right after the concert."

" 'Concert,' she calls it," Minotti said.

"Don't knock it, *babbo*. It pays the rent."

Oreo and Adriana on a traffic island

The light seemed to be in the running for longest in the embarrassed history of red. Oreo saw an opening between a beetling Volkswagen and a bounding Jaguar. She timed her move and darted to the other side of the street.

Adriana was stranded on the island. She waved to Oreo.

"Change at Forty-second Street!" she shouted. "Follow the arrows for the IRT!"

"Forty-second Street. Arrows," Oreo said, nodding her head. She waved her walking stick to Adriana. The last glimpse Oreo had of her was when a woman who looked like a Minerva flew onto the island, a racking Pinto narrowly missing her heels. The woman turned the smooth button eyes of an owl now toward Adriana, now away, her small hooked nose beaking this way and that as she gazed, unblinking, at the traffic.

Oreo underground at Forty-second Street

A horizontal rectangle with black letters told her:

PORT AUTHORITY BUS TERMINAL
← 8$^{\underline{TH}}$ AVE SUBWAY ←

A red sign said:

TRACK 3
SHUTTLE TO GRAND CENTRAL

↑ BMT LINES STRAIGHT AHEAD

said another red sign. A fairer sign gave one line each to complementary green and red:

GREEN ← FOR BWAY 7$^{\underline{TH}}$ AVE LINE
& MEZZANINE FOR BMT

·UPTOWN & DOWNTOWN BMT & IRT →

offered another. Under this, a *graffito* made a cross-cultural admission:

OH, BOY, AM I FARBLONDJET!—DAEDALUS

Oreo finally found the right train. She sat down and wiggled her perfect toes in anticipation of the about-to-be-revealed secret of her birth. As she moved Toro's carrying case a little to one side, she noticed the socks of the man opposite her. She started looking at sock patterns. Was there a pattern to the patterns on this car? Lisle of Manhattan offers so many diversions, she thought as she knitted her brow.

Oreo on her father's street again

She switched the carrier from her left to her right hand and her walking stick from her right to her left. As she looked down the street, she saw two things: a black girl in a white dress carrying what looked like a large lunchbox. Her father was waving at the girl. He turned his head and saw Oreo. He started to wave again and stopped in mid-wave. Oreo flashed on what was about to happen. She started to run. The other girl started to run. Their two black headbands sailed on oceans of air as they rushed toward each other. Samuel's double takes took up less and less lateral space as they got faster and faster. Oreo stopped short under his window, fearing that she would collide with the onrushing girl—who also stopped short. Oreo looked up in time to see Samuel falling toward her. His body brushed her right hand as he smashed onto the carrier, driving it to the ground. Oreo ran over to her father. She looked up open-mouthed at an openmouthed girl who looked just like her.

And then the mirror moved.

15 Pandion

Oreo's reaction to her father's death

She was more distressed over accident than essence — the fluki-
ness, not the fact of Samuel's death. The jive mirror of the new
people moving into his building, his landing on the carrying
case. The fall alone, from the second floor, would not have
killed him. No bones had been broken, but his plummet had
split the carrier and squashed poor Toro, whose rhinestone collar had left an intaglio coronet on Samuel's brow. Unmarked
except for his baron's band, he was dead nevertheless and (dear,
fatherless Jimmie C.) winnie-the-pooh. Oreo was sad but not
too. She felt about as she would if someone told her that Walter
Cronkite had said his last "Febewary" or that a fine old character actor she had thought for years was dead was dead.

When it happened, Oreo knew she had two unpleasant things
to do: break the news (banner head) to Mildred Schwartz and,
worse, break the news (sidebar) to Bovina Minotti. She left
worse for last. After the ambulance took Samuel away and the
ASPCA claimed what was left of Toro, Oreo waited for Mrs.

Schwartz outside her apartment until she and the boys came back from their track meet in the park. Mrs. Schwartz said nothing when she heard the news. Slowly, as if in benediction, her torch arm declined until it was level with her shoulder. One of the fingers that had encircled the invisible torch peeled off from her thumb and pointed to the telephone, to which she went directly and began dialing Samuel's *mishpocheh.* Marvin and Edgar cowered in a corner with their suitcases.

While Mrs. Schwartz was still talking to Samuel's relatives, Oreo went outside to find a pay phone and call the Minottis. She was relieved when Adriana answered. Oreo told her what had happened.

"Oh, God, poor Mr. Schwartz—how am I going to tell Mother about Toro?"

"I don't envy you."

"Listen, do you have the collar?"

"The what?"

"Toro's dog collar," said Adriana. "Do you have it?"

"Yes, the ambulance driver put it in a paper bag and gave it to me."

"Thank God. Call Dominic and give it to him."

"I don't have his number," Oreo said.

"I thought you were with the agency."

"What agency?"

"Dominic's agency. The ad agency. You know—Lovin' Cola."

"I don't know what the ham-fat you're talking about."

Adriana laughed. "Oh, wow, those people are really off the wall. They don't even tell their own couriers what's happening." After a few more chuckles, she said, "Look in the dog collar."

Odd choice of prepositions, Oreo thought. They talked a few more minutes, then Oreo called Dominic at the number Adriana had given her. A half hour later, he met her on the corner and took the paper bag. He did not look too happy as he rolled away. She did not know whether his gloom stemmed from Samuel's death or from the fact that he faced the prospect of building a campaign around a new Voice of Lovin' Cola.

Adriana had cleared up the mystery about Dominic, Toro, and the Minottis. Samuel had been mixed up not with gangsters (Oreo's surmise) but with industrial spies—or, rather, fear of industrial spies. He was to be the Voice of Lovin' Cola, a new soft drink its makers thought would flatten Dr. Pepper, Coke, and Pepsi. Keystone of the introduction of Lovin' Cola was the jingle Adriana had written about the beverage—a jingle the ad agency hoped could be adapted and released as a pop tune that would have pop heads fizzing Lovin' Cola's message, sub- or supraliminally, until the national fever for carbonation defervesced—around the thirty-third of Juvember. The agency did not want to break wind until it knew which way the breeze was blowing. One of the other gas companies might pull the old switcherino on the music and lyrics and come out with a carbonated copy before the Lovin' Cola people were ready to open the silo and push the button for their blitz spritz in the media.

Before Dominic trundled into view, Oreo snapped open the back of Toro's dog collar and found Adriana's demo tape and an onionskin with the typed lyrics of the jingle:

LOVIN' COLA

by

Adriana Minotti

(Dom: For pop version, sub ''oh-la'' for ''Cola'')

Lovin' Cola, Lovin', Lovin' Cola,
Lovin' Cola, Lovin', Lovin' Cola,
Get your fill, it's a thrill,
Lovin' Cola, Lovin', Lovin' Cola.

Oh, well, thought Oreo, the *tune* is probably unabashedly addictive:

Oreo at the door of 2-C

She had spent the night in the park. In the morning, she waited outside of Samuel's apartment building until she saw Mildred Schwartz leave for the funeral. The sun glanced away from the dragon hood ornament as the limousine turned the corner. The children were not with her. Oreo assumed that someone had been assigned to prevent their escape from the apartment. She had to get inside to go through her father's bookshelf. She was still a bit pissed off at Samuel for falling out of the fool window before he had told her the secret of her birth.

She heard gay laughter in 2-C. Her knock switched it off.

The door opened and before her stood a woman whose smooth facial planes gave her an expression so benign that she made Aunt Jemima look like a grouch. "Won't expecting nobody," the woman said. "Who you?" Her voice was soothing too. Marvin and Edgar had given up their death grip on their suitcases to garrote her skirts. After one lemur-look at Oreo, they hid behind the woman.

"I'm the . . . mother's helper," said Oreo.

"Madam didn't tell me, but come on in, chile. These kids running me crazy." The woman was wearing a starched white uniform and apron. She motioned Oreo to a seat. "Name's Hap. I'll be in the kitchen yet a while."

"Mine's Anna, Miss Hap," Oreo said politely, eyeing the voles.

Hap tried to shoo the children toward Oreo, but they bobbed around that rich broth of a woman like dumplings.

Oreo's eyes went to the bookshelf her father had pointed out. Before she was half the distance to it, the phone rang. Hap stepped out of the kitchen to answer it. "Schwartz residence," she said solemnly. Then she smiled sunnily and said, "How you, Nola?" She sat down in a straight chair just under the book-shelf. The spines of the volumes were just out of Oreo's reading range.

"Yeah, it right sad," said Hap into the phone. "Madam at the funeral now. . . . *Naw*, she just asked me to fix a little something, case anybody drop 'round after the burial. I'll cook it, but ain't nobody gon eat it. Don't nobody never come here, chile. You should see this living room, the mess she got 'round here. No wonder the children 'fraid of her. . . . Yeah, chile, scared to *death*. . . . The Millers? Chile, them people much rich. The madam in Florida now, and mister in Chicago on business. The two girls in Europe with they husbands. . . . Oh, sure, they ain't got nothing better to do than travel 'round."

It was too early for Oreo to tell whether Hap was of the this-job-is-a-piece-of-cake school or the these-people-are-stone-slave-drivers faction, but she was already dropping the time-honored phrases of the my-people-are-richer-than-yours bloc.

"*Who?*" Hap challenged the caller in outraged tones. "Are you kidding! I don't do *no* cleaning! I don't get down on *my* knees for *nobody*. No, chile. I don't even have no downstairs cleaning to do. They got a girl comes in to do that. Colored girl. She even clean *my* apartment for me every day. . . . No, Nola, I told you before, I only go out there the first two weeks in every month. I told the boss, 'Mr. Miller,' I say, 'I can't be staying out here all the time.' I say, 'Times have changed. You can have two weeks of my time, but the rest of my time have to be for other folks need me much as you do.' . . . I most certainly did. . . . Well-sir, I thought I would die when I caught that laundress down in that basement just filling up a box with meats and veg'tables. . . . *Naw,* she Irish woman. You know she always hinting 'round to the madam that I order extry food so I can take it home to my fam'ly. . . . *Who?* She bet' not say nothing to me 'bout it. Who they gon get to go way out there

and stay even for two weeks the way I do? . . . Yeah, is that
so? Is that *so?* That's the trouble with day work. They work
you to death for six fifty and carfare. I ain't done no day work
—no *cleaning* day work—for twenny years, chile. . . . No,
I'm a cook, and I *rule* my kitchen. If they come in *my* kitchen,
they *tiptoe* around. . . . What's that? . . . *Naw,* you don't
mean it? Well, these people are cheap too, chile. Guess that's
why they got so much. My sister Bessie been working for the
old man for how long now? You know as well as I do. . . .
Naw, it's longer than that. But whatever it is, it's umpteen
years. She been working for old man Schwartz since Hector
was a puppy—and he an *old* dog now. Been dusting them
plastic plants since before his wife died. And you know what he
give her last Christmas? A pair of sixty-nine-cent stockings. He
haven't even noticed after all these years that she don't even
wear no stockings. What she need stockings for? Now, the Millers, they give me ten dollars extry and a fifth. The girls gave
me perfume. One time they gave me a pocketbook. . . . *What?*
And as long as you been with them! . . . *Naw,* chile, all they
care 'bout is that *work.* . . . Retire? How can I retire? I got my
bills to pay. But I tell you one thing: I ain't gon die in no
kitchen like poor Henrietta did. No, sir. They ain't gon work
me to death. . . . Oh, she's a caution. She's really something.
You know she won't let that man have more than *one* egg for
breakfast? When she home, he eat like any *bird.* She won't let
him eat! Say she don't want no fat slob for a husband! Can you
beat that! But when she not around, I fix him a nice breakfast.
He just *gobble* it up. That's why he so nice to me. But her, she
something. I think she a little off. Yessir. You know, she fell
off a horse once. Yeah, fractured her skull. I think it made her a
little bit screwy. . . . Yeah? . . . Well, when I'm gon see you,
Nola? Why don't you stop by the house next Thursday. . . .
Yeah, after that, I be out to the Millers for two weeks, so come

on over. I'll have something good for you. . . . *Naw,* I'm not
gon tell you. You guess. . . . Yeah, that's right.'' Hap laughed.
"I'll look for you Thursday, then, Nola. . . . Yeah, so long.''

When Hap got off the phone, Oreo knew that here was a
mother lode of information that, properly worked, could grout
together some of the odd bits of information she had about her
father. Oreo sidled over to the kitchen. She glanced with just
the right look of longing at the arrangement of canapés Hap was
making.

Hap's hearty laughter was surrender. Her generous breasts,
transformed by her uniform into giant marshmallows, heaved,
sweetening the air above her apron. "Take one, chile, 'fore you
break my heart.'' (She meant a canapé, not a breast.)

Oreo popped a caviar cracker into her mouth. She praised it
overmuch for itself but just enough for her purposes. She went
on to sample and laud the other hors d'oeuvres Hap was preparing. A Louise she wasn't, but good enough for any *Almanach
de Gotha* kitchen below the rank of marquis—viscount would
be about right.

A few leading questions about the Schwartzes and Hap offered a verbal tidbit: "His first wife was a colored girl, chile.''

"Naw," said Oreo.

"Um-hm,'' confirmed Marvin and Edgar, who, Oreo found
out within the next few minutes, gossiped like *yentas*.

On Hap's return from her biweekly stints at the Howard Millers, her sister would fill her in on Jacob Schwartz's every burp;
the boys outdid Bessie in scope with detailed reports on
Mildred, Samuel, and the rest of the second floor. In this pin-
cers of prattle, the Schwartzes were squeezed dry.

Oreo had only one thing left to do. "I have to go to the
bathroom. Is it okay if I take a book in with me, Miss Hap?''

"Sure, chile, go on. Be a while yet 'fore she be back.''

Oreo stood in front of the bookshelf. She took her time. She looked long and hard. Finally, keeping in mind her late father's penchant for dumb clues, she narrowed the likely volumes down to two. "Eenie, meenie, miney, mo, catch a cracker by the toe . . ." She realized how unfair that was and revised the parochial rhyme. "Eenie, meenie, miney, mo, catch a honky by the toe . . ." She still could not decide. In a fit of impatience, she grabbed both books from the shelf and went into the bathroom. *Left-right, left-right, left-right* went her heart for the second time in two days.

Oreo in the bathroom

She made her first choice: *The Queen of Spades and Other Stories*. She riffled through Pushkin's pages. Nothing. She went through the book more slowly, this time looking for printed clues. Did the Table of Contents form an anagram, the first lines of the stories a coherent paragraph meant for her alone? Still nothing. She sighed and picked up the other book. This time she decided to leaf through page by page. Between pages 99 and 100 (symbolism again?), she found the sheet of paper. On it were two numbers—a telephone number and a span of nine digits, the latter separated, like a social security number, by dashes after the third and fifth integers. Under the numbers was one word: "Aegeus." She looked ruefully at the book title again. She had to face it. Samuel's brains had been in his *tuchis*. He had just had no class. The book was *The Egg and I*.

Oreo came out of the bathroom. She put the books back on the shelf. "I wonder what the weather's going to be like," she said for Hap's benefit as she dialed the phone number on the sheet of paper.

The voice on the other end of the line said, "GI. May we help you?"

Oreo hung up. She had read an article about GI in a newsmagazine. Which one?

"What they say?" asked Hap from the kitchen.

"Partly sunny," Oreo said abstractedly.

"Heard chance of rain on my radio this morning. They don't know no more about weather than my big toe. Less. At least my big toe know when it gon rain."

Oreo was not really listening. "I have to go in a few minutes. I was only hired until" — she looked at the clock on the far wall — "eleven." That gave her ten minutes to go through the family telephone book.

"Guess she figured that'd give me time to fix this here mess," Hap said.

"Guess so." Oreo found what she wanted on a page headed "Emergency Numbers." She copied down the three names and numbers. Then she looked in the white pages for the nearest branch of the public library. It was only a few blocks away.

Oreo said good-bye to Hap and the boys. As she closed the door to 2-C, she could hear Marvin telling Hap, "You know what? Anna was here yesterday and . . ."

Oreo on a pay phone

After an hour's research at St. Agnes, she had found what she wanted. It had taken almost that long to find a pay phone that wasn't broken. She made the first two calls knowing that, as usual, neither would be the one she wanted. But she did not know which number would be the last, and right, one until she had called the other two. The first of the three doctors turned out to be a dentist. Just before she hung up on his receptionist, Oreo told her that everything was fine—her cavity was at that very moment filling itself, and she no longer needed an appointment. The next doctor was Mildred Schwartz's voodoo consultant, Dr. Macumba. Oreo hung up after telling him that for three sundowns he must avoid spicy foods and women who did not shave their legs. She heard him choke on what sounded like a hot sausage or a hairy leg.

The third doctor was the right one, Dr. Resnick, the Schwartzes' family physician. She told him that she worked for the Schwartzes and that she desperately needed a strong prescription for her menstrual cramps, which were about to descend on her (or whatever direction they came from) that very day. He said, chuckling knowledgeably, that menstrual cramps were all in her head. She marveled at his knowledge, saying that just went to show how smart doctors were, because she had lo these many years thought the cramps were in her uterus. She pleaded with him to humor her, and he condescended to allow her to come to his office for a prescription. The *mitzvoth* he must perform daily, she exclaimed, thanking him, and was in his office in fifteen minutes. Five minutes after she arrived, she had a prescription for a placebo. She threw the top half into the nearest wastebasket. She also had an envelope and a sheet of stationery that she had stolen from Dr. Resnick on which were embossed, in dignified medico black, his name, address, and telephone number. She had one more stop to make before she went to GI.

Oreo at the Central Library, Fifth Avenue and Forty-second Street

She spent half an hour perfecting her forgery of Dr. Resnick's scrambled-egg signature. Then she rented a typewriter and composed a letter. Its chief paragraph was:

> The bearer is therefore authorized to withdraw any and all deposits made to account no. 865-30-2602.

Oreo at GI

She handed the sealed envelope to a man with a head as knobby as a potato and a shaggy, rounded snout of a beard that made him look like a botch of an American bison, the Wolfman, and Cocteau's Beast—an Irving. He slit open the envelope, read the letter, and subjected Oreo to untoward scrutiny. She tried to look dull-normal when he said what she had expected someone to say.

"I'll have to verify this with Dr. Resnick."

Oreo replaced dull-normal with sullen-hurt, the look of the congenitally insulted. "He jus' gib me de 'scription. Say fill it." She had decided to use Hap's economical sentence structure and Louise's down-home accent.

"I still have to verify it, miss," he said, smiling like a shaggy potato—almost imperceptibly.

"He jus' gib it to me," she repeated sullenly. "Say fill it."

Irving picked up the phone and dialed the number at the top of Oreo's letter. "Dr. Resnick? GI here. I have a young lady here." He put his hand over the mouthpiece. "What's your name, girlie?"

"Christie."

"A Miss Christie." He chuckled. "She says you just gave her a 'prescription' and told her to fill it."

Oreo could hear what sounded like angry barking at the other end.

Irving held the phone away from his ear. "Okay, okay, sir. You can't be too careful in these cases, you know. Just wanted to double-check."

"I work fo' 'em," Oreo said petulantly when he hung up. "Send me fo' 'scriptions all de time," she added, just loud enough to lead him to believe that she had not meant him to hear her.

"I have to run this through the computer," said Irving. "Only take a minute." He left the room.

Oreo counted the dots in the wallpaper design while he was gone. She got to 381 before he returned. She would have to tell Louise to play it.

"Now, just as a last, final check, what's the name of account number 865-30-2602?"

"Huh?" said Oreo dull-normally.

"The people you work for, what's their name?"

"Now, what Mr. Sam's las' name?" she asked herself. "Begin with a *S*. Don't tell me. I get it shortly." She bit her lip. "Schwartz," she said triumphantly. "That what it is—Schwartz."

Irving smiled his unseemly potato smile. "Good girl. It never hurts to check."

"Ain't it the truth," said Oreo, smiling her cookie smile.

Oreo leaving GI

She walked out of Generation, Incorporated, swinging her cane and whistling "Hatikvah." When she tired of that, she switched to "Lift Ev'ry Voice and Sing." A special shipping container, about the size of a breadbox, knocked against her leg as she walked. In the container were sixty vials of frozen sperm.

The story of Helen and Samuel, Oreo's version

Piecing together all she had learned from Hap, Marvin, and Edgar, what she had known and now knew, Oreo's scenario went like this: Helen and Samuel meet in college, lust after each other, make out like minks, get married, and make out like minks. In a moment of calm (while the sheets are being changed), they determine to give the world human evidence of their endearment. Jacob would *shep* such *naches* from his first grandchild, he would forgive, forget, and make a new will. "At the rate we're going, it's a wonder I'm not pregnant already," Helen says. "It's understandable, sweetheart," Samuel says, "up to now, we've been taking precautions." "Of course," says Helen, "what are you using, honey?" "What am *I* using?

I thought *you* were using something." Gravid pause. They decide to have checkups. "Low sperm count," says the doctor. "Sorry about that." Samuel is desolate. Then he sees an ad for New York City's first research center for artificial insemination. Samuel fills vial after vial with semen. GI centrifuges, concentrates, and freezes the issue in liquid nitrogen at minus 321 degrees Fahrenheit. *Superimpositions of symbolic swiving and sets of vials being defrosted.* Nine months later: "It's a girl!" But Jacob does not forgive, forget, or make a new will. In fact, he says, "This you call my *aynekel?* In any war between Israel and Egypt, may all the Arabs have eyes like you got." Perhaps a boy? They try—getting and spending and thawing for days on end. In the fullness of time, Jimmie C. is born. But even before that, Jacob has made clear: "Kosher *kinder* or you'll get *makkes.*" And even before *that,* Helen and Samuel have split up. Solely over Jacob's *gelt?* Perhaps, perhaps not. In any case, Samuel determines to make his own fortune. *Montage of* Variety *headlines of the "O's Pop Top Flop" genre.*

After years of floppolas, Samuel meets Mildred. Miraculously, his luck seems to change. He starts pulling down heavy change doing commercials. He marries his luck. He can qualify for Jacob's loot as soon as Mildred has a totsicle. What a *bulba:* Jacob hates her. Make that two *bulbas:* Samuel hates her. She's weird, with her arm in the air and her Lucretia Borgia lab. Samuel reasons: Why should I risk making another boo-boo and lose all that mazuma? Luck or no luck, I'll give her grounds for divorce. I'll even let Jacob pick my next wife. Why take chances? I have a potential fortune stored there at GI. All I need is the right oven and—hoo-ha!—bread!

Clues, shmues

One of Samuel's flops must have been a play about Theseus—hence his legendary clues. Of course, the clues had been meant only to make Oreo *think* of the legend of Theseus. They had had nothing to do with any of her actual adventures. But since from the beginning she had determined what each item on her list signified, she would complete her task and ascribe meaning now, at the end. She took out her list and crossed off "Lucky number" (865-30-2602); "Amazing," which she felt should have been "A-mazing" (trying to find her way through the labyrinth of the subway); and "Sails" (her black headband and its mirror image). The last she crossed off a bit sadly.

Samuel had chosen to style himself "Aegeus." Perhaps he had played the part. Oreo had refreshed her memory of the legend in the library. (She had also found the newsmagazine story on artificial insemination—an invaluable guide to making the withdrawal from the GI sperm bank.) Theseus could be said to have had two fathers—Aegeus and Poseidon. Oreo and Jimmie C. could also be said to have had two fathers—Samuel at room temperature and Samuel frozen. Had the freezing process brought to Samuel's *tsedoodelt* mind the god of flowing waters? His brains had definitely been in his *tuchis*—definitely.

Oreo planning her next move

Jacob deserved a few days to mourn in peace. Meanwhile, she would deposit Samuel's semen in the sperm bank of her choice. There was no rush. The frozen tadpoles would keep for at least five days in their special container. She had been tempted at first to destroy the vials. But she was not ready to see Samuel die twice in two days. She thought of her mother. Helen would probably say, "Your father's dead. Let him rest in peace," and urge her to spill the seed. Her grandfather James would probably tell her to soak Jacob for every cent she could get in return for the vials.

But why not give Jacob an opportunity for what she was pleased to call a Judeo-Négro concordat? He was, after all, her paternal grandfather. They shared misfortune. Perhaps, in these circumstances, he would greet his granddaughter as a *zayde* should, with love and affection. If he did, she might give him the vials as a present. It was no skin off her skin. If, on the other hand, Jacob's greeting was not all that she felt a grandfather's should be, well, then . . . She would have to think about how best to impress upon Jacob the full import of her actions, how make him appreciate her fleeting possession of divine caprice as she poured the last of his strain down the drain. It was all up to Jacob, of course. The way he acted would in large part determine the way she acted. She would allow for his still fresh grief, his shock when she told him who she was and how she got there. Yes, she would cut him some slack. But, for all that, she would not forget herself completely.

Oreo put her package down at the intersection, resting one sandaled foot lightly on top of it as she waited for the light to change. She idly twirled her walking stick, smiled her cookie smile, and whispered slowly and contentedly to herself, *"Nemo me impune lacessit."*

A Key for Speed Readers,
Nonclassicists, Etc.

Pandion and Pylia beget Aegeus. Pittheus and wife (let's call her Neglectedea) beget Aethra. Aegeus visits old friend Pittheus. On the same night, both Aegeus and randy sea-god Poseidon sleep with Aethra. Aethra conceives. Who's the father? Generous Poseidon to Aegeus: "I've got enough kids — he's yours." Aegeus to Aethra: "Well, I'll have to be getting back to Athens now. Send the kid to me when he can lift this rock and recover the sword and sandals I'm leaving under it."

Aethra names her son Theseus ("tokens deposited"). "Boy, it's hot in here," says visiting relative Heracles (Hercules), flinging off the skin of the Nemean lion he's slain. Young Theseus and playmates enter, see lion. Playmates panic. Theseus attacks lion. "Brave lad." Later, he invents wrestling.

When Theseus is sixteen, Aethra says, "I've got something to tell you." Theseus lifts rock, retrieves sword and sandals, and sets out to see his father. He decides to take the overland route because it's dangerous. He wants to be another Heracles.

Epidauris: Theseus kills the lame bandit Periphetes, who'd been dispatching tourists with a club of brass (or iron). Theseus confiscates the club (Heracles has one like it).

Isthmus of Corinth: Sinis likes to play games with people and trees. You bend this tree, see; then you tie . . . Theseus does unto Sinis what Sinis, etc.

Crommyon: Thesus kills a wild sow.

The Cliffs of Megaris: "Wash my feet," the bandit Sciron ("parasol") would say to passing strangers, and then he would punt them into the sea. Theseus does unto Sciron . . .

Eleusis: Cercyon likes to wrestle wayfarers to the death. Theseus invented wrestling, remember?

Corydallus: Procrustes has a long bed and a short bed (or one bed). He fits overnight guests to his bed(s) by racking or lopping. Theseus does unto Procrustes . . .

Cephissus River, Attica: Theseus has done unto so many that he takes time out for purification.

Temple of Apollo Delphinius (the Dolphin), Athens: Hard-hats building the temple make unseemly comments to Theseus, believing that our hero (in braids and white robe) is either a girl or gay. Theseus tosses their oxcart (or ox) over the temple.

The Palace, Athens: Aegeus has married Medea. She knows that Theseus is not just another stranger. If he's who she thinks he is her child(ren) won't get to sit on the throne. Medea to Aegeus about the Stranger: "He's dangerous, poison him." But Aegeus recognizes his token sword, knocks the poisoned cup to the ground. "My son!" General rejoicing. Medea and child(ren) take flight (she has a dragon-drawn chariot).

Months Later: Ambassadors from Crete come to Athens. "Well, here it is that time again. Where are the seven youths and seven maidens we need for the Minotaur's dinner, in tribute for [another story] the murder of Androgeus?" (Cretan king

Minos' wife Pasiphaë and a white bull were the proud progenitors of a fine half-bull, half-human with a taste for all-human flesh.) Theseus says, "I'll go with the gang and kill the Minotaur, Dad." "Son, be careful. And for Zeus' sake, change the black sails on this death ship to white ones if you're successfull." "Black sails to white—okay, Dad."

Crete: Theseus boasts, "I'm a son of Poseidon." "Who isn't?" says Minos. "But prove it." Minos tosses his ring into the sea. Theseus dives in and, with the help of Amphitrite and/or lesser Nereids, retrieves it, along with a golden (or jeweled) crown ("You have to lay it on thick with these Cretans"). Ariadne, Minos' daughter, ever a softy for a showboat, gives Theseus a sword and a ball of string so that he can find his way through the Minotaur's Labyrinth (built by Daedalus), kill it/him, and find his way out again.

All the baddies are killed; all the youths and maidens get away. Theseus abandons Ariadne on the island of Naxos. "I just can't stand to be in anyone's debt. Besides, Athena or Minerva or whatever her name is came to me in a dream and told me to do it. Now, was I supposed to change the sail if I was suc*cess*ful or *un*successful?"

Athens: Aegeus, seeing the black-sailed ship, flings himself into the sea—hence its name, Aegean.

White is the talismanic color in the Theseus legend, eight the magic number.

Further Adventures of the Hero: Theseus and the Amazons; Theseus and Phaedra and Hippolytus; Theseus and Pereithous and Helen and Hades.

Aegeus — Samuel Schwartz
Aethra — Helen Clark
Apollo Delphinius, Temple of —
  Apollo Theater

Ariadne — Adriana Minotti
Cephissus — Jordan Rivers' sauna
Cercyon — Kirk
Heracles — Uncle Herbert

Medea — Mildred Schwartz
Minos — Minotti
Minotaur — Toro the dog
Pandion — Jacob Schwartz
Pasiphaë — Bovina Minotti
Periphetes — Perry the *gonif*
Phaea — Pig killed by taxi

Pittheus — James Clark
Procrustes — Manager of Kropotkin's Shoe Store
Sciron — Parnell the pimp
Sinis — Joe Doe
Theseus — Oreo

Afterword

Under the banner of the Black Arts movement that emerged as the cultural component of Black Power politics of the 1960s and 1970s, African American writers and artists struggled to define and practice a distinctive black aesthetic that departed from traditions based in the history and values of European cultures. The Black Arts movement was fueled by the desire to use art to recover— or, if necessary, to create or reinvent—an authentic black culture based in the particular historical experience of Americans of African descent.

Like the Harlem Renaissance of the 1920s and 1930s, the Black Arts movement resulted in an outpouring of music, art, and literature, and inspired many educated and middle-class African Americans to re-evaluate and to identify themselves more closely with the vernacular culture associated with the black proletariat. At its best, the Black Arts movement stimulated a creative exploration of the folk, popular, and fine art traditions of a community in which diversity and unity, innovation and preservation are interactive forces. At its worst, in their eagerness to purge black identity of all traces of Europe, some critics and theorists

proposed narrow prescriptions for black art that resulted in for-
mulaic expression from some artists. Even this served to provoke
others to question and transgress the limits, while the thorough
exploration of blackness not only contributed to the collective
self-knowledge of African Americans, but also helped to redefine
the culture of the United States as a hybrid multicultural gumbo
rather than a white monocultural melting pot.

Paradoxically, as much as it was concerned with defining the
cultural distinctiveness of African Americans, the Black Arts
movement also helped to create unprecedented opportunities for
the creative expression of African Americans to enter and influence "mainstream" American culture. Sometimes the more
"black rage" was vented in the work, the more the writer was cel-
ebrated in the mainstream culture. In addition to this tense inter-
action of political, aesthetic, and commercial impulses, another
contradiction that the Black Arts movement posed for authors
was the idea that black Americans possessed no authentic literature or language of their own. Writers wrestled with the dilemma
that they were severed from the spoken languages and oral traditions of their African ancestors, and had no intrinsic connection
to the language and literature of their historical oppressors. The
English language itself was perceived by some as a tool of oppression. The more fluent in standard English, or other European
languages, the more immersed in established literary culture, the
more likely one might be accused of forsaking one's own traditions, or abandoning the black community—by writing works it
could not comprehend, or enjoy, or draw upon for inspiration in
the coming revolution that radical activists envisioned.

Fran Ross's novel, *Oreo*, was published in 1974, when the
Black Arts movement had reached the height of its influence. Yet,
as its title signals, *Oreo* does not claim to represent any singular-
ly authentic black experience. More eccentric than Afrocentric,
Ross's novel calls attention to the hybridity rather than the racial

or cultural purity of African Americans. Ross's playfully innovative novel displays a discursive spectrum engaged in by African American characters who express themselves in a variety of languages and dialects, including standard English, African American vernacular, and Yiddish.

Compared to more familiar works of African American literature, this book might seem at first glance bizarrely idiosyncratic, but precedents for it do exist. In certain respects it bears a striking resemblance to a text that was published in 1859, but not widely read until it was rediscovered and reprinted in 1983. The first known novel by an African American woman, Harriet E. Wilson's provocatively titled *Our Nig* is the story of a freeborn woman of color, the indentured servant of a white Northern family who is treated little better than a slave. Like Wilson's novel, Ross's *Oreo* challenges received opinion about African Americans. Oreo is a character whose linguistic and cultural competence allows her to travel between two distinct minority cultures, while enjoying the resources of the dominant culture and exploring her own identity. Both Wilson and Ross have created intelligent African American female characters whose strategic placement within the white household allows them intimate knowledge of America's family secrets. From a position at the intersection of black and white, both Wilson's Frado and Ross's Oreo articulate astute critiques of America's hypocrisy about race. The two novels share other features. In each story, a young, attractive, plucky, defiant biracial heroine, in the absence of protectors, learns to defend herself against the physical aggression of hostile antagonists. Both authors employ innovative narrative strategies, resulting in complexly discursive, generically hybrid texts. Both novels were originally published in small first editions that were largely ignored; and because their works found few receptive readers in their lifetime, both authors remained virtually unknown until their books were rediscovered.

Frances Dolores Ross was born June 25, 1935, in Philadelphia, the eldest child and only daughter of Gerald Ross of Littleton, North Carolina, and Bernetta Bass Ross of Petersburg, Virginia. Her father, a welder, died in an automobile accident returning home from work in New Jersey in 1954. Her mother worked as a store clerk after attending Saint Augustine College in North Carolina. Fran Ross, whose childhood nickname was "Frosty," is remembered as a precocious bookworm, an artistically inclined doodler, and a spirited athlete by her two younger brothers, Gerald Ross, Jr., and Richard Ross. Their maternal grandmother, Lena Bass Nelson, was employed as a cook for the Irish-American family of Arthur J. O'Neil, a Seagram's Company vice president. Fran Ross and her brother Gerald often spent weekends at the home of the O'Neil family, helping "Big Mom" when her employers had large dinner parties. During school vacations, Fran also occasionally accompanied her grandmother to the O'Neil summer home on Lake Winnipesaukee in New Hampshire. The Ross family lived in Philadelphia in a Pearl Street house owned by Lena Bass and attended Mount Carmel Baptist Church.

As a child, Fran Ross often heard Yiddish spoken by the family of Samuel Koltoff, the Russian Jewish immigrant proprietor of the next-door corner store. Another Jewish family, the Millers, employed her brother Gerald in their neighborhood "five and dime" store. Ross attended George Brooks Elementary School and Shoemaker Junior High School. A few days before her sixteenth birthday, she graduated with honors from Overbrook High School, where the student body at the time was predominantly white and Jewish. Her brother Gerald's classmate Wilt Chamberlain played varsity basketball in the same high school. Ross herself, a lifelong sports fan, played basketball at Camphor Memorial Church Center and with the Varsity Pantherettes at Richard Allen Youth Center. In high school, she was a member of the debate team, literary club, and art club; her interests included literature, drama, and cartoons. She received a full college scholarship and graduated in 1956 from Temple University with a B.S. degree in Communications, Journalism, and Theater. Ross sought work as a journalist and was employed for a time at Curtis Publishing Company, home of the *Saturday Evening Post*. Finding it difficult to get suitable employment in Philadelphia, she moved to New York in 1960. There she worked as a proofreader and copy editor at McGraw-Hill and later at Simon and Schuster, where, among other things, she proofread the first book written by Ed Koch, the mayor of New York City.

Oreo, Ross's only novel, was released by Greyfalcon House in 1974. Although Ross never published another novel, she continued to work as a freelance writer and editor, while living "a bagel's throw from Zabar's in a terrace apartment on Riverside Drive in the same building as Jules Feiffer" (*Essence*, 70). Ross wrote pieces for *Essence*, a magazine for black women, as well as for the feminist humor magazine *Titters*, and published a facetious article on black slang in *Playboy* magazine. Ross's freelance activity supplemented her income as part owner and vice president of a mail-order company that produced educational media.

In 1977, on the strength of her published novel and a few sample television scripts, she interviewed for a job as a comedy writer for the controversial and short-lived *Richard Pryor Show*. Encouraged by the producer Rocco Urbisci, Ross had hoped that income from television work might allow her to complete a second novel; but with the expenses of her move from New York to Los Angeles, she barely broke even on the venture. Having given up her New York apartment, Ross was distressed to learn that the star had misgivings about committing himself to a weekly television schedule and submitting to network censorship of his outspoken humor. At an emotionally intense meeting of the show's creators, Ross found herself pleading with the reluctant Pryor to go ahead with the network program, arguing that he could make an impact as a socially conscious black comedian. Although Pryor's associates Paul Mooney and Urbisci collaborated with the comedian on other projects after the show was canceled, Ross scrambled for work at other studios. She soon discovered that she was even more of an anomaly as a black woman comedy writer in Los Angeles than she had been as an editor and author in New York. She submitted sample scripts and tried unsuccessfully to interest network executives in her idea for a pilot program featuring an African American character. Rather than pursuing her only offer—a possible job writing for the *Pryor Show*'s competition, *Laverne and Shirley*—she returned to New York, where she continued to work in publishing and media until her death on September 17, 1985.

A black and white photograph of the author on the back of the novel's original dust jacket shows a youthful-looking black woman with full lips and a kinky Afro hairstyle, wearing hoop earrings, a necklace of large beads, and a garment that might be a dashiki. The epitome of Afrocentric style, the author's portrait seems to engage in a lively dialogue with the novel's title and the eye-catching cover design created by Ann Grifalconi, an award-winning writer and illustrator of multicultural books for children, and the publisher of the original *Oreo*. The artwork features a cropped Nefertiti-like image of a smiling black woman wearing a star of David pendant. In the photograph, Ross poses in front of a sunny window, holding eyeglasses and a pencil in one hand, gazing skeptically at the camera, as if daring the photographer to try to capture her soul, as if challenging the reader to solve the riddle of *Oreo*. Although the author herself warned readers that the book is fiction rather than autobiography, the novel does incorporate or allude to a few circumstantial facts that are known of Ross's life, including her education at Temple University (where Oreo's parents meet), her journey from her Philadelphia birthplace to New York City (like her heroine's odyssey), and her work in advertising and mass media (where Samuel Schwartz, Oreo's father, earns his living).

Oreo is one of a very few works of satire written by African American women. Historically, black women are far more likely to be the objects rather than the authors of parody and satire. Like William Melvin Kelley's *Dunsfords Travels Everywheres* (1970), which also combines vernacular dialects and literary invention in a Joycean romp through language, Ross's *Oreo* languishes in the purgatory or limbo of innovative works by black writers that have been overlooked in the formation of the African American literary canon. Although it is notable for its satirical response to the racial and sexual politics of the 1970s, *Oreo* apparently failed to find its audience, possibly because in the process of commingling two ghettoized vernaculars, African American and Yiddish, the novel also draws on material that both black and Jewish readers might find offensive, perplexing, or incomprehensible. Ross's double-edged satire includes a Jewish immigrant who retains a voodoo consultant named Dr. Macumba; a reverse-discrimination tale of an all-black suburb where a local ordinance is selectively enforced to keep white people from moving into the neighborhood; a black radio producer's script of an advertisement for Passover TV dinners; a joke about the heroine's odds of inheriting sickle-cell anemia and Tay-Sachs disease; and a fight in which Oreo beats a predatory pimp to a pulp while wearing only a pair of sandals, a brassiere, and a mezuzah. Ross frequently confronts her readers with conventional stereotypes encoded in familiar jokes. In *Oreo*, the stereotype is often made more conspicuous by an unexpected twist or inversion, forcing into consciousness the underlying assumptions of jokes about sex, race, and ethnicity.

With its mix of vernacular dialects, bilingual and ethnic humor, inside jokes, neologisms, verbal quirks, and linguistic oddities, Ross's novel dazzles by deliberately straining the abilities of its readers, as if she wrote for an audience that did not yet exist. Relatively few people in 1974 would have possessed the linguistic competence, multicultural literacy, and irreverently humorous attitude toward racial and ethnic identity that Ross demonstrates and expects of *Oreo*'s ideal audience. The more that today's readers have come to learn and understand about America's cultural diversity and the less constrained by narrow definitions of identity, the more likely we are to comprehend and appreciate Ross's satire, which seems to have arrived ahead of its time.

What makes this quirky novel accessible, despite its idiosyncrasy, is Ross's lively appropriation of popular culture genres, including jokes, cartoons, graffiti, advertising, palmistry, cookbooks, and dream books. Ross borrows as heavily from such sources as she does from the culture of high literacy represented by classical literature and "great books," dictionaries, thesauruses, and other reference works, as well as the scholarly essays, handbooks, and bureaucratic pamphlets of academics, technical writers, and other specialists. Oreo borrows without prejudice from elite as well as popular forms of writing and speech, just as she takes equal pleasure in European classical music and "singing telegrams well sung" (178). Ross exploits the double-edged humor of jokes incorporating Yiddish in particular and of "ethnic humor" in general. On the one hand, Yiddish is popularly associated with a certain brand of "Jewish humor"; on the other hand, Yiddish as a language of foreigners, immigrants, or ghettoized Jews may simply "sound funny" to non-Yiddish speakers. Ross also suggests that ethnic humor is a significant aspect of the serious business of constructing American identities within a mainstream culture that rejects some while appropriating other aspects of diverse ethnic groups. As the insider humor of a minority group crosses over into American popular culture, becoming ethnic humor, it allows some members of the marginalized community to make a living by laughing at what makes an ethnic minority group seem "funny" or strange or incomprehensible to others.

As often happens, one minority ethnic group can also be pitted against another when one group is comically portrayed or caricatured by the other. Ross satirically examines just such scenarios, although she departs from the cultural script with a wisecracking heroine who feels free to claim or discard whatever she wishes of African American, Jewish American, and "mainstream" American cultures. Like its eponymous heroine, *Oreo* is a hybrid, a product of racial and cultural miscegenation. While *Oreo* can claim a high-culture pedigree as an innovative literary work retelling a classical Greek myth, Ross also appropriates the lowbrow shtick practiced by performers of stand-up comedy, along with the brisk hucksterism brought to you by advertising copywriters who collaborate with actors and directors in the making of commercials for radio and television. Jokes, cartoons, graffiti, and advertising cohabit with linguistics, classical mythology, picaresque novels, and feminist manifestos as influences on the construction of the novel.

In *Oreo* the ancient Greek myth of Theseus' journey into the Labyrinth becomes a linguistically riotous feminist tall tale of a young black woman's passage from Philadelphia to New York in search of her white Jewish father. Ross's brain-teasing humor gives *Oreo* its distinctive wit. It is essentially a ludic text, full of verbal games, jokes, puns, and puzzles. Ross clearly delighted in inviting readers to play along with her rollicking parody of classical myth. However, there is also a serious aspect to her heroine's playful wrangling with language. The Labyrinth that Theseus entered was a kind of game created by Daedalus for King Minos of Crete; but the intricate maze served the serious purpose of corralling the violent Minotaur. In certain Greek myths, solving a riddle is a test of the hero's ingenuity, suggesting that life itself is a game of wits. Oreo's journey is not merely a whimsical comic adventure, but also a meaningful quest for self-knowledge. As she seeks the answer to the riddle of her origins, word games entertain the heroine in her solo journey, and keep her wits sharpened for verbal duels with the assorted characters she encounters on the streets of New York, who correspond to the bandits that Theseus slays on his overland journey from Troezen to Athens.

A satire on relations between African Americans and Jews, as well as a topsy-turvy treatment of racial and ethnic shibboleths and stereotypes in American popular culture, *Oreo* is also a formally inventive picaresque novel written as a series of language games, comic translations, bilingual wisecracks, and arch etymological puns that call to mind crazily erudite vaudeville routines performed by comedian Professor Irwin Corey; elaborately constructed shaggy dog stories with absurdly far-fetched punch lines delivered with the raised eyebrow of Groucho Marx; the high hipster monologues of Lord Buckley; and the X-rated comedy of Lenny Bruce, Redd Foxx, and Richard Pryor. Ross's linguistic range stretches from scholarly wit and airy erudition to vernacular dialects and stand-up comedy shtick. The author's etymological puns trace her tongue back to its Greek and Latin roots, at the same time that her novel updates an ancient myth with several new twists, including a heroic feminist protagonist whose Labyrinth is the New York subway system, and whose Minotaur is not a bull-headed man but a mannish bulldog named Toro. Like James Joyce's *Ulysses*, possibly one of its models, Ross's novel is, on a smaller scale, a zesty, pun-filled parody of a classical myth.

Oreo's tongue-in-cheek mimicry of the Greek hero underscores Ross's cheekiness as an African American woman who travesties both James Joyce and the Greeks while blithely seeking her place in a Western literary tradition. Ross's clever parody is wildly irreverent in many respects, drawing interesting parallels between the macho hero Theseus, who is credited with the invention of wrestling, and her militantly feminist heroine, Oreo, who uses verbal wit and martial arts to dispatch her male adversaries. Like Theseus, when Oreo comes of age, she sets off to find an absentee father who has left behind clues to the "secret of her birth" and tokens of a paternal legacy, "sword and sandals," traditionally passed from father to son.

If Theseus' entry into the Labyrinth suggests the masculine hero's return to the womb followed by the rebirth of a new self through the feminine power of his guide, Ariadne, Oreo's quest to meet her deadbeat dad suggests a feminist daughter's claim to self-knowledge as well as her determination to challenge patriarchy and to contest the phallic power of the male. Unlike Theseus and the Minotaur, who owe their existence to the perverse promiscuity of gods and aristocrats, Oreo is the legitimate offspring of a middle-class couple who happen to be of different races and religions; and unlike other feminist heroines of the 1970s, Oreo remains virginal throughout her often risky adventures. Although Ross stirs racy jokes and spicy sexual innuendo into the mix of *Oreo*, it is perhaps because of conventional strictures on the sexual expressiveness of black women that Ross prefers to demonstrate her heroine's physical and intellectual prowess in martial and verbal arts rather than in sexual adventures such as those of Erica Jong's Isadora Wing in *Fear of Flying*, or Rita Mae Brown's Molly Bolt in *Rubyfruit Jungle*, two novels published in the year before *Oreo* appeared.

As a literary heroine, Christine "Oreo" Clark is both particular in her individual and cultural identity and universal in her quest for self-knowledge. Though Oreo is a physically beautiful young woman, what is most striking is her ability to amuse herself in any situation, owing to her speculative intelligence and wry sense of humor. Her attention to verbal quirks and habits of speech defines her character and calls the reader's attention to the artifice of language as a cultural construct, demonstrating the materiality as opposed to the transparency of the spoken and written word. Christine Clark, nicknamed Oriole (the bird), but called Oreo (the cookie), is the offspring of an African American mother and a Jewish father. Oreo's parents divorce shortly after her younger brother is born, and she grows up knowing only the black side of her family: her African American mother, Helen, her brother, Moishe (called Jimmie C.), and her mother's parents, James and Louise Clark. Each member of the family has a different idiosyncratic relationship to language, thus contributing to Oreo's semiotic competence and opening the text to a variety of verbal experiments and variations on the spoken and written word.

James, Oreo's black grandfather, is speechless following an immobilizing stroke that occurs minutes after hearing that his daughter "was going to wed a Jew-boy" (3). Her grandmother Louise speaks an almost incomprehensible southern dialect. Helen, Oreo's mother, converses in standard English sprinkled with Yiddish she learned from her father, who before his stroke ran a mail-order publishing business selling religious publications to an exclusively Jewish clientele. Oreo's mother is a gifted professional musician and eccentric amateur mathematician who ponders whimsical "head equations" whenever she suffers from boredom or distress. Oreo's younger brother, Jimmie C., expresses himself with a secret musical language of his own invention, and prefers to sing rather than speak. When a neighbor's tomcat loses a fight with an alley cat, the woman announces, "My cat's a coward." The sensitive Jimmie C., who has put his fingers in his ears during the cat fight, hears "Mah cassa cowah," thus providing the family with a strange new idiolect:

> Jimmie C. was delighted. He decided to use this wonderful new expression as the radical for a radical second language. "Cha-key-

key-wah, mah-cassa-cowah," he would sing mysteriously in front of strangers. "Freck-a-louse-poop!"

Oreo recognized the value of Jimmie C.'s cha-key-key-wah language over the years. For her, it served the same purpose as black slang. She often used it on shopkeepers who lapsed into Yiddish or Italian. It was her way of saying, "Talk about mother tongues— try to figure out *this* one, you mothers." (42)

Ross's novel can be read as a deliberate extension of the possibilities for expression, humor, self-defense, intellectual stimulation, and aesthetic pleasure in the various mother tongues or invented languages that the heroine can claim as her own, from the almost unrepresentable dialect of her African American grandmother to the code-switching "Yidlish" that is the lingua franca of several relatives on both sides of her family. In addition to the vernaculars of her own blood kin, Oreo can also claim fluency in the salty street talk of hustlers, pimps, and prostitutes, as well as the obscure erudition of cranky scholars.

Oreo's ability to speak and communicate with a diverse cast of characters is a skill she cannot take for granted. Her grandfather is silent for much of the novel; her grandmother speaks a southern dialect alien to the northeast; her brother sings a secret invented language that resembles a cross between baby talk and the ooga-booga lingo of natives in old Tarzan movies. Oreo hears in his babbling a "radical" new language that serves as an extravagant means of self-expression and self-defense, like black slang or the arcane scat of bebop hipsters.

Ross seems to anticipate hip-hop culture's technologies of sampling and distorting sound at the same time that she satirizes the "mainstream" culture's marginalization and appropriation of racial and ethnic difference, when Oreo substitutes for her actor father in the Harlem studio of Slim Jackson, the mute "Mr. Soundman." Pitching the products of "Tante Ruchel's Kosher

Kitchen," she performs a shmaltzy shtick aimed at Jewish con-
sumers. At the very moment that she is searching for her Jewish
roots, tracing her father through the brothels and sound studios
that are his accustomed haunts, Oreo replays her father's sold-out
commercialism, even as her performance in the radio commercial
calls into question the whole idea of authentic ethnic identity.
With the close proximity of commercial recording studio and
bordello, Ross satirically notes the pimping of creativity that cap-
italist cultural production requires. Significantly, both establish-
ments are located in Harlem, where Oreo's father sells his talent
in order to buy time with black prostitutes and to provide his wife
with domestic help (also black women).

The satirical force of Ross's parodic inversions relies on the
reader's awareness of historical roles in which African Americans
and Jews have been cast in the making of popular culture. Oreo's
passable impersonation of a Jewish housewife inverts such popular culture scenarios as Al Jolson's performance in *The Jazz
Singer* as the son of a Jewish cantor who sings "jazz" in black-
face in the first major Hollywood film to incorporate syn-
chronous sound. Oreo's mimicry also brings to mind the radio
production of *Amos 'n' Andy*, in which characters speaking a
comical black vernacular dialect were played by white actors.
The roles of Slim Jackson and Samuel Schwartz invert the more
typical relations of white producers and managers of black talent
before the 1960s.

Ross aims her satire at the commercialization of culture that
tends to produce reductive and often degrading caricature, while
it deprives many Americans of a richer, livelier linguistic heritage. Although Oreo has an appreciation of the vernacular, she is
also aware of the power of the stereotype, which she manipulates
to her own tactical advantage. The closer Oreo comes to unravel-
ing the clues that will enable her to find her father and discover
"the secret of her birth," the more she relies on her talent for

improvisation and impersonation. She moves from her conventionally essentialist performance of Jewishness as the niece of "Tante Ruchel" to an equally stereotypical performance of blackness as a spy in her father's house. At one point she impersonates a domestic day-worker in order to glean insider information about the Schwartz family, pumping their black housekeeper for juicy details as they gossip together like yentas. Later, impersonating the family's trusted factotum and confronted with an officious medical professional, Oreo's acting combines African American vernacular with body language borrowed from Hollywood's stereotypical black servants, in a calculated ploy to dig deeper into the Schwartz family's business and discover the secret withheld by her father.

He slit open the envelope, read the letter, and subjected Oreo to untoward scrutiny. She tried to look dull-normal when he said what she had expected someone to say.

"I'll have to verify this with Dr. Resnick."

Oreo replaced dull-normal with sullen-hurt, the look of the congenitally insulted. "He jus' gib me de 'scription. Say fill it." She had decided to use [the housekeeper's] economical sentence structure and [her grandmother] Louise's down-home accent. (203)

Oreo's cynical manipulation of stereotypes underscores Ross's increasingly biting satire as the heroine enters the Schwartz household, not as a long-lost daughter, but as a trickster in the guise of a servant. At one point a friend of her father's even mistakes her for one of Samuel's "harlots of Harlem" (182–184). The extent to which identity, kinship, and heritage are constructed around race, culture, and economics may be the ultimate lesson of Oreo's quest, as Ross questions the "natural" bond presumed to exist between parent and child.

Finally, in the sections titled "The story of Helen and Samuel, Oreo's version" and "Clues, shmues," Oreo comes to her own conclusions about her origins, ultimately relying on her powers of interpretation to piece together and understand her family's history of strained relationships. Oreo imagines this story as a film treatment for a Hollywood biopic, a scenario complete with a requisite *"Montage of* Variety *headlines of the 'O's Pop Top Flop' genre"* (205). In the process, Ross describes her method of composing this novel. The myth of Theseus (also a search for paternal origin) generates a list of episodes, characters, and clues, which the novelist strings together in the labyrinthine twists and turns of her own parodic plot.

Is *Oreo* a black text? Ross was surely aware that, while Norman Mailer's jazz-influenced "White Negro" saw himself as the essence of hip sensibility, secular "black Jews" or any other African Americans who identify themselves intellectually as "people of the book" might be branded as oreos, when literary culture is associated with a "white" heritage. One of the novel's comic epigraphs quotes the most commonly repeated definition of "oreo": "Someone who," like the cookie, "is black on the outside and white on the inside." However, her protagonist is not a culturally whitewashed, deracinated, or "wannabe white" character who has assimilated European-American cultural styles in order to escape the supposed inferiority of African American culture, or to make herself more acceptable to the mainstream. Oreo claims no cookie-cutter identity; rather, she is a character whose cultural hybridity has given her an intimate view of two of the diverse subcultures that have made significant contributions to the production of American culture. Along with her biracial and bicultural identity, Oreo maintains an abiding interest in the mechanics of identity construction and cultural reproduction. Through Oreo's adventures, Ross depicts a complex negotiation of identity within a racial, ethnic, sociocultural, and linguistic heterogeneity that extends beyond black and white. While Oreo is visually identifiable and self-identified as African American, the content of her identity is formed dynamically, improvisationally, and contingently as she interacts with others, choosing from a diverse menu of sometimes competing possibilities and influences that vary from one encounter to another.

In Oreo's interactions with members of both sides of her family, as well as with neighbors, friends, acquaintances, and strangers, Ross's novel suggests that acculturation is not a one-way street, but is more like a subway system with graffiti-tagged cars that travel uptown as well as downtown, or even more like an interconnected network of multi-lane freeways. Particularly in racially diverse and integrated settings, immigrants of various races and national origins, on their way to becoming American, may emulate the cultural styles of black Americans, since African Americans, though a minority, are as much the founders of American culture as Anglo Americans. Anglos themselves are a minority of white Americans. Oreo's biracial and bicultural heritage is not so exceptional when one considers that most native-born Americans, regardless of skin color, are products of racial hybridity, just as American culture and language are products of cultural and linguistic hybridity. The significant contribution of black Americans to the national culture includes the problem and challenge that linguistic and cultural difference offer to American democracy, and to the creative production of African-American writers.

Entering the maze of Ross's imaginatively constructed novel, the reader is reminded that a labyrinth is "an intricate structure of interconnecting passages," much like the text of *Oreo*; and also that "labyrinth" is the name given to the internal architecture of the ear, the destination of the spoken word. In this unfortunately overlooked work, Fran Ross lends the reader a remarkable eye for the baffling absurdity of everyday life and a receptive ear for the noisy diversity of the American idiom. *Oreo* is a text that assumes the verbal intelligence, the linguistic and cultural competence of readers who appreciate the rich diversity that contributes to the complexity of their own identities.

HARRYETTE MULLEN

Biographical information was gathered from Gerald Ross, Jr., Richard Ross, Gerald Ross, III, Ann Grifalconi, and the Temple University Alumni Association. I gratefully acknowledge all these sources, and I especially appreciate the cooperation of the Ross family, who generously shared their memories and personal documents with me.

Works Cited

Brown, Rita Mae. *Rubyfruit Jungle*. New York: Bantam Books, 1973.

Ingram, Billy. "The Richard Pryor Show." http//www.tvparty.com/pryor.html.

Jong, Erica. *Fear of Flying*. New York: Holt, Rinehart and Winston, 1973.

Joyce, James. *Ulysses*. London: Secker and Warburg, 1994 (1922).

Kelley, William Melvin. *Dunsfords Travels Everywheres*. Garden City, N.Y.: Doubleday, 1970.

Mailer, Norman. *The White Negro*. San Francisco: City Lights Press, 1957.

Mullen, Harryette. "One Smart, Tough Cookie: The Lit, Grit, and Motherwit of Fran Ross's *Oreo*" (forthcoming article).

Ross, Fran. "Richard Pryor, Richard Pryor." *Essence*. April 1979: 70ff.

Wilson, Harriet. *Our Nig*. New York: Random House, 1983.